A SURFEIT OF SUSPICIONS

The elegant, elderly Sir Henry Peirson claimed to have Jane Woodley's good in mind when he introduced her to society and then to the handsome Mark Courtland.

The gallant, good-looking Lieutenant James Dancy claimed to have Jane's safety and future happiness in mind when he warned her against Mark and urged her to accept his own devotion and protection. Mark Courtland himself claimed to be an honest country gentleman in the face of mounting evidence that he was neither honest nor a gentleman.

In this maze of mischief and mystery, Jane could be sure of only one thing. She could not afford to blindly trust anyone or anything—most especially her own foolish heart. . . .

THE MISCHIEVOUS MATCHMAKER

SIGNET Titles for Your Reference Shelf

(0451)

☐ **WHY DIDN'T I THINK OF THAT!** by Robert L. Shook. Here are the true stories of those enterprising Americans who used ingenuity and the free enterprise system to make their fortunes. "An unabashed pitch for the glories of that freak of American free enterprise—the million-dollar idea!"—*Los Angeles Times*   (120760—$2.95)*

☐ **THE REAL ESTATE BOOK** by Robert L. Nessen. Revised edition. A complete guide to real estate investment including information on the latest tax laws, mortgage tables, and a glossary of terms. "Indespensable"—*Forbes* Magazine   (122372—$3.50)*

☐ **THE COMPLETE ESTATE PLANNING GUIDE** by Robert Brosterman. A renowned lawyer and estate planning expert tells how you can set up a long-range program that will not only benefit your heirs, but safeguard your own financial security in your lifetime. Newly revised and updated to incorporate new tax law changes.   (621263—$3.95)

☐ **HOW TO BUY YOUR OWN HOUSE WHEN YOU DON'T HAVE ENOUGH MONEY!** by Richard F. Gabriel. A real estate specialist's guide to creative financing, dollar stretching, low-cash buying techniques, and dozens of home-buying, money-raising-and-saving strategies.   (129903—$3.95)*

☐ **GET YOUR MONEY'S WORTH: The Book for People Who Are Tired of Paying More for Less** by Froma Joselow. Learn all the ways—and how easy it is—to make your money buy more and grow faster today. If you're tired of your living standard going down when your income is going up, now is the time to start to *Get Your Money's Worth!*   (121325—$2.95)*

*Prices slightly higher in Canada

BARBARA ALLISTER
THE
MISCHIEVOUS
MATCHMAKER

A SIGNET BOOK

NEW AMERICAN LIBRARY

SIGNET TRADEMARK REG. U.S. PAT. OFF. AND FOREIGN COUNTRIES
REGISTERED TRADEMARK—MARCA REGISTRADA
HECHO EN CHICAGO, U.S.A.

SIGNET, SIGNET CLASSIC, MENTOR, PLUME, MERIDIAN AND NAL BOOKS
are published by New American Library,
1633 Broadway, New York, New York 10019

First Printing, March, 1985

1   2   3   4   5   6   7   8   9

PRINTED IN THE UNITED STATES OF AMERICA

*To God who gave me the talent to write
and to my family and friends
who encouraged me to use it*

CHAPTER

1

As usual the door to the small salon stuck on the warped floor. For Jane Woodley it was one problem too many. After half an hour of biting her tongue to keep from insulting the squire and scandalizing his wife, Jane let her fury loose. As soon as she heard the front door close behind the departing couple, she kicked the door shut.

Muttering a decidedly unladylike oath under her breath, Jane hopped to a chair just inside the door. "You can come out, Mrs. Hawkins," she called. Curling her leg into her lap, she looked at her injured big toe. "That was foolish," she mumbled. "A broken toe won't solve anything, and the door didn't even slam."

"Miss Jane!" Mrs. Hawkins's appalled tone echoed throughout the small room. "What if someone should see you now?"

"Someone already has." At the older woman's frown, Jane reminded her, "You are here."

"None of your palavering, miss. What did the squire have to say?" The housekeeper looked at her mistress anxiously.

Jane straightened her gray skirts and said, "Just what we thought. When the lease runs out, we must leave here. Oh,

Mrs. Hawkins, you should have heard him.'' Her anger clearly revealed on her face, Jane mimicked, '' 'It wouldn't be right to rent this comfortable family house to a young spinster. Of course, if you are interested in something smaller . . .' Smaller! He wouldn't even listen to me. His wife told me that her cousin is to buy the house for his mother. Even if Papa were still alive, they would have found some way to make us move.'' A tear trickled down her cheek, and Jane reached up angrily to wipe it away.

''Now, now. After dealing with that man I know just what you need—a nice hot cup of tea. It will be ready in just a minute.'' Before Jane could utter another word, Mrs. Hawkins whisked out the door.

As she often did when she had a problem, Jane began to pace. For a time the only sound was the whisper of her gray skirts. As the late-October sun slanted across the room, Jane considered her problem until her head began to ache. As she walked up and down, deep in thought, she did not hear the door open. The housekeeper paused and then put the tray on a table. She watched her mistress fondly. From the first weeks when she had taken over the reins as housekeeper for the professor and his daughter, Mrs. Hawkins had taken secret pleasure in working for such a lady. Although not truly beautiful, Jane had a certain something that made people look at her a second time. Perhaps it was the way her sparkling gray eyes tilted up at the outside corners, or her unusual brown hair that in some lights seemed washed in silver. There was a certain elegance about her, from the top of cropped curls to the silk slippers that peeped out from her half mourning. Although she was only average in height, her slim figure was the envy of more beautiful girls in the neighborhood.

After watching Jane march up and down the room for a few minutes, Mrs. Hawkins said, ''Miss Jane, you are wearing a path in the rug. Sit down and drink your tea before it is cold.''

''Tea? Oh, tea. Thank you.'' Taking a deep breath, Jane smiled at the older woman, sat on the settee near the tea tray, and poured a cup of Bohea, Mrs. Hawkins's trustworthy restorative.

"And here is the post." She put the mail before her mistress and left the room.

Jane eagerly opened the first letter, one of her godmother's chatty and rambling summaries of her life. As usual it was filled with the latest gossip about people Jane did not know. After skimming a long passage about her godmother's annual move to Bath, she paused and began to read more slowly. One paragraph in particular she reread several times.

> And, my dear, you would not believe how lax the morals have become in Bath. I must tell you that I will follow the Prince's example and go to Brighton hereafter. Can you believe that just anyone can attend the assemblies? All they have to do is pay a subscription fee. Even a young woman, I hesitate to call her a lady, accompanied only by a hired companion was welcomed by the Master of Ceremonies. I was appalled, simply appalled.

Gradually the tension in Jane's shoulders began to drain away from her. A smile drifted across her lips. She read the paragraph again. Finishing it for a second time, she laid it carefully to one side. Scanning the rest of her post quickly, she returned to her godmother's letter. How strange that her godmother, who had refused to help her five years ago, should now provide a solution to her problem.

Still with a slight smile on her face, Jane crossed the room, her step much lighter than before. As she opened the door to the small room her father had called his library, she knew just what she would do.

Four weeks later, in spite of her determination and natural optimism, Jane felt downcast. Dark shadows of the late-November sun hung over the room as she lifted another armload of books from the almost empty shelves. Crossing to the fireplace, she put them carefully into an empty tea chest sitting on the hearth.

Wearily she glanced around the room, noting clearly the faded wallpaper, once blue but now dull gray, and the worn chairs. Only the bright blues and reds of the rug gave the room any life. She sank into a chair. As usual, this room depressed her. It was the last one whose contents she needed to pack, and she had deliberately left it for last.

Its heavy, polished desk, leather chairs, and shelves of books seemed to hold so many memories—memories of her few successes and many failures. It had been her father's hiding place, a sanctuary from a world he did not like, a sanctuary he had refused to allow her to change. After giving lessons, her father had retreated into a world of books and a study of the Exchange and his fortune.

She, however, had belonged nowhere. Had the social leaders known of her father's vast wealth, they would have welcomed her into their homes. But her father had a penchant for secrecy, and an unchaperoned daughter of a schoolmaster, no matter how wellborn, was not a person with whom the mothers of the neighborhood chose to have their daughters associate. Her appeal to the gentlemen of the neighborhood had distressed them. On the few occasions when she had persuaded her father to accept an invitation, she had had her role in society made clear for her. She was an example for those daughters who seemed to be wasting their chances— letting their beauty rot on the vine.

Finally the struggle had grown too much for her. She wanted to scream, ''It wasn't my choice. I want a chance to dance, to laugh, to enjoy myself, to marry. Don't shut me out!''

Only Sir Henry Peirson had understood. Newly returned from India, he was that rarity in the neighborhood, a wellborn man who had done well in trade. His black-and-silver hair, permanently sun-browned skin, and elegant if thin figure set him apart, as did the fact that he was a man who went his own way, who set his own fashions. Like Jane, he knew what it was to be different. Following his visit to see her father, whom he had known at school, he took Jane under his wing. He had taken her for rides in the country, had even planned dinner parties at which she had been the hostess, much to the dismay and scandal of the countryside. And how the gossips had enjoyed Jane's plight when he had left the area. Everyone for miles around knew she had been jilted.

Only Jane knew differently. How she had laughed at first when she had heard the rumors. She and Sir Henry? Sitting there in the library with shadows gathering around her, Jane chuckled. If only Sir Henry were here.

Shaking her skirts out, she hurried back to the shelves to pack the last few books. Only these and the few personal belongings in her bedroom and she would be ready to leave. She had her life all planned. First to London to interview a chaperon, then to Bath. Her only worry was her lack of relatives. But no matter—she planned to enjoy her life, to find something to entertain her before she was too old to enjoy it.

The last book carefully packed away, Jane closed the lid and stood, shaking the dust from her skirts. By tomorrow she would be on her way. Hesitating for a moment on the threshold, she looked back into the now gloomy room. "Goodbye, Papa," she whispered.

Turning back into the hallway, she paused as she heard a knock at the door. Another visit from the squire would be more than she could endure. Cautiously she crept to the head of the stairs that led to the kitchen. But the deep voice at the door was nothing like the squire's high-pitched squeak. Catching sight of her visitor, she dashed forward.

"Sir Henry!"

"Did you think I had forgotten you, my dear?" he asked as he bowed his silver-and-black head over her hand. His searching black eyes frowned at the pallor of her once rosy cheeks and the look of loneliness in her eyes. She was as attractive as ever, but those tip-tilted gray eyes needed something to make them sparkle.

Smiling up at him, she drew him into the almost empty library. "How fortunate you arrived today!"

Seating her carefully, Sir Henry settled himself and said, "Now tell me about this plan of yours. I came as soon as I received your letter."

As careful as he had been to keep his disapproval out of his voice, Jane reacted almost defensively. "I told you the squire expected us to move. Since I had to leave, I decided to find a more congenial place, a place where I could find amusements and friends. My godmother gave me the idea. I plan to see my lawyer in London soon and sign the papers on the house he has found for me to buy in Bath."

"Bath? All year round? It's become less fashionable of late. My dear, surely that would be a mistake. A woman as young as you needs more life and excitement than that old watering hole and its elderly guests can offer!" He paused and then asked, "Have you ever been to Bath? Especially in the winter?"

Jane hesitated. "No. But I want to go. My lawyer has made all the arrangements. And tomorrow or the next day I plan to leave for London to see him."

"Tomorrow?"

"Sir Henry . . . please wish me well. All I want is a chance to see the world, to have some excitement in my life." Jane's gray eyes begged him to agree with her.

The man who had been such a good friend of her father's crossed to her side and looked at her sadly. "Excitement, my dear?" he asked gently. "In Bath? The only excitement you will find now will be in providing the old gossips who live there a chance to tear a young lady like you to shreds."

"Young? I am twenty-five years old, and the most excitement I have had in the last few years has been going to church on Sunday. Since Papa died and I have been in mourning, no one even calls on me. Even providing ladies a chance to gossip about me will be more exciting than my life now."

"But your reputation! Who will chaperon you, introduce you

to the *ton*, sponsor your entry into society? Have you thought of that?'' His black eyes met her gray ones. ''You may simply be trading one difficult situation for another.''

Defiantly, hiding her own misgivings, Jane said quietly, ''I am planning to hire a companion.''

''Hire a companion.'' For a moment Sir Henry simply stood there. Then he asked, ''And where did you plan to find this paragon of virtue who will protect your innocence?''

''Papa's lawyer has made some inquiries for me and has arranged some interviews. I am certain I can find someone suitable.''

''Hah! What you will find is some old tabby who knows how to say 'Yes, ma'am' and does not have another intelligent idea in her head. Like most companions she will have been forgotten by her family and will have no entry into society at all. It will never do. You will simply have to come home with me.''

For a few minutes Jane looked at him as if stunned. And then she said, ''Come home with you? And create a scandal so that there will be no hope that either of us will ever be accepted by society again? No thank you! I appreciate the thought, but . . .''

''Jane, silly girl, I am not making an indecent proposal. My cousin's wife has put off her mourning. As soon as the Little Season is over, she will be returning to the Abbey. Hortense will be happy to introduce you to our neighbors. In fact, we are to meet her in London, and you can begin to enjoy *ton* parties.''

For a moment Jane allowed herself to hope. She really was dreading Bath, where she knew no one, and she knew better than to hope for support from her godmother. And then she remembered the way the squire's wife had reacted when she had seen Jane and Sir Henry together. She asked, ''And how shall we explain my arrival?'' Jane's usually soft tones were harsh. ''I am rather old to be your ward. I suppose you could introduce me as your future wife,'' she said sarcastically.

"My ward or my future wife? Hm. Well, either will do nicely," he said pleasantly.

"Sir Henry, I was only joking. Really, you must accept my plan. I will be perfectly safe in Bath. At least there I will be able to attend the theater and the assemblies and visit the libraries."

"But by yourself or with a dreary old companion," he said softly. "How much more fun to attend balls and dinner parties with all the eligible young men of the countryside. They will enjoy you, I am certain of that."

"But no one will believe that you are my guardian, and I would really rather not be engaged."

"Your father did ask me to serve as your financial adviser, Jane. In a sense that does make me your guardian."

"Then why have you ignored me until now?"

"You were in mourning, my dear, and had a perfectly adequate place to stay."

"So adequate that no one would talk to me or invite me into his home," Jane whispered unhappily. "If you wanted me to come to live with you, why did you wait until now?"

Sir Henry took her hand and pulled her from her chair. Putting a finger under her chin, he forced her to look at him. His voice was quiet and full of regret as he said, "With Hortense in mourning I could not ask you into my home. Your life would not have been much different had you been living with me. Polite society insists that ladies spend at least a year in mourning. At least here you had your own servants, your own books. You could run your life. I believed you would be happier here."

For a few moments Jane stood there. She had enjoyed being able to make her own decisions. The thought gave her courage. She said, "You are right. I did well on my own this year, and I can do well in Bath. Thank you, Sir Henry, but I will do as I planned."

"Jane, think of your alternatives. Some time in the *ton* and then a pleasant Christmas season with me. Or would you rather be alone at Christmas?"

Her face pale but determined, Jane refused to give in. Finally, Sir Henry made what he felt was his final appeal. "Jane, I need your help."

"My help?"

Sir Henry nodded and then said, "A young neighbor of mine, Mark Courtland, will be staying with me for some time. A short time ago his home, Courtland Place, caught fire. It will take some time to repair it. He has been so despondent that I cannot reach him. I thought perhaps a new and pretty face might do what I cannot."

"Me? But I don't even know the man." Jane crossed to sit in one of the worn leather chairs. Although she did not want to admit it, Jane was intrigued by the thought that she could help. Then she remembered the way Sir Henry liked to get his way. She jumped back up and looked at him. "No, I am going to Bath."

As their disagreement went on, both combatants began to lose their tempers and shout a bit. As their voices grew louder, they did not hear a timid scratching at the door. As if the person realized that the noise could not be heard over the loud voices, a loud rap sounded during one of the moments when both Jane and Sir Henry drew breath to begin again. Muttering an oath beneath his breath, Sir Henry stormed across the room, forgetting for the moment that he was not master of the house. "Yes?" he shouted at the timid maid who wanted nothing more than to disappear into the normal confusion of the kitchen.

"If it please, sir, a Mr. Mark Courtland said he was to meet you here," the girl mumbled.

"Show him in," he said, only to be interrupted by Jane, who was bristling with indignation.

"How dare you tell my servant who should be admitted to my presence? This is my home, at least until the end of this week, and I will decide whom I will or will not see, and not you." Her eyes flashed gray fire at him. Realizing what he had done, Sir Henry hurried toward her only to see her turn and flounce to the darkest corner of the room.

"Now, now, my dear. I am sorry for overstepping my bounds. But Mark Courtland is a good friend of mine, a man whom I am certain you will like."

"Mark Courtland? Ha! You did not think you would be enough to persuade me on your own. You had to bring in reinforcements."

Before she could continue, a quiet voice as rich and smooth as honey said, "I will return later, Sir Henry, when you are free."

Still angry with her friend and yet embarrassed by her churlish attitude before a stranger, Jane turned. Later Jane wondered if Mark had realized how long she had stared at him. With great effort, she lowered her eyes, amazed at her own reaction. What had caught her breath? She had seen more handsome men, but those shoulders—never had she seen such broad shoulders. She raised her eyes and more calmly regarded him again. From his sun-kissed brown hair to his lean hips, he glowed with the good health of a person who spent his days outside. His dark brown eyes surrounded by thick dark lashes caught hers, and she stood frozen for a few seconds. Hesitantly she smiled at him and then looked away.

"Mark, my boy. I was just telling Jane that you were staying with me. Now you can help persuade her to visit the Abbey." Remembering his manners, he paused. "Miss Jane Woodley, I would like to introduce Mr. Mark Courtland. Mark, Miss Woodley."

As he crossed the room to make his bow to her, Jane realized that he walked with a limp, a limp so slight that many people might not be aware of it. As he came closer, Jane wondered how he ever managed to get the close-fitting claret coat over those broad shoulders, and she enjoyed the way the biscuit-colored pantaloons clung to his lean hips and muscular legs. "Delighted to make your acquaintance," he said.

Jane could not help herself. The smile that twinkled in her eyes lit her face. "Welcome to my home, Mr. Courtland. I apologize for the scene you just saw. Arguing with Sir Henry always makes me forget I am a lady,'' she said, her voice a throaty purr.

His good manners helped Mark make the right reply as he gazed thoughtfully into the most intriguing laughing gray eyes he had ever seen. This was the daughter who had cared for her father until his death? The men in the area must have been blind, he decided. She was delightful. His rich voice seemed almost a caress as he said, ''I must certainly forgive both of you, since his coming here meant that I could meet you.''

Jane felt her heart fluttering as she looked into his eyes. She had forgotten about Sir Henry and anyone else who might enter the room.

Then Sir Henry reminded her of their quarrel. He said, ''Mark, you must help me convince Jane that the Abbey would be a far better place for her this winter than a dull house alone in Bath. This foolish girl refuses to listen to me any longer.''

''It is much more pleasant to share the season with someone else. I am certain you would enjoy the Abbey. Sir Henry is a marvelous host,'' Mark declared softly.

Jane tried her last weapon. ''But I have already had my lawyer draw up the purchase papers.'' The prospect of a visit to Sir Henry seemed more and more pleasant. ''And your cousin does not even know me. What would she think of a stranger descending on her?''

''Nonsense. Nothing could be more simple. Come to London with us and meet Hortense there. Leave Mrs. Hawkins to send off your goods to the Abbey. If you wish to remove to Bath later, you can have them sent from there easily.'' Sir Henry smiled down at her fondly. ''I even promise that if you decide you want to go to Bath I will ask Hortense to find you a suitable chaperon. Consider it, my dear. A few weeks of parties, even a ball or two. Maybe I can persuade Hortense to take you to London for the Season next spring.''

Mark's eyebrow tilted quizzically as he regarded his friend. Hortense would not be happy when she saw Jane.

With Mark's attention on Sir Henry, Jane had an opportunity to gaze at him from the corners of her eyes. The wine-colored coat hugged his shoulders like a caress. Ashamed of her thoughts, Jane glanced quickly away. Keeping her eyes determinedly on the floor, she missed the fond look that Sir Henry focused on her, but Mark did not. The young man looked thoughtfully at his friend.

"Well, Jane, what do you plan to do? First to London and then to the Abbey? Or will you persist in your foolish plan?" Sir Henry asked, beginning quite gently but forgetting his conciliatory tone at the end.

Hesitantly, Jane glanced first at Mark, who wore a slight frown, and then at her older friend. "If you think you will make a good guardian and your cousin does not object?"

"Object, nonsense. She will enjoy your company. What time can you be ready to leave tomorrow?"

CHAPTER

2

As the traveling carriage jolted down the road toward London, Jane gave a tired sigh and smiled at the men across from her. She smothered a yawn behind her hand. As hard as she tried, though, she could not stay awake.

Smiling paternally, Sir Henry carefully moved beside her, removing her bonnet, settling her head into the well-padded corner, and covering her with the fur lap robe. Mark too leaned back on the wine-colored squabs and lowered his eyelids so that it looked as though he were sleeping. Cautiously under his long eyelashes he watched the woman on the seat in front of him, fascinated by the sweep of dark lashes on the creamy cheek. When she was jostled by an unusually large bump, Sir Henry reached to steady her.

Opening his eyes, Mark asked, "Did Mrs. Morgan tell you whom we could expect to see while we are in town?"

"You must know Hortense better than that. All she told me was that the parties had been delightful and that everyone who was anyone was in town," his friend replied.

"Does she know about Jane?"

"I plan to surprise her. That way she won't have a choice.

After all, Jane has nowhere else to go." He laughed softly. "Besides, for the last six months Hortense has been complaining that I don't entertain enough. I plan to give her free rein to keep Jane amused. I want Jane to meet everyone."

Mark thought of the possessive way the older woman regarded Sir Henry. "But . . ."

"No, my boy, I am certain everything will work out beautifully. Leave it to me." Then he too leaned back into a corner and closed his eyes, hoping his predictions would come true. One could never tell about Hortense.

Neither the jostling of the coach nor the stops to change horses roused Jane. Because she was sleeping so deeply, the men let her sleep, using the few minutes while the horses were being changed to grab a scratch meal.

As they came closer to the capital, the traffic on the road began to increase. The rattling of wagons and the comments of the drivers finally roused Jane. "Are we already here?" she asked in amazement.

"Yes, my dear," Sir Henry said, laughing. "A nap makes any trip shorter."

"How could you let me go on sleeping?"

"What would you like to do first?" Sir Henry asked.

"Go shopping." Jane shook out the gray skirts of her traveling costume and said, "After gray and black for a year I want something bright, something pretty."

"Hortense will be able to help you there. I never met a woman so up to date in terms of fashion," said Sir Henry. "And while you two are spending money, Mark and I will consult some members of Parliament about a problem in our district." Smiling at her, he patted her hand affectionately. "You are to relax and enjoy yourself. I'll make sure of it."

Mark settled back in the seat and wondered how much Jane's shopping expedition would cost his friend. Of course, no matter what she spent, Sir Henry could afford it. According to the latest rumors, he had left India as wealthy as a rajah, quite a catch for a schoolmaster's daughter.

A short time later they pulled to a stop before an imposing

structure. After greeting Marsden, his butler, Sir Henry demanded, "Is my cousin at home?"

"No, sir, but she will return for tea. I expect her at any moment."

At Sir Henry's suggestion, Jane and Mark agreed they would like to be shown to their rooms. As Jane followed Mrs. Marsden, the housekeeper, up the imposing curved staircase, she smiled happily down at the older man, who beamed up at her. But his smile disappeared as he thought of the coming interview.

By the time Hortense arrived, he was ready. And Hortense gave him the opening he was looking for. "I am so happy that you and Mark have finally arrived. It has been so dull going to parties alone," she said in a voice filled with ennui.

"I have the perfect solution."

"Henry, I knew I could depend on you."

He continued as though she had not spoken. "You can take charge of my ward, Jane Woodley. She'll enjoy those parties immensely."

For a few moments Hortense was speechless. Her attractive face was marred by a deep frown. Then her deep blue eyes filled with tears that seemed on the brink of streaming down her pale cheeks. "How can you expect me, a woman who has so recently lost her husband, to take charge of a young girl? Henry, it is too much."

"Jane is a pleasant young lady who means a great deal to me. I have already told her that you would be happy to be her chaperon." His tone was as cold as ice. "And you have already returned to society. As the owner of this establishment I could ask someone else to be my hostess. But I was certain that you would willingly assist me in this way."

Hortense took a close look at his impassive face. "And who is this girl you wish me to sponsor? Who are her parents?"

"Her background is impeccable. Her father and I were in school together. She meets my standards. That's all you need to know."

Taking a firm grip on her distraught nerves, Hortense looked into his face once again. She knew that expression. There was no crossing him when he looked like that. She took a deep breath and asked, "When will she arrive?"

"She is upstairs freshening up. You can meet her before dinner."

His answer caused her to sink to the jade-green sofa in shock. The hand that she stretched out to pick up her teacup trembled slightly before she got it under control. Forcing a smile to her lips, she asked, "How long will she stay?"

"Oh, no date has been set. I told her you would bring her to London with you in the spring if she wants to come."

Hortense set her cup down with a clatter. She rose from her seat and moved to the door with her usual studied grace, movements that would have been better suited to a tall willowy young lady instead of a short plump lady of indeterminate age who seemed to bounce along. "I simply must go to my room. The excitement," she said. "I will never be ready for the evening without a rest. Tell your little ward that I'm looking forward to seeing her at dinner." She grimaced mentally at the thought of presenting a debutante. And at such an inconvenient time of year.

Before she left the room, Sir Henry stopped her. "You will need to take her shopping. She's been in mourning for her father. I told her you knew all the fashionable modistes." At his words Hortense preened slightly, forgetting her languid pose. "I thought tomorrow would be a good time to begin."

Hortense frowned as she reviewed the next day's obligations. "What is the limit on what she can spend? And who gets the bills?"

"Have the bills sent to her lawyer. And she will set her own limits."

"How delightful. And what is her name?"

"Jane, Jane Woodley," said Sir Henry impatiently.

Nodding her head, Hortense drifted slowly toward the stairs. A debutante in control of her own money. She knew what Henry had meant when he said she was important to him. Well, if the girl was presentable, she might just change that. With money anything was possible.

The subject of their discussion had spent the afternoon basking in luxury and worrying. From the moment the maid who had been assigned to her arrived, she had been cosseted. From the warm depths of the hip bath in front of a roaring fire to the delicate slices of chicken surrounded by the crispest tart apple slices and delectable tea cakes, her every need had been met even before she had acknowledged it.

Had she been less preoccupied with thoughts of meeting Sir Henry's cousin, she would have been in gales of laughter over the artless comments of Betty, the young maid who wanted to appear sophisticated. As it was, Jane spent the afternoon pacing. It was all right for Sir Henry to promise that his cousin would chaperon her, but she knew women. She should have gone to Bath.

Finally persuaded to sit long enough for Betty to comb her hair, she watched while the maid, exclaiming over the unusual highlights in her hair, carefully arranged the short curls in riotous disorder and arranged the long back locks into an elaborate knot. She would be pleasant to the older woman no matter how difficult it was. And if things did not work out, she could still go to Bath.

Anxious not to keep her hostess waiting, Jane arrived to an almost empty room. At first not realizing that anyone was there, she glanced around the jade-and-gold room that had obviously just been redone in the latest Chinese fashion. Sinking onto one of the gold-covered chairs, she smiled wryly. "A perfect beginning. As usual I'm the first one here," she said to herself.

"Oh, but you're not," a deep voice assured her.

Jane's cheeks burned with color as she looked into Mark's amused face. Before she could overcome her embarrassment and reply, Sir Henry swept in.

"Jane, Mark, I am sorry that I was not here to greet you. Are your rooms comfortable? Hortense will be down shortly.

She has agreed to chaperon you as I knew she would. You are to spend tomorrow morning shopping. Now, don't be misled by Hortense's languid manners. She has more energy than any three other people I know, if she is interested in something. Don't you agree, Mark?''

''Mrs. Morgan does seem to be able to accomplish remarkable feats if she is allowed to do things her own way,'' the young man agreed. ''Do you remember the hunt she organized this fall?''

''Do I? I was the one who was caught up in that whirlwind.'' Before Sir Henry could continue, the door opened. Slightly confused by the description she had been given, Jane turned toward the door. As she caught her first glimpse of her chaperon, Jane's big gray eyes grew enormous. This fussy little lady covered in shawls and lace was Sir Henry's cousin?

''Here she is, Hortense. My ward, Jane Woodley. Isn't she lovely,'' Sir Henry said, his voice filled with pride and his face beaming.

Like Jane, Hortense was shocked. This was no green girl who would be easily disposed of. Glancing quickly at her cousin, she noted his doting smile. Composing herself, she extended her small plump hand and smiled. ''How delightful of Henry to relieve my boredom in such an unusual way. And all I really hoped for was his escort to parties,'' she said in so low and slow a manner that Jane had to concentrate to follow her words.

Before Jane could do more than curtsy, Hortense walked closer for a more thorough inspection. She circled Jane slowly. ''Yes, you will do nicely. You may call me Cousin Hortense.''

Controlling her temper with difficulty, Jane smiled at the older woman. ''I appreciate your kindness.'' Privately she wondered at the lady's motives.

Sir Henry winked at Mark, who was watching the two women warily. For the rest of the evening, Jane felt she was being watched constantly, but every time she glanced at Hortense the lady was deep in conversation. Finally weary from the strain and determined to contact her lawyer as soon as possible, Jane refused tea and went up to bed.

The next morning Jane prepared for the shopping expedition. No matter what happened, she needed clothes. Dressed in her best spencer and bonnet, Jane made her way to the front entry, where her hostess waited. To Jane's surprise, the lady she met was not the languid, slightly disorganized woman of the night before. Finally she understood Mark's description of Hortense. The lady now swathed in furs rather than shawls had assembled a shopping list of truly remarkable proportions.

"I think I need to see a modiste first," Jane said firmly as she walked toward the waiting carriage, shivering slightly in the cold breeze.

"Certainly. Exactly what I would have chosen for you." Having given the direction, Hortense settled back into her seat. "And after that, bonnets, shoes." She looked at Jane closely for a moment and then said, "Furs, yes, you must have furs. Perhaps Madame Camille can help there." Those details taken care of, she turned to look at Jane. "Henry is a delightful person, but he rarely tells me what I need to know. I know your father was a friend of his but very little else of your background. Where did your mother come from? And where have you been living?"

By the time they arrived at the modiste's shop, Jane felt as though Hortense were a master spy for Napoleon. Surely only a professional could ask so many questions in such a short time.

Hortense, on the other hand, was pleasantly surprised. She and Jane's mother had attended the same school in Bath, unfortunately not at the same time. With her knowledge of the *ton* she should be able to find Jane someone closer to her own age. Why, Jane was closer to Mark Courtland's age than to her guardian's. A smile remained on her face as she drifted into the select dressmaking establishment she had chosen.

"Ah, madame, such a pleasure to see you again," the modiste said, delighted to see a customer who spent vast sums on her clothing. "Something for you today? I have an elegant amethyst velvet that just arrived. Or perhaps something for the young lady?"

"For Miss Woodley." As Hortense sank into a nearby chair and picked up the fashion plates of clothing suitable for ladies Jane's age, Jane took a deep breath.

Realizing that Hortense had no idea how much she resented the thought of someone else selecting her clothing, Jane controlled her anger. Turning to the waiting modiste, she smiled coldly. "I need a complete new wardrobe to replace the mourning I have been wearing. I hope you will be able to help me."

Recognizing the difficulty, Madame Camille turned her attention to the younger woman. "But of course. I have the latest in fashions and fabrics. Something to wear now or later? Here are the fashion plates. Let us see what you like and then we will take measurements."

For the next few hours, Jane immersed herself in fashion and fabric in a myriad of colors. Fortunately Madame knew of a milliner who was happy to come and bring a few samples of her bonnets.

As Jane reviewed her purchases, she asked, "The wine velvet riding habit—you don't think that black velvet hat with the plume will be thought too dashing?"

"My dear, the men will admire it, and the ladies will gnash their teeth that they did not think of it first," Hortense assured her. "Are you certain you have ordered enough gowns for evening? The Christmas season is a very busy one."

"I've ordered five today. And Madame Camille has assured me that another shipment of fabric will arrive later this week so that I can order more then. Will that interfere with your plans?"

"That's a wise move." Hortense turned to the modiste. "The aqua crepe? It will be ready by this evening?"

"Without fail. Madamoiselle will be one of the loveliest ladies at the theater."

The two ladies continued with their shopping, visiting a shoemaker and the Pantheon Bazaar before returning to the house on Grosvenor Square. As Hortense prepared for her afternoon calls, Jane made ready for her meeting with her lawyer, Mr. Green. Promptly at three, Marsden showed him into the library.

"Miss Woodley," Mr. Green began, "how delighted I was to hear of your new arrangements. I suppose that you will not need the house in Bath now." He smiled at her; he had been as opposed to her idea as Sir Henry was.

Jane's gray eyes flashed. "No, Mr. Green. My instructions are for you to complete the purchase as quickly as possible."

"But Sir Henry . . ."

"Do you work for me or for Sir Henry?" she asked with a steely glint in her eye.

One look from his client was enough to quiet him. "Of course. And how soon do you plan to take occupancy? Should I arrange for servants?"

"A small staff. Just enough to keep it in proper condition. I'll let you know when I expect to arrive." When the lawyer left some time later, he was still muttering to himself. Jane spent the rest of the afternoon in the library waiting for Sir Henry. But by the time her gown for that evening had been delivered, he had not returned.

To her dismay, neither of the gentlemen returned for dinner. Although she would not quite admit it to herself, she was disappointed not to see Mark again.

All the way through dinner Jane lectured herself. She would not show her annoyance at being deserted by the men. She would enjoy her evening. By the time they reached the theater and their box, she had relaxed. As Hortense nodded first to one friend and to another, she explained to Jane, "Had I known that the gentlemen would be busy I would have arranged an escort. I do hope they arrive before the last interval."

Hortense's program to introduce Jane to a variety of eligible young men had already begun. A few words dropped into the right places had ensured that Jane's situation was known. The first interval gave Jane a taste of the attention she had been missing.

"My dear, let me introduce you to one of my closest friends, Lady Hastings, and her son Lord Denham. My cousin's ward, Miss Jane Woodley." Hortense beamed at her as if presenting Jane had been her own idea.

When Sir Henry and Mark entered the box a short time later, they were just in time to hear Lord Denham tell Jane, "From the other side of the theater your hair seemed spun silver. I had to know who the captivating woman was." Jane sent his head reeling further as she flashed an impish smile at him.

"Henry! You've finally arrived." As her friends left, Hortense turned to face her cousin. But before she could begin her complaint, Jane said to Sir Henry, "I need to talk to you, sir. I had quite an interesting conversation with my lawyer today."

"Now, Jane."

"Shall we discuss this later?" Hortense said too sweetly. "We are disturbing our neighbors."

Settling back in her chair, Jane was embarrassed to notice the attention they were receiving. Not only were the people in the next box staring, but Mark had a frown on his forehead. Forcing her attention to the stage, Jane nodded. At the next interval, Sir Henry and Mark escorted the ladies into the corridor.

"I think you and I should have a talk," Jane said quietly to her older friend. "Can you spare me some time tomorrow morning?" Her voice was cold and decisive.

"Tomorrow? Jane, I have appointments all day," Sir Henry said. Before she could answer, the bell that marked the end of the interval rang. As she walked back to the box on Sir Henry's arm, she was surprised to notice a look of disapproval on Mark's face.

*   *   *

Jane's days fell into a regular but frustrating pattern. She went shopping in the morning, on visits with Hortense in the afternoon, and to at least one party or engagement every evening. But somehow there was never any time to talk to Sir Henry. If she came down to breakfast, he had just left. If they went out to dinner, he stayed in. The only time she saw him was in company.

Almost a week after Jane had arrived in the city, she was again one of the first down for dinner. To her surprise, Mark was waiting for her. As he saw her come in the door, he stopped as if in a daze. She was so lovely in her deep blue gown sewn with pearls. The candlelight gave her hair its silver glint, and her gray eyes had a blue cast. Assuming his usual teasing attitude, he said, "You will be the envy of all the young ladies there tonight. Whom do you plan to enchant?"

Jane smiled at him. "Perhaps you, sir. Shall I save you a dance?"

"The supper dance, if it's not already bespoken." Ah, well, he might as well be hung for a wolf as a sheep. Just then the door opened and Sir Henry entered. Guiltily Mark retreated, a dismayed look crossing his face.

Jane, her heart beating wildly, looked at Mark in confusion. And then she realized what her friend had said. "By this time next week, we'll be at the Abbey."

"The Abbey? Sir Henry, you and I must talk. Soon." Jane's eyes flashed.

By that time Hortense had come in, the last one down as usual. As she glanced at the other participants in her little drama, her eyes brightened. The way that Mark was looking at Jane held promise. And Jane was not exactly indifferent to him.

Conversation at dinner that evening was unusually stilted. Every member of the party seemed engrossed in his own affairs. When the ladies retired and left the men to their port, Mark sighed and relaxed.

"Did you have a chance to see your man today?" the older man asked.

"No. But Lord Sefton said he would probably be at the ball this evening. What kind of luck did you have?"

"The same as usual. No one will commit himself. That duel and the trial have left everyone afraid of his shadow. It's no wonder the country has problems. The people leading it are incompetent. They'd never have lasted in India."

"Someone has got to be made to help."

"Tonight may be our last opportunity. Keep your ears open." Sir Henry stood up and sighed, "We mustn't keep the ladies waiting any longer."

As Jane sat close beside Mark in the darkness of the coach, she sensed the tension in him, tension that seemed to grow worse as they inched their way up the crowded staircase to the ballroom above. She herself was filled with anticipation. Sir Henry had been right when he said she would enjoy the balls and parties. She had.

As the musicians struck the opening notes for the first set, Jane was claimed by her dancing partner, a handsome young man who did much to relieve the faint worry that troubled her. Laughing up at her escort, she allowed him to sweep her into the figures of the dance.

Two hours later as Mark emerged grim-faced from the meeting he had been seeking for days, the first couple he saw were Sir Henry and Jane. His head thrown back, the older man seemed convulsed with laughter as he whirled his partner about the floor. Jane, her eyelashes fluttering wildly, flirted with him as though he were her lover.

The music ended, Sir Henry led Jane to Mark. As they approached, he heard Sir Henry ask, "Well, my dear, do you regret your decision?"

"Tonight? No. But in the morning, perhaps. You wouldn't want me to make a rash judgment, would you? I'll talk about it tomorrow."

"You minx! Determined to keep me in suspense a while longer, eh?" He handed her over to Mark. "I advise you to keep a careful eye on her, sir. She's a wicked little thing."

He smiled at them both. "Go on. The supper dance will be beginning shortly."

Stiffly, Mark led Jane to the floor, smoothing the frown from his face. How dare this little chit lead his friend on! he thought. Why, even the clothes on her back came from Sir Henry.

The dance Jane had been looking forward to was a disappointment. Mark was an excellent dancer, but he seemed so far away. His distance and his disapproval continued throughout supper.

That disapproval was a factor in her conversation with Sir Henry the next morning. She had made certain that he would not escape her, instructing her maid to call her as soon as anyone in the household started stirring. When Sir Henry entered the breakfast room, he stopped in surprise. "Up rather early for the belle of the ball, aren't you, my dear?"

"I might have missed you if I weren't."

Sir Henry took a deep breath and promised, "After breakfast, without fail. But first I must have my coffee." A short while later he was as good as his word. "Well, my dear, what is the problem?"

"I was rather disturbed to learn that you have discussed my plans with my man of business, Sir Henry."

"Your father would have wanted me to do it."

"I doubt it. Other than wanting to keep me at home—more for his comfort than mine, I might add—my father allowed me to make my own decisions."

"About what to wear and your reading material. Not about your reputation."

"My father never gave a thought to my reputation."

"You're right. He didn't. And that's part of the problem."

"What do you mean?"

Sir Henry stood looking into the roaring fire. Then he faced Jane, his countenance unusually grave. "Had your father cared more about you and less about his comfort he would have seen to your presentation years ago. I tried to reason with him, but he simply refused to listen."

"You tried to get him to present me?" Jane asked, stunned. "Why didn't you say anything?"

"He refused to allow me to mention it. You know what he was like. There was no further reason to talk about it once he had made up his mind."

"When did this happen?"

"Shortly after I moved into your neighborhood. Jane, I couldn't do anything then. Let me help you now. Please?"

"Hortense doesn't really want to present me. And all Mark does is frown at me."

"That's an improvement over his indifference. Remember, if you still want to remove to Bath in the spring, I'll have Hortense find you a companion. Just stay until spring. You don't want to spend Christmas alone." He smiled at her encouragingly.

Remembering her last Christmas, she looked at him and smiled. "Just until spring."

CHAPTER
3

When Jane awoke several mornings later, she breathed a sigh of relief as she looked around her. The soft blue wallpaper with its thin silver stripes and the matching blue curtains and bed hangings were clean, soothing, and best of all, still. The roads to Dorset had been less than good even in Sir Henry's well-sprung carriage. More than once she had regretted her decision to winter in the country, and more than once she had envied the gentlemen their horses.

Stretching, Jane winced. Not even the soft feather bed protected her bruises. She was reaching for the bellpull when her door swung open to reveal her maid. "I've brought your tea, miss. Mrs. Morgan is breakfasting in her room this morning, and the gentlemen have already left." Betty placed the tray carefully on her mistress's lap, then crossed the room to pull back the curtains. "Here's a note Sir Henry's man asked me to give you."

Jane took the note from her maid, carefully placing the delicate cup back on her breakfast tray. As she broke the seal and opened the note, she smiled. As the words sank in, her smile changed. He had arranged for Mark to show her the countryside. They would leave after luncheon if she wished to go. "Take the tray, Betty. No, I've had quite enough. My robe, please." She crossed to the pretty writing desk beneath the windows and dashed off her reply. "Make certain Sir Henry gets this as soon as he returns. And hurry back, please."

An afternoon with the most fascinating man she had ever met, a man who disapproved of her. Well, she wouldn't be bored. Sir Henry had promised her that. For the few minutes she was alone, Jane did an impulsive waltz around the room. "Sir Henry, you are a darling!" she said, laughing as she danced past the door to the hall.

Mark, returning from a discouraging inspection of his own home, stopped beside the slightly open door. Cursing himself for his feeling of desolation, he pulled his shoulders erect and walked slowly toward the stairs to his suite, his face a grim mask.

As Jane donned her new wine velvet riding habit and had her maid arrange her hair to fit under the rakish hat that completed the ensemble, Hortense gathered the reins of the household back into her capable hands. "The menus will be fine with the additions I have suggested. Do remind Alberto that Sir Henry must not eat strawberries. They give him a terrible rash. I'm certain it was only an oversight last evening. Fortunately, I tasted the jam cakes first."

As Mrs. Marsden nodded her head in understanding, Hortense continued, "We will be entertaining more than usual this season. As soon as Sir Henry gives me all the details, we will make the arrangements." Hortense smiled at the housekeeper and nodded her dismissal. As the woman hurried from the room, eager to dismay the encroaching individual who reigned over the kitchen, Hortense sighed despondently. She did so enjoy running this establishment.

As the bell for luncheon sounded, the only one in the group with high spirits was Jane.

After a luncheon of fluffy omelets bursting with mushrooms and herbs, baked trout with almonds, and rich cake with sherry sauce, Mark seemed in much better spirits. Pulling out his pocket watch, he looked at it pointedly and then at Jane.

Taking the hint, Jane dashed off to put on her hat. Tripping down the stairs to the entryway where Mark and Sir Henry waited, she heard Sir Henry say, "Here's your riding partner now. Now, off with you. Enjoy yourselves."

For both Jane and Mark, the afternoon was a revelation. To Mark's surprise, Jane was interested in every detail of country life. She enjoyed meeting the tenants and asked intelligent questions about problems in the area.

For the next few days, they spent hours together. Every morning Mark would visit his home, and every afternoon he escorted her around the district. To his delight, the cliffs looking over the Channel, his favorite spot, was the one place she always asked to see once more. After visiting the farms and barns in the outlying district, they would swing by his home and then on to the cliffs above the beach where he moored his yacht.

After several visits, Jane asked, "Come spring may I go out with you?"

"Have you ever sailed before?"

"In the center of England? No, of course not. But I've longed to. To roam the world under snapping canvas. It sounds so exciting."

"And dangerous."

"But so is riding a horse. And thousands of people do that. Please, Mark, just once?"

Unable to resist the pleading gray eyes with the wicked sparkle, he agreed. "But only if Sir Henry approves."

"He will. Especially when I tell him how much I want to go."

And she probably is right, he thought cynically. She has only to smile at him and he does what she wants. And then he laughed at himself. And so do I.

Jane and Mark cantered up to the abbey steps and dismounted. "Oh, it is so beautiful here," said Jane with a lift in her voice.

"Beautiful? With all the fields bare. Come now." Mark mocked her.

"Not the fields. The sea. It's so glorious. So wild and free."

"Trying to recruit another sailor, my boy?" Sir Henry asked.

"Can you imagine? Jane had never seen the sea before she came here."

"Not everyone has had your experience."

Suddenly Mark was no longer the laughing, carefree man he had been only moments before. "And I don't want anyone to have."

"What do you mean?" Jane asked, puzzled by the suppressed anger in Mark's voice.

Hastily Sir Henry drew her to one side. "I'll explain it to you later," he whispered. He continued in a louder tone. "Shortly after you left, Jane, several packages arrived for you from London. From Madame Camille's, I believe."

"The rest of my clothes! Excuse me, gentlemen." Turning, she ran lightly up the stairs, one hand holding the long skirts of her riding habit out of the way. As she reached the bend in the stairs, she waved. For a moment she paused, puzzled by Mark's clearly disapproving face. Slowly, thoughtfully, she continued on her way.

"More clothes?" Mark asked, his voice as disapproving as his face.

"Yes. Poor child, her father allowed her such a pittance for clothes when he was alive. With all the parties this winter, she needs a much larger wardrobe." As he spoke Sir Henry led the way into the library, a comfortable room filled with leather furniture and the musty smell of books.

As Mark followed, he reviewed the outfits he had already seen and made an awed guess at the total cost of Jane's shopping expeditions. "Damn fripperies," he muttered, remembering the way the feather on her rakish black hat caressed her ear.

"Now what have you found?" the older man asked, settling into his favorite chair.

"Just what we suspected. Most of the grain is gone. Within a week or two we'll have animals starving. And then it will be people!" Mark leaned against the mantel, his despair evident. "There should be a law."

"There is. And it favors those bloodsuckers in London. Pull yourself together, man. We have a stopgap, the grain we bought in London."

"And after it's gone?"

"There has to be a way."

While Mark and Sir Henry tried to find solutions to their problems, Jane was unpacking the massive array of boxes. But in the back of her mind was the look on Mark's face.

CHAPTER

4

Dinner that evening was depressing. Hortense was at her most languid. Her eyes seemed so heavy at times Jane thought she was asleep. Even her speech was slower than usual.

Mark, too, seemed affected by some malady. His usual quiet deep voice had a sharp edge to it as he refused yet another dish. And when Sir Henry complimented Jane on her new mauve wool frock, Mark's eyes positively glowered at the pair. Time after time, the older man tried to draw Mark and Hortense into the conversation, but between them they managed little more than a sentence.

As the last course was removed from the table, Sir Henry gave up his efforts and devoted his attention to Jane.

"Yes, it's so different from what I've been used to, so quiet and peaceful."

"Have you had a chance to meet any of the people?" he asked.

"Some of your and Mark's tenants. Oh, Sir Henry, they seem so worried. Isn't there anything you can do?"

"We're trying, my dear," he said soothingly. "But the problems are so widespread. A bad harvest affects everyone."

"If everyone is finished," Hortense drawled, "let us retire to the small salon, Jane. The gentlemen undoubtedly wish time with their port and their tobacco." Seeing her hostess rise, Jane had little choice but to follow.

Within a few minutes Sir Henry had joined them. Crossing the room to a chair opposite the settee where the two ladies were seated, he said, "Hortense, with the Christmas season approaching, the county will be ablaze with parties. We must be sure to introduce Jane at once."

"How soon would you suggest, Henry?" she asked. "Next week is still open. Perhaps by then Jane will have found time to make some calls with me."

Jane blushed at the criticism in Hortense's voice. "I would be most happy to accompany you, ma'am, whenever you suggest. I will cancel my ride with Mark for tomorrow so that I will be free."

At that, Sir Henry cleared his throat and rose to pace the floor. "Well, yes. Perhaps we should discuss that later, my dear."

"Don't let my presence disturb you," said Hortense smoothly. "With a party to plan I have more than enough to occupy my time."

"If there is anything I can help you with . . ."

Hortense gave Jane a keen look and then nodded. Keeping a firm control on her emotions, she rose and drifted toward the door. "I will see you at breakfast then," she said quietly.

As soon as the door had closed behind her, Jane turned toward Sir Henry. "What is the problem, sir?" Sir Henry refused to look her in the eye. "Please don't try to fob me off with a Banbury tale."

Squaring his shoulders and clearing his throat, her friend said in a rush, "It's about your rides." He paused as if trying to find some new words. "Mark asked me to express his regrets. The work at his home is progressing at such a slow rate that he feels he must spend more time supervising."

As she understood what he was trying to say, her face assumed the mask that he had seen many times before. A sweet smile did not hide the disappointment that she kept carefully hidden in her voice. "How demanding he must think me. Of course, I quite understand." She blinked rapidly to dissolve the tears that gathered. "His home must be his first consideration." Shaking her skirts out, she rose. "And now, if you will excuse me. It's been a long day." With a quick curtsy she was gone with only a flick of her mauve skirt to mark her passage.

"Damn!" The echo of the oath followed her up the stairs. By the time she had reached her room, Jane's tears flowed freely. Pacing the floor in front of the hearth, she sobbed. Finally she sank to the floor and buried her head in her arms. Not since her father's death had she felt so alone, so bereft.

Determined to hide her feelings, Jane appeared to be her usual bright self as she entered the breakfast room the next morning. Even Mark's curt "Good morning" did little more than cause her a momentary hesitation.

"What may I help you with today?" she asked, a slightly forced laugh in her voice, as she greeted Hortense.

Hortense waved her to her seat. "If you've a readable hand, our first job will be the invitations," she said as if conferring a great honor.

Nodding her agreement, Jane sank into her chair and smiled at the tall man who waited for her orders. "Some tea, a slice of ham, and one of those delicious rolls will be fine."

As he watched her smile at the footman, Mark frowned. Flirting in front of Sir Henry, and with a footman, too.

While Jane made a determined effort to contribute her share of the conversation, Mark was noticeably quiet. Hurriedly he downed the last of his ale and made his escape.

Almost every day was a repeat of that one. Mark glowered at her through breakfast and then disappeared for the rest of the day. But Jane did not have time to worry about it. Almost before she finished the first task, Hortense would find a new one. As Jane fell into bed each evening, she wondered what new plans Hortense had made. And plans there were. After supervising the maids, there was the linen check, the meeting with the irascible gardner, and a quick trip to the village for extra ribbon for the meringue baskets. At times it seemed almost as if Hortense were testing her.

After years of longing for parties, Jane was beginning to change her mind. Not that it wasn't exciting. It was. But she longed for a moment to herself.

At breakfast the morning of the party, the men quickly made their escape. Like a general marshaling her troops, Hortense checked each detail, from the appointments of the dinner table to the champagne supper she planned to serve at midnight.

Finally Jane made her escape. Breathing a sigh of relief, she shut the door to her room behind her. As she shed her clothes to enjoy the steaming tub before the fire, she deliberately shut out all the noise and relaxed. Only when the water had cooled did she emerge to sit before the fire. As Betty brushed her hair, Jane smiled, the remnants of the tension of the last few days slipping from her.

Working with Hortense had been enlightening. The lady was a power to reckon with. Attending parties and the theater with her in London had been delightful. The rides with Mark had provided a welcome distraction. But during the last few days Jane had been frustrated. Even when her father was alive, she had gone her own way, been the mistress of the house. And although she had not realized it at the time, she had enjoyed her power. As she had helped prepare for the party she had had to watch her tongue. Hortense had said, time after time, "Jane, how clever. But that's not the way I prefer it done." Gritting her teeth, she had wanted to scream. She had promised Sir Henry that she would stay until spring. After that—well, she would decide that when the time came.

Betty was putting the last pin in place in the elaborate confection of riotous curls and intricate coils of hair when someone scratched on the door.

"For the young lady," said Sir Henry's valet with a bow.

Jane opened the small flat velvet box. There on a nest of

satin lay a beautifully matched set of pink pearls with a rose-shaped diamond clasp. Slowly, she opened the accompanying note. "In place of a nosegay, will you accept this rose? Your 'guardian.' "

"Oh, miss, how lovely. They match your dress."

Thinking of how closely her friend had questioned her about what she was going to wear, Jane smiled. "Help me with my dress. I want to see how they look."

The last hook in place, the last button on her long gloves buttoned, Jane stood before the mirror. She knew she had never looked better. From the tips of her silver-gilt curls to her silver slippers she glowed. The soft dusty rose of her dress made her cheeks come alive with color, her eyes sparkle. The deep neckline trimmed in silver lace made her neck and shoulders seem alabaster-white, a perfect foil for the soft pink pearls.

'You'll be the toast of the evening," Betty said, her voice ringing with pride.

Jane smiled at her maid, glanced at the clock, and hurried from the room. Entering the large drawing room a few minutes later, Jane drew a breath of relief. She had thought she was late. She crossed to the mantel where Sir Henry was standing and dropped him a curtsy. Rising, she leaned up and placed a soft kiss on his sun-browned cheek. "Thank you, my friend, but I wonder if I should accept them."

"We'll let Hortense be your guide," he said, leading her to the chair where the older woman stood. "Hortense, is it proper for a guardian to give his ward pearls for a party in her honor?" he asked, one eyebrow slightly raised.

"Pearls? Quite unexceptional and quite correct," she replied, pleased that her dismay was not evident in her voice. She sank to the ivory settee, carefully settling her soft amethyst skirts. She held out a hand sparkling with diamonds. "Come, let me see them, my dear."

"See what?" asked Mark as he entered the room, his dark looks enhanced by his Corbeau-colored coat.

"Her pearls. Sir Henry gave them to her. Aren't they lovely?"

For a moment Mark stood completely still, an accusing look in his eyes. Taking a deep breath, he advanced, bowed, and said formally, "They are a lovely addition to a lovely lady." Before Jane could do more than smile at him, he had turned to Hortense. "And you too are a vision tonight. Don't you agree, Sir Henry, that we will be the envy of the gentlemen in the district?"

As Hortense smiled up at him delighted, Jane, through long years of practice, kept her smile. Marsden's entrance to announce the first guests helped to give her time to hide her confusion. By the time dinner was announced, Jane had captivated more than one gentleman and won the approval of several of the ladies and the distrust of at least one matchmaking mother. The food was a gastronomic delight, and her dinner partners were interesting. The man on her right, an older bachelor who owned a small property nearby, took one look at her and said, "Quite rare, you know."

"I beg your pardon?"

"Pearls that color. Must have taken some time to match. Good investment, too."

"They were a gift."

"Wise person. Just the right color for your skin. Too many people want only the silver-white ones. Not good with everyone's skin."

"Are pearls supposed to match skin?"

"Certainly. But a person needs to be an expert to tell," he explained. "My hobby, collecting gems. Especially natural stones such as pearls and amber. Coral, too."

By the end of the soup, Jane had learned the complete process of the development of a pearl. As she turned her attention to her young dinner partner on the left, she was delighted when he uttered a complete sentence. "Miss Woodley, I have been admiring you all evening. I am not too late to request a dance?"

"I should warn you that I've had little practice," she said

laughingly. Accepting a lobster patty, she suggested, "Perhaps you should wait until you've seen me on the floor."

"A lady as graceful as you could not be less than a superb dancer."

Content for the moment to smile her most captivating smile and allow the young man to drown her in compliments, Jane forgot about the frown on Mark's face. "Where did you learn to turn such a pretty phrase?" she asked, her eyelashes sweeping her blushing cheeks and then fluttering up again.

"At Oxford."

"Are you certain? All Oxford taught my father was the classics."

"Oh, but times have changed."

"And so have the students."

From compliments to gems to compliments again, Jane nibbled on the roast partridge, refused the turbot soufflé, selected a spoonful of green peas, and finished with a morsel of spongecake. By the time Hortense signaled the ladies to retire, she had two devoted admirers who would have been happy to monopolize every dance. Later as the party moved into the ballroom to await the other guests, Jane took her place in the receiving line beside Hortense and Sir Henry. As the remaining guests were introduced, Jane smiled until she thought her face would crack. She had almost decided to plead faintness to escape from the crowded ballroom when Marsden announced, "Lieutenant James Dancy."

As the man moved from a gracious but overly polite Sir Henry to a clearly delighted Hortense, Jane thought she had never seen such a handsome man. His guinea-gold curls à la Brutus glinted in the light of the reflected candles. Although his shoulders were not as impressive as Mark's, he had an admirable figure. As Hortense introduced him to Jane, he bowed and then looked into her clear gray eyes with his own midnight-blue ones. For a few seconds his smile held her prisoner. Finally realizing that the man was still holding her hand, Jane pulled it loose.

Hortense's whispered "Jane, here are the next guests"

forced her attention to an older couple. As one group after another were introduced, Jane caught herself searching the floor for a man with golden curls and deep blue eyes in a dark blue coat.

When Sir Henry gave the signal for the orchestra to begin the first dance, Jane turned expectantly toward him.

"Your first dance is free?"

"Yes, for my host."

"No, here is your partner now." Sir Henry smiled at Mark, who was crossing to his side. The frown that had been so evident on Mark's face earlier in the evening was absent, but to Jane it was evident that he was there because of his sense of duty.

"Sir Henry," Jane asked quietly, "did you ask?"

"Mark to be your partner for the first dance? Certainly. He's a much better dancer than I."

Her heart beating madly, Jane smiled breathlessly at the man who bowed to her.

"Miss Woodley," he said formally as he offered her his arm to lead her to the floor. His dark eyes seemed to search her face carefully. As his hand closed over her waist for the waltz that Hortense had declared must be the first dance of the evening, Jane caught her breath. As they circled the room with every eye on them, it was all she could do to breathe. After one circuit of the floor, other couples joined them, creating a kaleidoscope of colors.

Taking a deep breath, she asked, "How is the work on your house progressing? I hope I didn't contribute to its delay."

If Jane had expected Mark to admit how much he had enjoyed their rides, she was soon corrected. "Fortunately the days I showed you around the countryside also enabled me to check on my tenants. I would have had to do that in any case. Although I had neglected my home, the work is now progressing on schedule." His voice was cold.

Caught in his arms, Jane froze and almost stumbled. Quickly she regained control. Although she didn't lose her smile, it changed. The last strains of the lilting music faded away as Mark released her conveniently near the spot where Hortense and Sir Henry stood.

"Thank you," Mark said stiltedly.

Remembering her manners, Jane replied, "It was my pleasure." As he turned and walked away, his limp slightly more pronounced than usual, she turned toward the older couple, determined to maintain her poise. Before she had taken more than two steps, her new partner had arrived and swept her into a set that was forming.

For the next hour Jane was passed from one gentleman to another, each trying to entertain her, to amuse her, to capture her attention. And she let them. But no matter how hard she tried she could not ignore the way Mark was dancing attendance on a willowy redhead in a daring pomona-green crepe over a white satin slip. Although he had only danced with the redhead once, Mark had brought her punch before sitting out another dance. Frantically reviewing the people she had been introduced to, Jane tried to remember the lady's name.

As she sat out a dance to catch her breath, her partner hastened toward the punch bowl.

"Alone, Miss Woodley?" a voice asked, its accent holding a hint of mystery.

"Only for a moment, Lieutenant Dancy. My partner will be returning shortly."

"A few minutes will do nicely."

"Nicely? For what?"

"For me to request a dance. Never say you've already promised them all."

"There is one." Jane glanced at the chairs where Mark sat, his eyes never leaving the redhead in green.

"Good." Scribbling his name on her card, he rose as her partner returned.

Shortly afterward Hortense made her way to her side.

"Have you promised a dance to Lieutenant Dancy?" she asked. At Jane's nod, she whispered, "Which one? A waltz I hope."

"No." Jane paused and then rushed on. "Who is that lovely redhead in the green crepe?"

"You must mean Miss Sybil Westmoreland. Isn't she delightful? I can quite understand why Mark is so captivated by her." She leaned closer to Jane. "She's a heiress, you know."

At that moment Jane smiled up at her next partner and escaped onto the floor. And there she stayed, being handed from one partner to another, hoping that she would remember their names when next they appeared.

The man whose name she knew she would remember was Lieutenant James Dancy. As he led her through the figures of the set, his blue eyes laughed and flashed at her. "I refuse to be ignored," he said in her ear.

"Ignored?"

"As you have most of your previous partners."

"I haven't," she said, her gray eyes flashing with indignation.

"Perhaps 'ignored' was too strong. 'Dismissed,' then."

"What?"

"You're magnificent," he said. "Without a doubt you're the most outstanding lady in the room."

"And the rudest?"

"That is not what I said."

"But it's what you meant." Gradually the other dancers in the set realized that an argument was building. As more and more attention focused on her, Jane bit her tongue. Fuming but quiet, she walked from the floor as the music ended.

"May I call tomorrow?" Dancy asked.

"Call? On a lady who is rude?" Jane asked sarcastically.

"On the most beautiful lady in the room, a lady who will not soon forget me. I promised myself I would make you remember my name. You didn't seem to pay attention when I complimented you."

"I'm not certain I care for your methods."

"But you will see me again? You can be sure I'll never bore you."

"Bore me, no. Anger me, yes."

"And which is best? A morning or afternoon call?"

"Afternoon." She stopped and then laughed ruefully. "Yes, lieutenant, you may call tomorrow."

For the rest of the evening Jane was aware of a pair of blue eyes that laughed at her across the room. For a lady who had longed for attention, it was a heady feeling.

As long as the music played, she danced and laughed. Eventually, though, the musicians put their instruments away, the guests departed, and she was alone in her bedroom once more.

Then it was not the anger that Lieutenant Dancy had caused or the rush of pride from the heady compliments she had been given that she remembered. No, as tired as she was, she lay awake hearing over and over again Mark's cutting words, watching him laugh with Miss Westmoreland.

CHAPTER
5

Long before anyone else was up, Jane was awake. Glancing at the clock on the mantel, she yawned. She had been asleep for only two hours. As she tossed and turned trying to get comfortable, she realized that although she was still tired she would not be able to go right back to sleep.

Climbing out of bed, Jane retrieved her warm robe. She paused to light a few candles and to throw a log on the fire, shivering in the frosty air. Quickly she hopped back in bed and drew the covers close around her.

Once she was warm again, the memories of the previous evening surrounded her. Lieutenant Dancy was so handsome. Those blue eyes. But no matter how hard Jane tried to concentrate on the dashing officer a pair of disapproving dark brown eyes intervened. "I won't think about him. I won't," Jane muttered through clenched teeth. In spite of her efforts, guinea-gold curls gave way to broad shoulders and lean hips.

"No, I don't care about him! I couldn't!" she cried futilely into her soft pillows, sobs wrenching her body. Finally, exhausted by her tears, she drifted off to a sleep troubled by dreams.

When she awoke several hours later, her head ached and her eyes were swollen. As soon as her maid realized Jane was awake, her chatter filled the room. "What a wonderful party it was, Miss Jane! After supper was served, we had a midnight supper of our own. Did you ever see so many wonderful dishes? My mouth fairly watered, it did. And one of the coachmen brought his squeeze box. It was smashing." As Betty bustled about the room, Jane lay quietly, a hand over her eyes. "Mrs. Morgan told everyone to sleep late this morning. Why, we slept past the rising bell. A positive disgrace, according to Mrs. Marsden. A day after a party is almost as frantic as the actual day. Are you ready to dress now?" she asked.

Her voice slightly husky, Jane said, "Betty, check with Henshaw, Mrs. Morgan's dresser, to see what is planned for today."

For the first time that morning the maid glanced at her mistress. Startled by her red eyes, Betty nodded and hurried away. By the time Jane had slipped out of bed and made her way to the tea tray in the sitting room, Betty was back. "According to Henshaw, the mistress is still abed. She's not to be disturbed before luncheon. She'll be down in time to receive afternoon callers, though."

Needing some time to herself, Jane smiled her thanks. "You can take this away." She gestured to the tea tray. "And I think I'll follow Mrs. Morgan's example. I'll ring when I need you."

When she was finally alone again, Jane sat at the writing desk and stared out the window. After a few minutes she rose and began her pacing, muttering to herself.

Finally, as though the words were a flood she was helpless to stop, as if she had to explain to herself, she said, "The toast of the evening! A belle! Just what you always wanted!" She paused and looked out the window, catching a brief glimpse of Mark mounted on a tall black gelding heading across the fields to his home. Her breath caught on a sob.

"For six years you've dreamed of dancing the night away.

Of being noticed.'' She leaned against the windowpane hoping to catch one last glimpse of that rider, but he was gone.

"Six years I've waited." The resentment Jane had tried so hard to repress came flooding back. She hadn't wanted to leave their home in Oxford for the small market village, but her father had given her no choice. It was as if her witty and sometimes irrascible father had been replaced by a dour stranger who begrudged her his time and the little money she required for the housekeeping.

Jane glanced around at her comfortable rooms. She had been so hungry for beautiful surroundings. Had Mrs. Hawkins not told her of the talk in the village she would have refurnished the squire's house during her year of mourning. Thinking of those drab furnishings she had been forced to live with, she grew angry at the way her father had sold her mother's belongings. Jane's eyes filled with tears as she remembered begging him, "Just her piano, Father. Let me keep her piano." But it as well as the rest of her mother's favorites had been sold. The few pieces she had bought this last year had done little to compensate for their loss.

"Oh, Father, I loved you so. Why did you shut yourself away?" she whispered sadly. Only Sir Henry had had any success reaching him, and even he had known his limits.

"Sir Henry." Jane stopped her pacing for a few minutes. She was going to have to have a serious discussion with him shortly. That speculative gleam in his eye as he had watched Mark and her dancing last evening had put her on edge.

"Mark," she said yearningly. Giving herself a shake, she began to pace again. Granted, he captivated her. But he also disapproved of her. "It should be just as easy to learn to care for someone who admires me," she told herself. A rather secretive smile lit her face as she reached for the bellpull.

The afternoon provided her a perfect opportunity to test her decision. As Hortense drifted languidly toward the settee, Marsden announced the first guest. "Lady Brough and Miss Westmoreland," said Marsden in his most formal voice.

"How delightful you look, Miss Westmoreland," Hortense said, greeting the pair. "Do you remember Miss Woodley?"

As the ladies smiled and took their seats, Jane noticed a slight frown cross the younger woman's face.

"Are you recovered from your long evening? I vowed that nothing would bring me out today but my dear Hortense. I am quite exhausted," Lady Bourne said, her smile slightly forced.

"Yes, parties are so fatiguing. And somehow the gentlemen never understand," Hortense agreed.

"Yes, they simply are insensitive. Have they deserted you, Miss Woodley? I would have thought that a guest in the house would expect some attention from them." Lady Brough's tones were as coldly condescending as those Jane had heard for six years from the squire's wife.

"I refuse to be greedy, Lady Brough. After all, I did have Mr. Courtland to myself until it was time to help prepare for my party. And, of course, Sir Henry is always attentive," Jane said, almost smugly. She smiled at the older woman.

"Of course, they've both been so busy," Hortense added. "Why, even today Mark is at his home overseeing the renovations."

"He is? But when Mama and I were there . . .."

"An errand my husband asked us to do for him," her mother said hastily. "So important to be on good terms with your neighbors, don't you agree?"

"Naturally. We were so delighted when Mark agreed to stay here at the Abbey. He's such a wonderfully thoughtful person," Hortense said.

Much to the younger girl's annoyance, Jane simply smiled.

As the afternoon slipped away, Hortense was gratified by the number of callers. But Jane was waiting. Just as she had almost given up hope, he was there.

"Good afternoon, Miss Woodley," he said after greeting his hostess.

"Lieutenant Dancy."

"You remembered my name." He took a chair close to

hers and leaned closer to whisper. "Now dismiss these others so that we can talk."

"You presume too much, sir." Jane drew back, frowning.

"Have I offended you? Would you prefer me to lie, to pay attention to others?"

"I think you should be less personal, sir. I hardly know you." Jane's voice was as crisp and cold as the December air.

As the lieutenant leaned over to continue his conversation, Hortense said coyly, "Oh, Lieutenant Dancy, it is so reassuring to have you in charge of our district. One hears such frightful stories of smugglers in other places. Since you arrived last summer, there has been scarcely a rumor of them here."

"And no French brandy either," muttered one of the gentlemen in the background.

"Your superiors must be so pleased with you," Hortense said, giving him her slow smile.

"Thank you for your support. My men and I try to keep control. I take defeat personally." He smiled at Jane. She moved restlessly, uncomfortable at the possessive gleam in his eye.

When the door opened and Sir Henry walked in, Jane smiled and crossed the room. Sliding her arm through his, she stayed by his side as he greeted his guests. As if his appearance had been the signal for the callers to leave, one by one they made their farewells.

Whether by accident or design, Lieutenant Dancy was the last to leave. "I'll see you again soon," he promised Jane as he bowed to her. "I want us to become better acquainted." The last words were said so softly that only Jane heard them. Startled, she looked straight into his eyes and shivered.

As soon as the door closed behind him, Sir Henry, his face stormy, asked, "And who invited that encroaching bully here?"

"Now, Henry. You know Lieutenant Dancy is invited everywhere," Hortense began.

"To parties. Not to call on the ladies of the household."

"Lady Brough receives him. If she does, I do not see that we can do less. It would be tantamount to an insult."

"Well, I don't like him."

Jane, although she had her own reservations about the man, wasn't ready to give up a gentleman who had made his preference so clear. "And he's so handsome," she said, a smile in her voice.

"Handsome! Ha!"

"Henry, if you have some specific reason for disliking the man, I'm certain Jane and I will respect your wishes." Hortense looked over at the younger lady, who nodded her agreement.

"He's—he's—blast!"

"Until then I see no harm in permitting his calls." Hortense smiled calmly. "Now, Jane, don't you think we should retire to dress for dinner? It's been such a long afternoon."

That evening Jane dressed carefully. The soft burgundy velvet with its long sleeves was both warm and lovely. Once again she wore the pearls Sir Henry had given her. Glancing in the mirror before she left her dressing room, she compared herself to the person she had been only two short months ago. In place of the drab, colorless girl stood a person glowing with anticipation, her hair expertly coiffed, her eyes sparkling. Laughing softly, she ran down the stairs and came to a sudden halt outside the slightly open door to the small salon.

"Now, Sir Henry."

"I saw his type time after time in India. Out for himself. A worthless cad with no money and no morals."

"We'll keep an eye on him. Don't worry. I'm certain Jane is too fond of you ever to get involved with someone like him." Mark kept his voice calm and steady.

"But, women, my boy, women."

"Yes, Sir Henry?" Jane asked, slipping through the door.

For a moment he hummed and stuttered, "Yes, women, oh, women add such enjoyment to men's lives. How lovely you look tonight. Mark, isn't she delightful?"

"Delightful." Once again Mark's compliment seemed more of an insult. His bow, however, was as courteous as ever.

"Thank you, sir." She smiled at him, determined that he would not make her lose her temper. "How are the repairs coming? Lady Brough and Miss Westmoreland were quite disappointed not to find you at Courtland Place this afternoon."

"Yes, well, I had to visit one of my tenants. A problem with a roof," Mark explained hurriedly, his eyes shifting from hers to Sir Henry's.

"We thought it must be something like that. I know how you dislike anything that takes you away from the work on your house," she said, her voice full of concern. Her flashing eyes, however, told him she had not yet forgiven him for canceling their rides.

"Yes, the dear boy works so hard," Hortense said as she came in. "Everyone asked about you this afternoon."

"Especially Miss Westmoreland," Jane added.

By the time dinner was over Mark was happy to escape into the library with Sir Henry. Jane, left alone with Hortense, found she was more sympathetic with the woman than ever before. Until it was time for the tea tray, Hortense detailed their plans for the next few days: shopping at a nearby town for the last few Christmas gifts, overseeing the details for the tenants' party, afternoon visits of their own, and the beginning of the Christmas parties.

"I hope you won't mind my advice," Hortense said. "Henry simply is not an authority on young men. If you like Lieutenant Dancy, don't allow Henry to discourage him."

"But, Cousin Hortense!"

"No. Just remember that women are much better judges of character than men. Especially when the man being judged is so handsome. Don't you agree?"

Jane smiled and nodded, thinking of how distinguished his uniform made him. If he weren't so—so pushy, she thought.

Although London had been exciting, the party Sir Henry had given for her marked the beginning of the life Jane had always wanted. She enjoyed the shopping in spite of the limited selection in the village stores. Even helping Hortense prepare for the tenants' party was not as difficult as she had feared it would be. But the afternoon calls and the parties were exactly what she had hoped for. Under Hortense's chaperonage she was received by the best families of the countryside, not just received but welcomed. Only Lady Brough showed any reserve.

Quickly Jane established a growing circle of friends, the gentlemen who made certain she never lacked a partner as well as some of the younger married ladies who were delighted to open their circle to her.

One evening as Betty was brushing her hair, Jane smiled and whispered, "Sir Henry was right. Bath would never be like this."

"What, miss?"

"Nothing." Jane looked at herself in the mirror and almost laughed. How grand she had become.

The only dark cloud on Jane's horizon was Mark. He seemed never to be at home. If she rose early for breakfast, she might see him, but more often than not he was already away. For the last few days he had also missed dinner.

One morning after Jane had spent what seemed like hours listening to Hortense and Mrs. Marsden discussing the menu for the tenants' party for the third day in a row, Jane made her escape. Whisking down the back stairs to avoid Hortense's inevitable suggestions for a new project, Jane thought longingly of those quiet mornings she had enjoyed in the past. Quietly she made her way down. With Mark gone and Sir Henry meeting with his bailiff in the office the library would be deserted. And it was one place Hortense would not think to look.

Jane had just passed the bend in the stairs when she heard a noise in the hallway beneath her. Slipping back around the corner, she peered cautiously down the stairs. It was Mark. Furtively he glanced down the hall and then slipped toward the library. Although it was a clear day, he was wet and shivering. Slipping down the stairs as quietly as she could, she watched Mark open the door of the library and slide inside.

Curious, Jane followed. Hearing the low rumble of voices inside the room, she quietly turned the latch, all the while reproaching herself for her curiosity. With the door open enough for her to peek through, she hesitated.

She had just begun to close the door when she heard Sir Henry ask, "What happened? I expected you back last evening. Was it a success?"

"Of sorts. We ran into some problems. I'm sure that lieutenant suspects something. His patrols were out all night," Mark said, his voice tired.

"What about your men?"

"Safe. And loyal to the man."

"The cargo?"

"Safe. Let me have some more of that brandy. I thought the boat was going to be swamped, the waves were so high."

"Any trouble in Holland?" Sir Henry paused, looking at the tired and wet man standing on the hearth. "Listen to me—I sound like a veritable judge. Come on, my boy, we need to get you into some dry clothes. I imagine you need some rest too. Later we can talk about distributing the goods."

CHAPTER

6

Startled, Jane gasped. Before she had time to escape, Sir Henry was on her. Seizing her arm, he pulled her into the library and shut the door.

"How long have you been there?" he demanded, his face more stern than Jane had ever seen it. She trembled at the look in his snapping black eyes.

"Too long. She obviously heard something," Mark said, tossing off the last of his brandy and putting the glass on the table. He had pulled off his wet shirt and stood before the fire, his broad chest covered with dark curls; he was drying himself with the cloth from the serving table.

Jane, after one brief glance, kept her eyes on the floor. Her cheeks flamed.

"Well, what do you have to say for yourself, miss?" Sir Henry asked.

Jane tried to speak, but only a squeak came out. Clearing her throat, she was finally able to whisper. "I'm sorry. Please believe me. I won't tell anyone. But why? Oh, Sir Henry, do you need money?"

"Money? Gad, girl, just what do you think is happening?"

"I don't doubt she has already decided. Haven't you?" asked Mark silkily. Friends who had known him for years would have warned Jane that his deep purr meant danger.

"Oh, how could you? And taking others into danger. You're despicable," she said, her voice angry.

"Despicable, am I? Well, at least I don't go listening at keyholes."

"No, you're helping the enemy."

The men looked at each other, puzzled.

"Jane, wait," Sir Henry said. "Exactly what did you hear?"

She drew herself up to her tallest height. "I heard you discuss hiding from Lieutenant Dancy and his patrols. I know what that means. You're smugglers. Sir Henry, as your guest I feel I cannot inform on you. But I can no longer remain here. I will be leaving tomorrow."

"And rush straight to that officer and tell him everything, I wager," Mark said, his eyes never leaving her face.

"You have my word."

"The word of a snoop."

"Better a snoop than a smuggler."

Tiring of the bickering, Sir Henry said, "Stop." Although quiet, his voice carried a tone of command that could have quelled a riot. Startled, both Jane and Mark hushed and looked at him.

"Mark, you go and change. Jane and I will wait here until you return," he ordered. Mark, recognizing the good sense of this, pulled his damp shirt over his head and hurried from the room. As Jane opened her mouth, Sir Henry motioned her to a chair. "I think you'll be comfortable here. Would you care for some tea?"

She sank into the large leather chair by the hearth and shook her head. Her heart was racing madly. Under her long lashes, she looked at the older man who stood before her on the hearth, his face an unsmiling mask.

Just as she thought she would have to jump up and run out of the room, Mark returned. His hair, usually brushed smooth, now curled slightly. And instead of a cravat he wore a Belcher scarf hurriedly knotted.

"Take a seat, Mark," Sir Henry said, waving him to a seat near the fireplace. "This may take some time." Then he turned his attention to Jane. Totally surprising her, he asked, "What did you think of the farmers in the area as you rode around with Mark?"

"They seemed good, hardworking people." She paused. "Almost too hardworking."

"And the fields?"

"Bare and dry."

"You know what kind of harvest they had?"

"Yes, it was poor." Her voice revealed her confusion.

"It was bad. As you noted, the fields are dry. Too dry to produce much. And a small harvest means problems. Where will they get the grain to feed their families and their stock?"

"Buy it?" she asked, puzzled.

"With no money? What dream world have you been living in?" Mark asked sarcastically.

"How should I know? I've always lived in town." Jane refused to allow him to intimidate her. She was fast changing her once favorable impression of him.

"Even if they had money, which they don't, there's another problem," Sir Henry said.

"I don't understand what this has to do with your smuggling," Jane said, staring at the older man with a determined look on her face.

"It has everything to do with it," he said. "Even though Mark and I, with a few others, were willing to put up the money to buy the grain, there was none to be had."

"Remember London?" Mark asked, crossing to stand immediately in front of her. "We talked to anyone who would listen. And there weren't many of those around. With the turmoil in government this year all they're interested in is keeping their jobs." His eyes flashed, and his face was stormy as he remembered the hopes and then the frustrations of those weeks.

"One man made a suggestion—not officially, of course. He gave us the name of a man who had connections in Holland," said Sir Henry.

"Holland? But doesn't Napoleon control the Low Country?" Before Mark's steady stare her eyes fell. "Oh," she said self-consciously.

"Jane, you're right in thinking us smugglers. But we have to be. The people in our district need grain for themselves and their animals if they are to survive. And if Holland is the only place we can get it, we will." In Sir Henry's voice Jane recognized the steely quality and the masterful attitude that had earned him one of the top administrative posts in India, tremendous wealth, and finally a knighthood.

"But smuggling! Aren't you taking a tremendous chance?" Jane asked, not quite certain what her reaction should be.

"Mark is an accomplished sailor. Knows these waters like the back of his hand. And when he was in the navy he helped patrol the Channel and the North Sea."

"The navy?"

One look at Mark's angry face told Sir Henry that he had better retreat, and quickly. "Jane, we can't have you leave. Everyone knows you expected to stay for some months. We simply cannot afford to create any suspicion, especially since that officer has been visiting so regularly."

"But smuggling!" Jane said again.

"For all intents and purposes, the smuggling is over," Mark said soothingly.

"Does that mean this is a one-time solution to the problem?" she asked, her voice revealing her skepticism.

"With luck, yes," Mark assured her.

She looked at him in disbelief. "Smugglers. I can hardly believe it."

"For a lady who was willing to go beyond the pale and set up housekeeping alone in Bath, your objections are hardly valid," Mark reminded her.

"But I wasn't breaking any laws."

"Only the laws of respectability."

Jane jumped to her feet, her face stormy. But before she could reply, Sir Henry intervened. "The cases are far from similar, Mark, and you know it. If we are to achieve our goal successfully, we need Jane's help. Instead of trying to antagonize her, do you think you could try to be agreeable?" Mark, a rather sheepish look on his face, nodded.

As Jane smiled smugly at his discomfort, Sir Henry turned his attention to her. "And you, miss, just what do you plan to do? Will you leave here because our actions offend your self-righteous little soul, or will you help us to help those less fortunate?"

Before the blaze in his black eyes, Jane flushed. Then her self-control reasserted itself. "Naturally I'm willing to help. But I don't see what I can do. You've already gotten the grain, haven't you?"

The older man seated her carefully. "First you must promise to stay here as you had planned and keep this story to yourself."

"Humph."

"She will, Mark. She can be trusted, can't you, my dear?"

"Of course." She shot a flashing look at the young man, who was staring at her in disbelief.

"If she encourages Dancy to hang around, we'll be in trouble for sure," Mark said.

"In trouble? Never. Think how simple it will be to keep up with his actions," said Sir Henry, smiling. "You won't mind, will you, Jane? It's your chance to help us out." He looked at her expectantly, his face serious.

Jane could tell by the way he held his shoulders so perfectly straight that he was nervous. Had his self-control been weaker she was certain he would have been toying with the fob that hung on his watch chain. As she considered the question, Jane thought about what she knew of the two men. Sir Henry believed in duty and loyalty. If he said he was smuggling only to help people, she could believe him. Mark was a different story. But he was popular with his tenants. That had to mean something.

She looked from Sir Henry, his black-clad shoulders straight and still, to the pacing figure of the younger man. Mark's dark green coat was creased as though he had simply thrown it on. Somehow the knowledge that his worry about the situation had caused him to appear in such disarray when he was usually the model of perfection reassured her. She cleared her throat, and both men turned expectantly. "I'll do it—even to entertaining Lieutenant Dancy."

Sir Henry's shoulder relaxed, but Mark still had a worried look on his face. "There's nothing to worry about, my boy. If Jane makes a promise, she keeps it."

Still not completely convinced, Mark sat in a chair on the opposite side of the fireplace. "I suppose we have to take a chance on her. We have no other choice." He glanced over to where Jane sat, her brown curls burnished by the bright morning sun, her gray eyes enormous in her excitement. The deep blue-green of her wool dress provided a perfect contrast to her creamy white skin. As he looked at her with a longing he kept determinedly to himself, Mark was lecturing himself. She's a snoop and a flirt and too argumentative, he thought. Just the type you usually avoid. Besides, think of those pearls.

Gradually the tension that had filled the room relaxed; Sir Henry summoned his butler. "We'll have some light refreshments, Marsden. If my cousin inquires, we're making plans for Courtland Place. And Marsden, tell them to bring that food quickly." When the butler had left, he turned back to the other two, who were determinedly not looking at one another. "Since Jane has discovered our secret, we have some plans to make."

"Well, if I'm going to be involved, and it appears I am, I want to know more than what you have already told me," Jane said, her voice firm. "How have you explained Mark's absence?" She paused and looked at the younger man lounging in his chair before the fire. "How long was he gone?"

Dismissing Mark's snort of annoyance, Sir Henry nodded.

"Quite right. You wouldn't want to slip up in front of that bounder Dancy. You might as well explain, Mark."

Reluctantly he began, seated at first and then walking around the room. "After we got back from London, I made a fast trip to Holland." He turned toward Jane. "I had to cancel our rides to give me time, and the preparations for the party helped cover my absence," he said as if apologizing. Immediately Jane's heart began to beat faster. "The arrangements were as simple as we had been told. With gold, we could have as much grain as we needed." He paused. "Fortunately those of us involved had already withdrawn sufficient funds to finance the venture. My sailors were ready. We sailed with a small crew, only those the captain could personally vouch for, and four of my tenants to help load and unload." His voice was so rich and dark Jane thought she could listen to it forever.

Before he could continue, there was a scratching at the door. Marsden and a footman entered with tea, a wedge of cheese, some beef, bread, and cakes. For a few minutes the adventurous tale was put aside for more practical considerations.

Their hunger satisfied, they turned their attention to the problem at hand. Mark continued his story. "We chose our time carefully. There was no moon, but it was fairly calm. At least, we thought it was calm. There was no problem with our connection. He did warn us, though, that the French were more active than in the past. But we didn't see any. After only a few hours, we were back in the Channel without a sight of a French vessel. Then the storm struck—a squall, really."

"You didn't mention this earlier," Sir Henry said. "Is everyone all right? Everything went well?"

"Bruises and scrapes, nothing more," Mark assured him. "But it slowed us down. I guess it was just as well, as things turned out."

"What do you mean?" Jane asked.

Mark glanced at Sir Henry, who gestured for him to explain. He shrugged his shoulders and said, "The clouds gave us additional darkness. When we finally made landfall, we were able to slip along the shore without being seen.'' He paused and gave a rueful laugh. "We were so pleased with ourselves we were almost caught. Stupid, that's what it was! Those blasted patrols ruined everything!''

"But you weren't caught. You didn't lose the grain, did you?'' Jane asked.

"No, it's stored in a barn on my property.''

"In a barn? But Mark!'' Sir Henry's voice revealed his anxiety.

"I know, I know. The grain should already have been distributed. We were lucky to sneak into harbor before dawn this morning and unload. But we missed the rendezvous.''

"Had the troops been to your mooring?'' asked Sir Henry.

"Of course. But I think I managed to put them off the scent. After we unloaded, we went back out, minus my tenants. When we returned this morning, we made certain we were seen. My crew made sure they were overheard complaining about men who have nothing better to do than go sailing in the winter. We also brought in some fish. I sent some to Alberto for dinner.''

Jane smiled at Mark, delighted with the ingenious way he had provided an alibi. But Sir Henry wasn't smiling. He looked at Mark closely, noting the dark circles under his eyes and the other signs of exhaustion in his face. "Enough for now, my boy. Get some rest. We'll discuss this later.'' Mark, now that his story was told, felt drained. He nodded and walked toward the stairs, only the thought of his bed pulling him along. Slowly he pulled himself up the stairs to his room.

When there were only the two of them left in the library, Jane asked, "What more do we need to discuss? What can I do to help?''

Sir Henry smiled at her. "I knew I could count on you. But I'm not certain you'll be able to do anything.'' He paused, his face thoughtful. "Last night we planned to send the grain to several places around the district, places where our tenants would have a reason to go. Since Mark had to store it in a barn on his property, we need a reason to visit there, especially since we'll need several wagons for each estate's share." He gave a rather worried smile. "Go along, now. I'm certain Hortense is looking for you."

"Remember, Sir Henry, I'm a part of this now. I won't be left out," Jane said firmly.

"Naturally, my dear."

The problem of how to deliver the grain bothered Jane as she stood in the entryway of the Abbey watching footmen load baskets of food into the carriage. The gray clouds that had displaced the bright sunshine of the morning matched her thoughts. She pulled her warmest cloak about her and followed Hortense into the carriage.

As soon as they were under way Hortense said, "I appreciate your going with me this afternoon. The families we will visit need to know someone cares. At the first the mother is still in bed after her sixth child. Her oldest is only eight."

"Eight? Is there anyone to help her?"

"Only neighbors. And they have families of their own. Perhaps the basket Mrs. Marsden has prepared will help until she's on her feet again. The other two families have older children. At one I want to make certain a scythe wound is healing properly or arrange for the doctor; at the other is an old lady who used to be my husband's nurse."

As Hortense chatted on about the errands that afternoon, Jane looked at her with new understanding. She did care about people. She helped where she could.

With only a nod from Jane, Hortense hurried on. "Some landowners like to give the tenants gifts at the Christmas party. But I don't do mine that way. Oh, I do give little gifts, but I think it's important to visit each family personally. So often a personal visit can help if there is a problem, and it makes everyone feel special."

Jane observed the details of each visit carefully. Hortense and she would enter followed by a footman carrying the basket. The coachman and a groom waited with the horses. Usually before they had entered the house, someone from the family met them, took the basket, and escorted them inside. The footman returned to the carriage to wait. After twenty or thirty minutes, longer with Mr. Morgan's nurse, Hortense and she returned to the carriage and set off again.

Their last basket delivered, they set off to the vicarage for tea. Jane's face was thoughtful as she greeted the vicar, Mr. Langley, and his wife. Over tea as the two older women discussed finding help for the family whose mother was still weak, Jane turned to the vicar. "What kind of service do you have for the children during this season?"

The minister smiled at her, his eyes deeply blue under his white shock of hair. "We encourage caroling," he said. "But in a country parish?" He shrugged his shoulders.

Returning his smile, Jane asked, "Have you ever thought of having the children take part in the Christmas story?"

"Take part in? You mean act it out?"

"Yes."

"These children are needed to work on their parents' land. I doubt they would have time for something like that. Besides, how would they get here?"

"The children I've seen today seemed bored. They were working around their houses, always busy, but surely this season is not one of the busiest?"

"You're right. But there is still the problem of getting them here for practice."

"And if I found a way?"

"If you found a way, Miss Woodley, I would gladly take part. But what about costumes?"

"My responsibility, I think," Jane assured him. "How many practices do you think you would need?" The longer Jane talked the more enthusiastic the Reverend Mr. Langley became.

At only one point did he raise serious objections. "Animals? Live animals? My dear, there is no place to keep them. And I know nothing about their care. I really must object."

"For a country Christmas story? And there are animals mentioned in the Bible," she reminded him.

By this time the other two ladies were listening attentively. "What a wonderful way to teach the Christmas story! Would the children need to learn any verses?" asked Mrs. Langley.

"If they wanted, or there could be one person reading the story while the children acted it out. But there must be music," Jane said.

"The angel choir. Oh, yes."

"What may I do to help?" asked Hortense. "These children have so little pleasure we must encourage them whenever we can."

The visit that they had allotted an hour for stretched to two hours. Finally, refusing an invitation to supper, Hortense and Jane drove back to the Abbey.

"Shall I ask them to delay dinner, ma'am?" asked Marsden, looking at the clock on the first landing.

"I shall rush," said Hortense. "Can you be ready, Jane?"

Nodding her agreement, Jane hurried up the stairs.

Taking only a few minutes to wash up, change into her soft mauve dress, and smooth her hair, she dashed downstairs to the small salon. Finding Sir Henry and Mark alone, she said excitedly, "I think I have a solution to our problem." The men turned toward her, a questioning look in their eyes. Before she could continue, Hortense swept in followed almost immediately by Marsden.

CHAPTER

7

Never had a dinner dragged on so long. Jane fidgeted through one course after another until Sir Henry gave her a stern look. Only Mark's encouraging smile helped her gain control.

Even after dinner was over, the wait seemed unending. First there were the tea tray and the hand of whist that Hortense insisted on. Finally, stifling a yawn, Hortense gathered her shawl about her and said goodnight.

Almost before the door had closed behind her, Jane was pouring out her idea. "Isn't there someone on every estate who visits the tenants?"

"Well, yes, but . . ." Sir Henry began.

"They could deliver the grain. They wouldn't even have to know what they were doing."

"I'm not certain I understand your logic," Mark said, his forehead creased.

Jane carefully outlined what she had seen at each tenant's home that afternoon—the footman with the basket, the carriage left in charge of the servants, the farmers who merely greeted them and then disappeared.

"While the ladies are dispensing their usual baskets, the

footman and the farmer would unload the grain,'' the older man said thoughtfully. ''Yes, it might work. But the servants would have to be completely trustworthy.''

''Choose someone whose family lives in the area. He would be less likely to harm his own by gossiping,'' she said.

While Sir Henry and Jane were congratulating each other on such a clever plan, Mark still looked doubtful. He said, ''It's a good plan, Jane. I see only one flaw.''

''A flaw?'' Sir Henry asked.

''How will we get the grain to the estates so that it can be delivered? A parade of wagons to my barn would be more than slightly suspicious.''

''Oh!'' Jane exclaimed. ''How stupid of me! I assumed you knew. Remember the Christmas play Hortense told you about?'' The two men nodded, more puzzled than before. ''That's how we can move the grain.''

''Certainly. I can just see it now. 'Come to the Christmas play and pick up your smuggled grain,' the invitations will read. Jane, you'll have the soldiers on us in a heartbeat.''

Jane looked at Mark disgustedly. ''Wait until I finish. We need to cover our actions. And my plan should work.''

''Go on, my dear,'' Sir Henry said encouragingly.

''In order to have the play, someone on each estate will need to bring the children to each rehearsal. I think wagons filled with straw should provide a good hiding place, don't you?''

''Getting the grain to the estates isn't the only problem,'' Mark reminded her. ''How do you plan to get it out of my barn?''

''That's the best part.'' She smiled broadly. ''What's usually stored there?''

''Hay and some straw.''

''The perfect solution,'' she said, laughing. Noting the two men's still dubious looks, she continued, ''Since this is a country play, we are going to have real animals—a flock of sheep, some cows and horses, even a few chickens and such. I hope you don't object, but I told Mr. Langley you two would provide the animals and their feed.'' She looked from one to the other delightedly.

''Their feed?''

''Naturally. Of course we'll provide their feed—won't we, Sir Henry?'' Mark said, as excited as if he had thought of the idea himself. ''Jane, you're marvelous. Wagons of feed and wagons of children. What could be better?'' He grabbed her and swung her around the room as if waltzing.

Sir Henry smiled at their exuberance and then frowned. ''Does Mr. Langley know of your plan?'' he asked. ''We can't store the grain at the church without his permission.'' Mark stopped abruptly and took two steps back.

''No. But from what he said today, I think he'll agree. Without your approval I didn't feel that I could tell him anything,'' Jane said. ''Is that all right?''

The two men looked at each other and breathed a sigh of relief. The minister was a good, honest man, maybe too honest to support them. But he was very much interested in his people.

''When are the rehearsals to begin?'' asked Mark.

''Not for about a week. We thought the Saturday before Christmas would be a good time for the play. In the afternoon, so that everyone will have an opportunity to finish his chores before the families come to churchyard. Will that give you enough time?''

''If Mr. Langley agrees, we will be ready,'' Sir Henry promised.

As Jane waited for the men to talk to the minister, she was more nervous than she had ever been before. By concentrating, Jane was able to help Hortense with wrapping the presents to be given the children at the tenants' party, to start two maids working on the costumes for the Christmas play, and to be charming to Lieutenant Dancy, who called no fewer than three times a week.

The first time he arrived unexpectedly, Jane was sitting in the small salon finishing the hem on a wise man's costume.

Hortense, sitting at a table nearby, was painstakingly gluing feathers over stiffened cloth.

"Shut that door quickly, Marsden. There's too much of a draft. Oh, they're everywhere."

"Lieutenant Dancy," Marsden announced, dusting the feathers from his waistcoat.

"Here, let me help," the lieutenant said, kneeling to gather the swirling white down before it blew in the fire. As he captured one handful after another and placed it back on the table, Hortense muttered under her breath and once more reached for the glue pot.

As soon as most of the feathers had been restored to their proper place, Lieutenant Dancy drew a chair close to Jane's. "Every house in the countryside is busy with preparations for this play. Someone said it was your idea," he said.

"Yes, and the children here are looking forward to it so much. Mr. Langley said that the interest in learning Bible verses is greater than it ever has been."

"I hope you will still have time for me with all the preparations. Someone as angelic as you," he said with a wicked gleam in his eyes as he picked up the halo she had just finished, "needs a wicked gentleman such as I am to reform. With the right encouragement maybe I can grow less devilish." He leaned over as if to whisper in her ear.

"Jane, Jane, are you in there?" called Mark, flinging open the door to the salon just as Marsden opened the outer door. This time the feathers swirled over everything. "Oh, are we in the midst of a snowstorm?"

"Shut that door and help us pick them up again," Hortense demanded. "You young men are so impetuous. I suppose I will have to wait and work on these later."

For a few minutes everyone was too busy recapturing the feathers to talk. Finally most were safely tucked away in a bag. "What did you want, Mark?" Jane asked.

Glancing over at the lieutenant, Mark shrugged. "Nothing important. I'll talk to you later." Once more apologizing to Hortense, he left the room.

"You call him Mark and are still so formal with me," Lieutenant Dancy complained, his voice so low only Jane could hear him.

"I have known him longer than I have known you. Also, being houseguests under the same roof makes life more informal."

"Not too informal, I hope?"

"I do not believe my actions are any concern of yours, lieutenant," Jane reminded him, straightening her blue wool skirt carefully.

His blue eyes sparkling, the officer leaned even closer and whispered, "Not now, but someday they will be. I promise you."

"Sir, you presume too much!"

"Miss Woodley, if I must not call you Jane, face the inevitable. Someday you will be mine," he said firmly. Jane shivered slightly, but she wasn't certain why.

"Secrets, lieutenant? How rude!" said Hortense coyly. But her comments forced him to turn his attention to her.

After that, Jane made certain that she was never alone during any of his visits. Generally Hortense kept them company, but Jane once had to use Sir Henry to divert him.

The officer was charming. His attentions were flattering. But Jane was uneasy.

As the rehearsal for the play proceeded, she was away from home more and more frequently. The grain transfer was proceeding smoothly, thanks to Mark's and the minister's careful plans. Every day she and Mark would ride to the church, she to work with the children and Mark to check on the animals.

As the day for the performance grew closer, Lieutenant Dancy began stopping by the church to see her. At first she was certain he knew something. He was interested in everything. However, as time went on, she relaxed. He wandered around, but he was only following her. Finally she put him to work keeping the children in their places. The children were very quiet around Lieutenant Dancy; they responded differently to Mark, whom they obeyed happily and were always glad to see.

The Saturday before Christmas finally arrived. The day was all they had hoped for, clear and cold.

The party from the Abbey arrived early. Hortense, Mrs. Langley, and a few other ladies had provided cider, tea, and cakes for the children and their families after the play.

Mark, much to his own amazement, had taken charge of the shepherds and the young grooms of horses portraying camels. He wasn't certain how the animals would react, but the boys he had trained could be trusted to keep the animals under control. Although he hadn't planned to do so, he spent as much time as Jane preparing. Never having had much to do with children before, he was surprised by how much he liked them.

Of all of them, though, it was Jane who had found the most happiness. Instead of being merely a way to distribute the grain, the activity was what she had longed for. She loved the children, and they responded to her as flowers will to the sun. From the littlest angel to the tallest king, they listened to her, followed her around like disciples, and obeyed her every command. But most of all they loved her. In her soft velvet riding dresses she was their ideal of perfection. As Mark watched the faces as Jane checked each one's costume, he marveled at the difference she made.

From his vantage point with the minister, Sir Henry beamed as he watched wagon after wagon arrive. Even some of the other gentry had chosen to come. Finally a hush fell over the audience as Mr. Langley began the first words of the story from Luke.

Not even the fistcuffs that broke out between two small shepherds when a sheep dashed into the audience could mar the atmosphere. The smallest angel lost her halo, and someone in the angel chorus was off-key, but the alleluias echoed throughout the crowd as the minister read the final verse and the children froze into place.

The hush that fell over the crowd was broken when a small

goat gnawed through its lead and began nibbling on the trimming on an angel's robe. "You leave that alone," she screamed. "Miss Jane said I could keep it."

The blow she had directed at the goat hit a boy who was in charge of the horses. As the boy turned toward the angel, he dropped the reins. The ensuing disaster would make news in the district for weeks to come.

"Children," Jane called, trying to calm them.

"Don't let those animals loose. Keep them in a bunch," Mark yelled as he plunged into the bedlam to keep the flock of sheep together.

Finally the audience began to enter the fray. Here one father took charge of a cow or two while several others guided the sheep back to their temporary pen. The horses proved to be the hardest to catch, but the older boys enjoyed trying.

"Here, let's get those creatures in here," said Mark, opening the gate to the pen he and his men had built. Lieutenant Dancy, who had joined the group, pulled one old ewe in, and the others followed.

As soon as the sheep were safely inside, Mark left to help with the horses. Lieutenant Dancy was latching the gate when he saw a heavy cloth sack. Before shutting the gate, he picked it up. After a moment he folded it, walked to where his horse stood, and stowed the sack in one of his saddlebags.

At last every animal was safely locked up. Hortense and her group served refreshments, and everyone slowly drifted home. Comfortably tired, Jane, Mark, Hortense, and Sir Henry entered their carriage and settled back for the ride home.

After the noise of the afternoon, the quiet was satisfying. Then Jane began giggling and broke into laughter. "Remember the look on Mr. Langley's face when the sheep tried to run between his legs, and he sat down on it?"

"Or Lady Brough when that goat saw those cherries on her bonnet?" By then Mark was laughing as hard as Jane.

'' 'Miss Jane said I could have it!' '' Sir Henry said, his voice a high treble.

"You're wicked. That's what you three are. I'll never be able to face those people at Lady Brough's tonight," Hortense said as she dissolved in laughter. "The way that hump kept wobbling on that horse."

"Stop making fun of my camels. It was the best I could do," Mark said, but he was laughing so hard it was almost impossible to understand him. By the time they reached the Abbey to dress for the evening's entertainment, they had laughed so much they could hardly stand up.

Although there were parties planned for each night until Christmas Eve, the next Thursday, nothing matched the Christmas play. The favored few who had actually seen it spread the story to all corners of the district.

"You do plan to help stage another one next year, Miss Woodley?" asked the gem expert. "I missed this one."

One enterprising young matron even presented Lady Brough with a new bunch of cherries, "to replace the ones lost in the adventure."

By the time Christmas Eve arrived, both Jane and Mark were happy to put aside the social occasions for the religious one. Not sure of his reaction to the weekend disaster, both had visited Mr. Langley to make certain he had forgiven them. "The most excitement those people have had for years," he assured them. "It was wonderful." As they joined their neighbors at the Christmas Eve service, there was a sense of peace, a shared accomplishment, that linked them. Mark watched proudly as one farmer after another stopped Jane to thank her. The rich silver velvet of her newest spencer made her blushes even more apparent. The next morning the Yule log and the presents were merely small advantages compared to being a part of a caring circle of friends. However, for the first time in several years Jane had masses of presents, including a new scent and a lovely scarf from Hortense, and a painted fan with ivory sticks and a new novel by her favorite author from Mark. Sir Henry had saved two of his presents until last.

"For my favorite ward."

"Your only one." She smiled as she opened the largest. As Jane lifted the new burgundy cloak lined and trimmed in sable, Hortense gasped. When she opened the flat box containing the lovely aquamarine and diamond set, Mark's face grew bleak.

"It's too much, my friend," she whispered, tears sparkling in her big gray eyes.

"Nonsense. They took less thought than what you gave me," Sir Henry assured her, as he gestured to the set of leather-bound books she had so painstakingly searched for in London. Hortense, who had also received jewelry, said enviously, "Try on your cloak. When it snows, it will be just the thing over thin ball gowns."

Jane wrapped the cloak about her and rubbed her face against the dark fur that edged the hood. It was as soft as down.

"Perfect," her host declared, beaming proudly. Mark silently agreed.

The peace Mark and Jane had shared at the evening service the day before began to crumble in the days that followed. Mark stood up with her at country dances, rode with her if Sir Henry accompanied them. He was usually present when visitors called, especially Lieutenant Dancy. But his reserve was back.

When snow and an ice storm blocked the roads, the four quickly evolved a routine for their amusements. Mornings were their own. But the afternoons and most evenings were shared.

The first day went by rapidly. After the men helped dig a path to the barn and the other outbuildings, Hortense and Jane ventured outside for a few minutes to marvel at the changed landscape and piles of snow, in some places as high as their waists. Against the blinding white, Jane was vivid in her new cloak.

"Are the animals all right?" asked Jane, her breath frosty.

"Mostly. We'll have some losses, but most of our farmers have good weather eyes," Mark said, pleased at her concern.

"The farmers. At least they'll have something to eat. Everyone did get some grain?" Jane looked from one to the other, seeking their assurance.

"Grain? What grain?" asked Hortense, walking up to the three of them.

Mark glared at Jane while Sir Henry said hastily, "Rain. Jane asked if this would be as good as rain for the farmers."

Hortense glanced from one to another as if in disbelief. But she didn't say anything.

"I'm cold," Mark said. "Let's go back to the house." Pulling Jane by the arm, he soon was a long distance in front of the older pair.

"I knew you wouldn't be able to keep your promise. Do you know what you almost did?"

"But I didn't mean to. It just slipped out."

"And we could be transported or hanged as spies if Hortense talks to the wrong person."

"She won't."

"And how do you know, Miss Can't Keep a Secret?"

"Ohh!" Jane pulled away from him, her breasts heaving. Her eyes flashed. "Anyone can make a mistake, Mark Courtland, even you. You're the one who was almost caught by the patrols." Turning her back on him, she stormed into the house.

As Hortense and Sir Henry followed them up the path, Sir Henry chortled. "Look at the pair of them. Squabbling like children or a married couple. They seem fairly well matched, wouldn't you say?"

"Matched? Those two? I thought . . ." Hortense paused.

"Thought what?"

"Nothing important. But at the moment the match seems highly unlikely."

"Notice the way he watches her," he said, chuckling.

"It's better than a play. But not a word to either of them. Wouldn't want to put them off."

"You have my word." Hortense smiled up at him as she entered the house, totally at ease for the first time in weeks.

That evening they played cards, Sir Henry and Hortense against the young people. While Sir Henry totaled the last hand, Jane could contain herself no longer. "How long has it been since you played whist? Perhaps you would have rather played silver loo?" she asked Mark.

"Me? I wasn't the one who discarded wildly. If I had had a partner who knew what she was doing . . ."

"Oh! I will not play with that man again. Do you hear me, Sir Henry? Never again."

"Nor I with you," Mark said, his voice an angry snarl. "Goodnight!" He stormed out of the room and up the stairs.

"Isn't he magnificent when he's angry? Those shoulders . . ." Hortense said, her voice as languid as Jane had ever heard it.

"Magnificent! If I weren't a lady I'd tell you what he is!" Her teeth clenched, Jane rose hastily and slowly, as if counting to herself, made her way to her room.

After a day or so of renewed storms, the weather began to improve. But neither Jane nor Mark seemed warmer to one another. One afternoon as everyone sat in the library listening to Jane read the last of Scott's *Lady of the Lake*, they started when the knocker on the door sounded.

"Lieutenant Dancy," the butler announced.

"Why, lieutenant. How did you manage? I understood the roads were still impassable," said Hortense, smiling and gesturing him to a chair close to Jane's.

"The roads are not too bad, especially since I have a sleigh."

"A sleigh. What a wonderful idea," said Jane. "But wasn't the snow too deep for the horse?"

"Obviously not, or he wouldn't be here," said Mark. "What has been happening in the world?" For once he was happy to see the officer whom he heartily disliked.

"Quiet, very quiet. This has been the first day we've—I've—been able to get out, but I promise it won't be the last," he said as he smiled at Jane.

"Humph!"

"On a cold day like this you need something to warm you up. You will stay for tea, won't you?" asked Sir Henry. His voice, though polite, was not cordial.

That visit was only the first that week. Although no one else took the animals out, Lieutenant Dancy visited every afternoon shortly after luncheon. On the third day he rode, reporting that people all over the district were once again free of the ice and snow.

Sir Henry had been closed in the office all day. But Mark was very much in evidence as Hortense and Jane entertained the dashing officer.

Using her eyes and eyelashes, Jane kept Dancy's attention right where she wanted it—on her. He whispered in her ear, and she blushed. He complimented her, and she laughed.

Mark gritted his teeth and tried to tell himself that she was only following their plan. By the time Dancy left, Mark could no longer contain his jealousy. As soon as Hortense left to rest before dinner, he turned to Jane. "We told you to flirt with him, not to let him paw you."

"What?" At first Jane's voice was merely pleasantly incredulous.

"You heard me! How can you treat Sir Henry in such a way?"

"Sir Henry? What are you talking about?"

"You know what I mean. All you have to do is look at the presents he's given you."

"Mark, what are you trying to say?"

"Don't play me for a fool, Jane. Sir Henry is old and wealthy, but you want someone younger, more handsome too. What kind of arrangement have you made with Dancy?"

"Dancy?" She paused and looked him in the eyes. "What are you accusing me of?"

"I know your type. You flirt with an older man like Sir

Henry, a man noted for his fortune. But his admiration isn't enough. You also need someone younger, more handsome.''

"Are you accusing me of enjoying Sir Henry's company because of money?''

"That's right.''

She broke into laughter.

"You think it's funny! Well, we will see about that. When I tell him how you're leading Dancy on, it may hurt him, but at least he'll see you for what you are.'' Mark stormed out of the room. "Marsden, my coat,'' he called.

For a moment Jane was stunned. By the time she followed him into the hall, he was in his coat and through the door.

"Mark! Mark! Wait, please!''

CHAPTER

8

Although he heard Jane calling to him, Mark did not even pause. He headed straight to the barn.

"Saddle my horse," he called to a groom.

The head groom came forward swiftly. "He's thrown a shoe, sir."

"Then saddle any of the others. Make sure it's a strong one, though. I'll be riding across the fields, and the snow may be deep in places."

"Yes, sir."

Soon Mark was in the saddle of a deep-chested bay, crossing the fields that led to his home. The pounding rhythm of the hoofbeats kept beat with his pulse. "Flirts! That's all women are." He sighed deeply, thinking of the disappointment he was certain his friend would have to face. "Just like Lucinda."

Nine years earlier he had spent his first university recess in London at a friend's home. For a boy used to school it had been exciting, invigorating. Added to the excitement of boxing with Jackson, winning at faro, and pinching a dancer, there was Lucinda.

At twenty Lucinda was an acknowledged beauty. Petite, sparkling, she flirted her way from party to party, quickly captivating her brother's houseguest. Her dark curls and sparkling blue eyes, her softly rounded figure and her laughing little girl's voice had won his heart.

The first time he had seen her was at a ball. Her parents as the host and hostess had insisted on their son's presence, and Mark felt bound by hospitality to bear him company. The moment that Lucinda had entered the drawing room where he stood—nervous, unsure he was dressed properly—he had been in love.

Because she was in her third season, Lucinda was permitted to avoid the pastels that did little to enhance her dark beauty. That evening she was in a ruby satin dress trimmed with silver roses and worn over a slip of pearl gray. Almost frightened by his own daring, he made his way to her side. Even then he had been used to women staring at his shoulders, and Lucinda was no exception. By the time she raised her eyes to his face, she had promised a dance to him.

At first she had been amused by him. After that first dance his feelings had been so obvious. Later at other parties they had attended she usually gave him a dance, encouraging him to pour out what he thought were eloquent compliments.

When the season neared its close and she learned her parents would not finance a fourth one, everything changed. She no longer had time for him. And instead of filling her card with the younger gentlemen of the *ton* she was choosing older titled gentlemen as her partners.

One evening after they had returned from a ball, he had sat brooding on the sill of his window. As the moon broke from behind a cloud he caught sight of a movement in the street below. Quietly opening the window, he leaned out. Just before she pulled her hood over her head, he had a good look at her face. It was Lucinda.

Each night from his vantage point he watched while Lucinda, dressed in a black cloak, slipped from the side entrance and into a coach waiting for her down the block. Curiously he had watched to see when she returned. Hours later she crept back into the house.

One night he followed her. He was waiting in a doorway when the coach arrived. As soon as Lucinda was inside, he jumped on the back and held on.

As soon as the door shut behind her, the coachman set off. And so did Lucinda. Trapped as he was by his position, he had no choice but to listen, his heart growing sicker by the moment.

"Oh, it's been so long."

"Only a few hours." The sounds of moans and passionate kisses echoed in the darkness.

Then the man's voice asked softly, "What do you want? Tell me!"

"You. Now!" Lucinda almost screamed.

"You'll have to be more specific," the man's voice replied.

To Mark's horror, Lucinda did just that, using words that he had only heard from the stable hands. By the time the scene had been played to its end, the carriage had stopped.

"Get in quickly, my lord," the coachman said as he opened the door. "Press gangs are out tonight."

The light from the opened doorway told Mark what he already suspected. Lucinda's lover was a man known for his licentious behavior and his ill-treatment of his wealthy wife. Forgetting the light would illumine him too, Mark swung around the side of the carriage.

"Mark! Do something, Robert! He'll ruin everything!" Lucinda said, her face twisted in anger.

Before Mark knew what was happening, he was bound. "My engagement to Lord Beasley is to be announced later this week. If he tells old Beasley what he's seen—and he will—the engagement will be off," Lucinda said to her lover.

"Engagement? What engagement?" Mark tried to say, but the coachman slapped him.

"He won't say a word." Robert turned to the coachman, a large rough-looking man. "Find one of those press gangs and make certain they take him," the man ordered.

"No, you can't," Mark had cried. The last thing he remembered was Lucinda's delighted laugh. When he woke up . . . he wouldn't think of that.

For all her good qualities, Jane was a manipulator, as Lucinda had been. As soon as he returned to the Abbey, he would have to tell Sir Henry what he had seen. Lucinda had been right, he realized; he would have told Lord Beasley what he had seen that night.

As he rode up the drive to his own home, Mark was pleased to see a wagon pulled up before the entry. He had been afraid that the weather was still keeping the men away.

"Good afternoon, Mr. Courtland. We've missed you," Johnson said. The butler wore a heavy coat and a muffler.

"How did you make out in the storm, Johnson? I was worried because the roof still hasn't been completed."

"Just fine, Mr. Courtland. Our rooms are snug and warm. I must admit, though, that the snow did pile up in some of the others. Quite a mess it was."

"Who is here today? I saw the wagon outside."

"Only Mr. Adams and two of his men. They brought some paneling for the picture gallery. I believe they're up there now. Shall I tell him you've arrived?"

"No, I'll go up myself. You go back and get warm." Mark pulled his own greatcoat more closely around him and ran up the stairs. "Adams?" he called.

"Mr. Courtland. I had thought to visit the Abbey tomorrow to see you," his bailiff said, waving the other two men down the stairs.

"Something wrong?"

"Two tenant's roofs were damaged by the snow and ice. With your permission I'd like to get started on them right away."

"Immediately. Now, how are the repairs coming here?"

"Slowly, sir, slowly." Adams hurried on as he saw the frown cross Mark's brow. "As soon as the roads are dry enough for the wagon to travel without sinking, the roofing supplies will be here. In the next few days, I expect. I had the men postpone any work until the cold becomes less bitter. Once we get the roof completed, we'll be able to provide some heat, and the work will go faster.''

Mark nodded his approval. "How long do you think it will be before my suite is ready?" Mark asked, thinking of the day when he could avoid Jane completely. If Sir Henry and she . . ..

"Your suite? A week after the roofers are finished."

The bleak look that Mark had worn disappeared.

"But there'll be no place for servants for at least a month."

"What about the guest rooms?"

"Not even begun. The structural damage is all repaired, but we've hardly touched the interior. And if we have any more bad weather . . .''

"Yes, I know." Mark squared his shoulders and resigned himself to an extended visit at the Abbey. "Whose cottages were damaged? I'll ride by there on the way to the Abbey. Let's see if Johnson has any tea for us in the kitchen. I'd like some more information about what has been happening here." Mark led the way down the stairs.

Some time later he was once more on horseback. Glancing at the quickly fading sun, he spurred his mount. The inspection of the two cottages was as brief as he could make it. "If that roof gets any worse or if there's another storm, go to Courtland Place and tell Johnson to send for me," he told the farmer with the worst roof. "Adams should have the thatchers here in a day or so."

Although it was not yet five, the sky was already gray when he started across the fields to the Abbey. Topping a slight rise, he noticed a roof to his left and veered toward it. While most of the grain had been delivered, there were a few sacks still stored in that barn, as well as the seed grain. If the storm had damaged that roof, he'd have to act fast.

The low drum of the hoofbeats seemed to echo in the graying twilight. Cautiously Mark slowed the horse. No sense in taking any chances with a borrowed horse, he thought.

As Mark drew closer to the barn, he noticed that the snow

around the gray stone structure was not as clean as the snow in the fields. He reined in and swung to the ground, leading his horse closer. Even in the semidarkness Mark could see the packed and dirty snow. A group of people with horses and wagons had recently been there.

Stroking his horse's nose to keep it from betraying him, he glanced around the structure cautiously. Only the waves hitting the shore and the pounding of his heart could be heard.

Pulling the reins tighter, he led the horse closer to the building. Every few feet he stopped to listen. The closer he got to the door, the stronger a strange odor seemed to grow. Calmly, deliberately, he put his hand on the right side of the wide wooden door.

CHAPTER

9

Watching Mark plunge out of the house, Jane was furious. "Men," she said disgustedly as she turned to ascend the stairs. The farther she climbed the angrier she became. When she reached her room, she slammed the door, making a dreadful clatter. She smiled slightly in satisfaction.

"Miss Jane? Is there something the matter?" her maid asked fearfully.

Jane started. She had assumed she was alone. "No. I'll ring later if I need you, Betty," she said curtly.

"Yes, miss." Dropping her mistress a curtsy, the maid whisked out of the room.

As the door closed, Jane loosed the rein she had been holding on her temper. The anger she had been repressing boiled over into words. "How dare that man accuse me? Who does he think he is?"

She began pacing in front of the fireplace. The faster she walked the warmer she grew. She ran her hand around the high neck of the blue wool dress she had chosen for warmth that morning. Suddenly it was choking her.

Berating herself for having dismissed Betty before having

her unhook the dress, Jane managed to release the top three hooks and breathed a sigh of relief. The buttons on her sleeves quickly followed. However, as she worked on the other hooks that descended her back, she became more and more frustrated. All she had to do was reach for the bellpull and Betty would be there. But she was determined to get out of the dress on her own. "You did it on your own for years, ninny. You should be able to do it now," she told herself, forgetting that then most of her dresses had buttoned up the front.

By twisting and pulling, she was able to release one or two more hooks. They were enough to allow her to slip out of the sleeves and turn the dress around so that she could undo the rest. Finally, clad only in her petticoats and chemise, Jane tossed her dress and corset across her bed and breathed freely again.

If only she could solve the problem with Mark that easily. Why did she have to care so much about him? Lieutenant Dancy was far more handsome. "And he says he cares for me," she whispered. "Are you so willing to be hurt that you would let yourself care for a man who accuses you of having the lowest morals?" Her voice rose in anger.

For a moment the question echoed around the room. Almost before the last syllable was out, Jane knew the answer, had known it all long. "Yes," she said, her voice broken. "Oh, yes!" The tears she had been trying to avert ever since she had realized that Mark was serious in his accusations welled up and engulfed her. Throwing herself on her bed, she was wrenched with sobs.

Finally she lay there exhausted, the blue silk under her face drenched with her tears. Taking deep breaths to try to still the sobs that were more reflex than tears, she sat up and wiped her eyes.

Jane had learned years ago the fruitlessness of tears. She had cried when they left Oxford. She had sobbed in loneliness when it became apparent that a schoolmaster's daughter was to be ignored. She had cried when her father had shut himself away from her. Her tears had done no good then. They would do no good now.

Her jaw jutted out as she thought of her own weakness. Well, Mark Courtland had better be on guard. "Accusing me of liking Sir Henry for his money! Ha!" She slid off the bed and began pacing again. By the time Jane joined the others for dinner, her righteous anger had put a renewed sparkle in her eyes. They had more of a pixie tilt than ever. She had dressed with great deliberation. Her soft brown hair arranged in curls and a Psyche knot glistened with a silvery tinge in the candlelight. The rose color that glowed in her cheeks owed nothing to artifice but much to her anger and her figured rose crepe dress. The silk shawl embroidered in rose and silver added warmth and elegance. She swept into the small salon with her head held high.

"Jane, how lovely you look," Hortense said, her voice soft and slow. "You must ask Madame Camille to make you more gowns in that color. Don't you agree, Henry?" Hortense, as usual, was draped with an assortment of shawls seemingly flung one on top of another, held together by brooches. For that evening she had added a pouf of a cap that perched on top of her curls.

"Certainly, my dear. That color is most becoming," he said absently, pulling his pocket watch out to compare with the clock on the mantel. He put it carefully back into his waistcoat pocket and straightened his dark blue jacket. "Have either of you seen Mark this afternoon? Marsden said he left earlier and has not returned. So unlike him not to let us know whether to wait dinner on him."

Jane cleared her throat and said, "I saw him before he left."

"When was that?"

"Right after luncheon."

"He didn't say anything?"

"Well . . ."

"Did he tell you when we could expect him?" Sir Henry asked.

"No, but we had . . ." Before Jane could explain further, Marsden appeared in the doorway.

"Shall I ask Cook to postpone dinner, sir?" he asked.

"No. We'll go ahead. But tell Alberto to be ready to serve Mr. Courtland a warm meal when he returns."

Marsden, thinking of the threats the Italian cook had been screaming at the prospect of his dinner being ruined, breathed a sigh of relief. "Certainly, sir. Now, if you please, dinner is served."

Expecting to be interrupted at any moment, they drank their rich chicken soup heavy with cream and herbs. As Jane was served the poached fish, she hesitated and turned toward the door, but the noise was merely the wind.

Sir Henry, too, seemed on edge, listening for a sound that never came. He ate only a few bites of the beef roasted with vegetables, usually his favorite.

Only Hortense seemed undisturbed by Mark's absence. "I am certain Mark is taking dinner at his own home," she told them. "According to Marsden, the grooms said that was where he was going. As soon as the moon comes up, he'll return."

A frown suddenly creased Jane's brow as she took a bite of custard.

"That isn't sour, is it, Jane?" Hortense asked anxiously. "I wouldn't want anyone to become ill."

"Sour?" For a moment Jane was confused.

"The pudding?"

"No, it's fine."

"Then why were you frowning? You aren't ill, are you?"

"No, Cousin Hortense. The custard was cold on my teeth for a minute," Jane said, trying to hide her anxiety. Surely Mark wouldn't leave the Abbey permanently without saying goodbye to Sir Henry.

Although she wanted to make her excuses and run to Mark's suite to check to see if his clothes and valet were still there, Jane removed to the salon with Hortense and Sir Henry. After her few moments of panic, she knew he would not go without proper leavetaking. Besides, he had said he was going to talk to Sir Henry when he returned.

Jane turned to the couple sitting in chairs beside the fire. Maybe he had already done so. "Sir Henry, has Mark said anything about me to you?"

"Fishing for compliments, are you?" the older man asked teasingly.

"No!" The word came out so forcefully that Hortense jumped. "I beg your pardon," Jane said, embarrassed. She hurried on. "Before he left this afternoon, he mentioned that he wanted to talk to you."

"He did?" Sir Henry's voice was almost smug.

"He didn't see you, then?"

"No, my dear, but I will be happy to see him whenever he arrives," he said reassuringly.

Jane hesitated, not anxious to explain what Mark had planned to talk about yet not happy to deceive her friend. She crossed to the window and moved the curtain aside. She could hear the quiet conversation behind her, but it seemed so far away.

She leaned against the windowpane watching the play of shadow and moonshine on the snow that remained. The cold against her forehead seemed to isolate her from the warmth of the pair by the fire. Almost hypnotized, she watched the soft flakes fall slowly and begin to build up on the sill. They were so beautiful, so quiet, so cold.

Jane pulled herself back from the window, startled. "It's starting to snow again," she said, calling the other two to come and see.

"Just when we were able to get out," Hortense said in despair.

"Maybe it won't last long. Look at how slowly the flakes are falling," said Sir Henry, trying to comfort her.

"And what do you know of snow? All those years in India you never even saw it."

"That's not true. We had some incredibly high mountains there, and they had snow year-round."

''They did?'' Hortense asked as if she didn't believe a word he was saying. ''Did you visit them often?''

''Visit? Well, no. But we could see them, and the travelers to the interior told stories about how whole caravans disappeared into them, disappeared forever.'' His voice was hushed.

''Disappeared?'' Jane echoed, frightened by the thought. ''Oh, Sir Henry, you don't think that could have happened to Mark, do you?''

''Nonsense! The boy knows this district like the back of his hand. He simply stayed at Courtland Place too long and decided to wait for moonlight to ride back.''

Sir Henry tugged his waistcoat into place and walked closer to look out the window. The snow still drifted slowly down, gradually covering the ground. Still if the boy didn't show up soon . . . No, he put that thought firmly out of his mind. ''Come, what about a hand of cards?'' he asked.

''With only three players? Henry, do be sensible. Of course, two of us could play,'' Hortense said wistfully.

''You and Sir Henry play if you like,'' Jane said. ''I left my book in the library this afternoon. I'll go after it and then sit here and read.''

''If you don't mind?''

''Not at all, I assure you.''

Jane slipped into the library as the other two sat down at the table. Lighting a branch of candles from the taper she carried, she searched for the romance she had discarded when Lieutenant Dancy had been shown in. She paused as she thought of the way Mark reacted to the officer. The lieutenant seemed almost too perfect to be true. His perfection—that was it, she thought to herself.

Jane sank into one of the large leather chairs, cold now since there was no fire in the room. Why couldn't she and Mark get along for longer than a few days? He liked her. She amended the thought. At least he had seemed to like her during their rides. Then they had worked together so well on the Christmas play. After that he had changed. A shiver ran through her. Looking at the candles she had lit, she realized she had been sitting there in the cold for some time. Hurrying back into the small salon, she stood before the fire until she stopped shivering, listening to the older couple, who seemed not to have noticed her absence.

A few minutes later the door opened. She glanced up expecting to see Mark glowering at her. Instead it was Marsden and the tea tray. Startled, she glanced at the clock on the mantel. It couldn't be so late!

Her voice carefully casual, Jane asked, "Has Mr. Courtland returned, Marsden?"

"No, miss." He turned toward Sir Henry. "Shall I tell Alberto not to expect him, sir? Or shall we keep the kitchen in readiness?"

"This late? Tell them to go on to bed," Sir Henry said. After Marsden had left the room, he said in a worried tone, "This is not like the boy, not like him at all." He shook his head. A disturbed frown marred his usually smiling face.

Jane crossed to the window and stared out. She knew she would have to tell Sir Henry what had happened that afternoon.

She was just gathering her courage when Hortense rose. "Goodnight. Don't spend too long reading, Jane. You know how damaging it can be to the eyes. Henry, you play a good game of cards even if you do cheat," she said laughingly.

"Cheat! I'll have you know . . ."

"How else could you beat me?" Hortense asked as she sailed from the room.

"Cheat! That woman!" he said, sputtering.

"Sir Henry," Jane began, only to be interrupted.

"Henry! Henry! Come here quickly," called Hortense, obviously very disturbed. Both Sir Henry and Jane dashed into the entryway.

"Tell him what you just told me!" Hortense demanded.

"Mr. Courtland's horse, sir. It just came back to the stable." The head groom stood twisting his hat in his hands, his eyes firmly fixed on the floor.

"Mark's horse? Returned here?"

"The horse he was riding. The bay," the groom explained, looking at his master.

"Any sign of a fall? Was the horse injured?"

"No, sir." The man's voice dropped as if he wanted to say something else.

"Out with it man!" Sir Henry demanded.

The groom looked quickly at the two women and then back at Sir Henry. "The horse is all right, sir. But—but there's blood on the saddle."

CHAPTER

10

"Blood?" Jane froze, her heart fluttering. All color had left her face. Sir Henry, his own hands shaking, put an arm around her to support her.

"What do you mean?" he asked. "Give us more details!"

"Mr. Courtland borrowed your bay because his horse had thrown a shoe."

"Not about the horse. Tell us more about the blood!"

"There's not much to tell, sir. The horse came back a few minutes ago, its reins looking as though they'd been cut. When the stable boy went to take the saddle off and found the splotches of blood, he called me. I came to check with Marsden. When he said Mr. Courtland wasn't back, I knew something had happened." The man drew a sleeve over his sweating face and then straightened the hat in his hands.

"Get some men together. Better bring some lanterns too. If we don't find him before the moon goes down, we'll need them," Sir Henry said. "Some blankets and brandy." He paused. "Better get everyone you can."

As soon as the groom had disappeared, he turned to the women. "Hortense, you and Jane get everything ready here."

"No!" Jane said firmly. Both Sir Henry and Hortense stared at her. "I'm not waiting here. I'm going with you."

"My dear, I appreciate your desire to help, but—"

"I'm coming." Jane's voice was like steel.

"It's too dangerous," Sir Henry said firmly. "If your horse falls . . ."

"It won't."

"Anything can happen on a night like this. A sidesaddle is too dangerous."

"I'll ride astride. One of my habits has a divided skirt."

"No."

Ignoring him, Jane turned and ran up the stairs. As she reached the next floor, she turned. "If you leave without me, I'll simply follow you."

"Let her go, Henry. I believe she means it," Hortense said.

He sighed and shrugged his shoulders. "It seems I have no choice." He put that problem behind him for a time. "Hortense, send for the doctor." He paused.

"Go on, change," she said. "I'll have hot soup and a warm bedchamber waiting. You'll find him, Henry. You must."

When Jane came down a few minutes later, she found Hortense and Mrs. Marsden in conference. "Has Sir Henry left yet?" Jane asked.

"No," Hortense assured her. "He's still changing." Noting the fur-lined cloak Jane had over her arm, Hortense nodded.

Jane pulled on her gloves. She tossed her cloak over her shoulders and fastened it securely. When she heard footsteps on the stairs, she whirled around, the rich burgundy and black of her cloak circling around her.

"Let's go," Sir Henry said, drawing his greatcoat over his shoulders. Jane, nodding, pulled her hood up and waited by the door.

"Jane." Hortense's soft voice stopped her just before she

went through the door. "He'll be all right," the older woman said.

For the first few minutes of the ride that promise gave Jane hope. As the cold began to creep in, so did her fears. The moonlight on the fresh snow was bright, as bright as day at times. But the shadows cast strange shapes over the fields, transforming hedgerows into traps for the unwary. Slowly, carefully, they followed the tracks the bay had made in the snow.

Every few minutes Jane glanced at Sir Henry. His face was frozen into a harsh mask. But sometimes Jane saw him clench and relax his jaw as if he had to prevent himself from crying out.

His eyes sweeping the countryside, Sir Henry also kept an eye on the tracks that seemed to go on endlessly. What had happened to that boy? He had to be all right. What if they didn't find him? He had probably taken a fall, been stunned.

He thought of the first day he had met Mark. He had only recently moved to the Abbey, and Mark had come to call. The thirty minutes that they had spent together that day had made a firm impression on the older man. At first Mark had seemed too solemn. But the more they had talked, the more they had found in common. And these past few months with Mark sharing his home had given him a taste of family life that he had missed.

He had such plans for that young man. Sir Henry drew in a deep breath and forced himself to exhale slowly. No sense in getting himself too worked up, he thought.

By the time they reached Courtland Place, Johnson had heard them. He stood at the entrance.

"Is your master here?" Sir Henry asked, his voice rough with worry.

"No, sir." The hope that had been keeping Jane from despair dissolved. Her shoulders slumped forward.

"Did you see him today?"

"Oh yes, sir. He had tea with Mr. Adams before he left."

"Did he say where he was going?" Sir Henry asked, his voice hammering out the questions.

Although Johnson didn't remember exactly whom his master had been planning to visit, he was able to give them a general direction. Several grooms from Courtland Place joined the search.

As little as five hours earlier Mark had been well, Jane reminded herself. He was probably all right. But as her worry began to mount, so did her anger. How dare he frighten them so badly?

Her anger lasted until they knocked on the second cottage door. Mark wasn't there, but he had been. He had left hours before to return to the Abbey.

Brushing her tears away, Jane gathered up her reins. She yanked her hood, which had fallen around her neck, over her head once more. As the men milled around her, she breathed a prayer. "Don't let him be dead, Lord." Even if he hated her, she wanted to see him, to hear the deep velvet of his voice. He couldn't be dead.

Quickly Sir Henry outlined his plan. Working systematically, they would fan out in a semicircle heading toward the Abbey. Each group would be responsible for covering specific ground. If—when—Mark was found, they would fire three shots. And then repeat them. The men began to break into groups. "Jane, you'll come with me," he said firmly before turning to the others. "If we haven't found him in two hours, return here. We'll go in the other direction then."

As each team combed its area and more and more time passed, Jane had almost given up. Surely it was time to turn back and start again, she thought.

She had just turned to call to Sir Henry when the cold, still darkness was broken by three shots. "That way," Sir Henry pointed and spurred his horse forward. Jane was fast behind him.

With more shots to guide them, they covered the half mile rapidly. "Here, sir," a man shouted, waving his cap in the lantern light that had replaced the bright moonlight. "Over here!"

Sir Henry and Jane plunged off their horses, thrusting the reins into the hands of the other men. Hampered by the snowdrifts around some low bushes, they made their way to where the groom stood.

"Just by accident, sir. It was just by accident," the man said excitedly. "He was almost hidden under that bush."

"Have you moved him?"

"No, sir. Just put blankets about him, that's all. Thought someone should check him first."

"Here, let me through!" Jane demanded, shoving past the groom and Sir Henry. "No!" she cried as she caught sight of Mark's bloody head cradled on a worn blanket.

CHAPTER

11

Jane dropped to the snow, now trampled and bloodstained. Cautiously, she put out a shaking hand to touch his cool throat.

"He's alive," she said, her tears streaming down her face.

"Here, miss, let me look at him," said a groom known for his skill in treating the animals at Courtland Place. Reluctantly Jane gave way to him, positioning herself at Mark's head.

As the two men checked Mark's body carefully, she stroked his blood-matted dark hair, whispering to him so softly that no one else could hear. "When can we move him?"

"Nothing broken that I can see. Of course, with a head injury . . ." The groom hesitated.

"Well, he can't stay here," said Jane, who had managed to gain control of her tears. "Shall we send for a wagon?"

"My dear, our first task will be to get him some place warm. He'll have to ride," Sir Henry said.

"Ride?"

"At least be on the horse in front of someone."

"I'll take him," she said, volunteering. She stood up and walked to where the horses were being held.

"Jane, be serious. It will have to be someone strong, stronger than either of us." Sir Henry glanced around at the men standing nearby. "Get somebody mounted up who thinks he can hold him. It's going to be a rough ride for everyone."

As they carefully handed Mark to the chosen groom, he groaned, causing Jane to run to his side. "Is he conscious?" she asked.

"No, miss."

For the rest of her life Jane remembered that ride through the darkness. The jarring hoofbeats were accompanied by groans. Jane's face dripped tears that she brushed away before they became ice. A few paces behind the groom carrying Mark, she kept her eyes fixed on his still body, trusting her horse to find its way.

Sir Henry, too, rode close beside him. But while Jane sought for signs of returning consciousness, Sir Henry prayed that they would be at the Abbey before Mark roused. His injuries had not seemed severe, but the fact that he was still unconscious worried the older man.

After what seemed like hours to the two who watched Mark so closely, the lights of the Abbey sparkled in the distance. By the time they arrived with Mark, Marsden and Hortense stood at the entrance.

"Carefully now, men," Sir Henry said, overseeing Mark's transfer from horseback to the waiting arms of several footmen.

"Take him straight up. The doctor is waiting in Mr. Courtland's rooms," Hortense said. She spoiled the reassurance Jane and Sir Henry felt as she added, almost under her breath, "Little good though the man may do."

"What do you mean?" asked Sir Henry.

"He's foxed."

Jane, stiff from her hours in the saddle, stumbled toward them. "Who's foxed?"

"The doctor."

"No! Then who'll look after Mark?" she asked, her voice shaking.

"He'll manage. He always does," Hortense said, trying to calm her down.

"Who is with them? We have to be there!"

"Jane, it would be most improper if either of us were there. Henry will go up and check on them."

"Of course. I'll give them a few minutes to get him into bed and then go on up," he said, leaning against the newel post at the bottom of the staircase. His normally sunbrowned face was almost pale, and his voice shook with weariness.

"Sir Henry, you go and change. I'll look after Mark," Jane said, a determined note in her voice. She tossed her cloak to a waiting footman and started up the stairs.

Hortense and Sir Henry looked at each other and sighed. Neither had the heart to argue with her. Slowly they followed her up the stairs.

"You go on," Hortense said, urging the older man toward his own suite of rooms. "I'll stay with her. Besides, Mark's valet is there."

She watched in satisfaction as Sir Henry did as she suggested.

"I'll join you shortly," he promised.

By the time Hortense arrived, the doctor was pulling the sheet back over Mark's chest. "Hmm. Yes," he said, slurring his syllables. "Slow but steady."

Jane, fast regaining her warmth, tapped her foot in impatience. If she hadn't wanted to keep a close eye on the doctor, she would have been pacing. She glared at him and said, "Well, what do you suggest?"

Turning to the older woman as though he hadn't heard Jane's words, the doctor said, "No real injuries except the blow to the head. He should wake shortly. I'll just cup him; then I'll go."

"No!" Jane's refusal echoed through the chamber.

"So you're a doctor, now, miss?" the man asked insolently, turning back to the bed. Hortense opened her mouth to agree with him, but Jane cut her off.

"No. But I've read Harvey. Have you?"

"Harvey? That quack. No one listens to him," the doctor said scornfully, his voice more slurred than it had been.

"I do, and I won't let you touch him." Jane put herself between the doctor and his patient, her hand clasping Mark's.

"Be it on your head, then, if he succumbs to fever. I wash my hands of this case." The doctor folded up his instruments and repacked his bag. Shrugging into his coat, he turned to Hortense. "If you come to your senses, call me. But keep her away." He made his bow to Hortense and stumbled to the door, almost knocking Sir Henry to the floor as he swung it open. "You'll get my bill, sir," the doctor added, his face so close to Sir Henry's that the older man gasped at the stench of brandy and bad breath.

"What's going on?" Sir Henry asked as the door closed behind the doctor. As the two women explained, Mark's valet, Smythe, bustled around the room. "No! Hortense, I must agree with Jane. Don't you? In fact, haven't I heard you say you wouldn't have that man treat you?" At her nod, he continued, "Now our problem seems to be what to do."

"Excuse me, sir. May I recommend that all of you get some sleep while I keep watch. The doctor seemed to think my master will awaken naturally in a few hours," the valet suggested. He crossed to the bed and adjusted one of the red silk curtains so that there was no longer a draft. Recognizing the good sense of his words, Sir Henry and Hortense agreed and swept Jane with them.

Before Jane had a chance to think of a good argument, she was in the hall and at her room. "Goodnight, my dear. Sleep well. We will call you when he awakens. I promise," Sir Henry said as he opened the door to her room.

Every time Jane opened her mouth to answer, Sir Henry cut her off. Finally she nodded, her eyes faintly shadowed by worry, and closed her door.

Her eyes were closed in weariness and her cheeks were wet with tears as she leaned against the door. He was so still. Slowly Jane began unbuttoning the jacket to her riding dress.

"Let me do that, Miss Jane," Betty said, her voice giving her mistress a start.

As soon as the last button was undone, the last pin removed from her hair, Jane dismissed Betty. When the door closed behind her, the silence engulfed her, allowing Jane's ravaged nerves a moment of peace.

Slowly, her legs and back already aching from her long ride in an unaccustomed saddle, Jane moved toward the bed that waited so invitingly. Even the step up to the bed hurt. As she sank into the soft feathers, Jane welcomed the relief the bed gave her, yet resented her need of it. Tears slowly running down her cheeks and a prayer on her lips, she drifted off to sleep.

As deep as her sleep was, Jane must have been waiting to be called to Mark's bedside, for as soon as a maid entered to start the fire she awoke. Her memories flooding back, she sat up and moaned. The aches of the evening before were agony. With effort she reached for the bellpull.

By the time Betty arrived, Jane was out of bed and walking around. "I'll wear something simple, Betty. And just knot my hair." She paused and asked hesitantly, "Has Smythe left Mr. Courtland's chambers?"

"No, Miss Jane." Betty slid the last pin in place and stepped back to look at her mistress's hair. "Here's your dress." She held out a lovely velvet day dress.

"No, that's too elaborate," said Jane, crossing to the wardrobe where her clothes were kept. "I'll wear this." She pulled out a gray wool, one of the dresses she had worn when she was in mourning. Looking at Jane's face, Betty did not utter the protest she had been considering.

"Shall I serve your breakfast here, Miss Jane?"

"No, I'll ring when I want something. I want to check on Mr. Courtland."

Later Jane was thankful for the sleep she had gotten, but when she entered the room that morning and saw Smythe's worried face, she was certain she had been wrong to leave him.

"How is he, Smythe?" she asked, her voice scarcely louder than a whisper. She moved closer to the bed.

"I'm not certain, miss. He hasn't regained consciousness, and he seems to have a fever." The valet's voice was carefully noncommittal, but his eyes seemed to reprove her for her presence.

"Has he moved, cried out, anything?"

"Not once. Of course, the laudanum the doctor gave him naturally kept him quiet for a time."

"Laudanum? When?"

"Last night, before you came in."

Taking deep breaths to calm herself, Jane remained quiet. Finally, her composure under control, she said, "You get some rest, Smythe. I'll stay with him."

"But it wouldn't be right. What would Mrs. Morgan say?" said the valet, his moral sense outraged.

She stared at Smythe until he dropped his eyes. "I'm staying. If you want to stay too, that's fine with me. But if he doesn't get better, we'll need you rested and ready to help."

When Sir Henry entered two hours later, he found Jane alone standing by Mark's bedside, removing a compress from his head. "Jane, what are you doing here? I thought . . ."

"Sir Henry, I admire and respect you. But if you are going to tell me I shouldn't be here, please don't. I'm here and I'm staying."

Never before had her friend heard such a determined note in her voice. Quickly changing his mind, he said, "Fine, my dear. Just as you wish. How is he?"

"Not good." Now that she had won her battle, her voice was shaky. "He's so hot, and he hasn't regained consciousness. Oh, Sir Henry, was I wrong to refuse to let that quack cup him?"

"Nonsense. Cupping simply weakens a person. Come and tell me what you've done."

Before she could begin, a low moan drew them closer to the bedside. "I've been trying to get him to drink some barley water when he does this," Jane said as she lifted

Mark's head and held the glass to his lips. "Sometimes he takes a sip or two."

When Hortense joined them a few minutes later, Jane and Sir Henry were resettling Mark on his pillows. Taking a look at Jane's disturbed face, Hortense decided she would wait to voice her objections. "Marsden tells me that Mark has not regained consciousness. Let me see him." She crossed to the bed and felt his pulse. "Hmm." She laid her hand on his brow. A disturbed look on her face, she said, "Send someone to bring Mrs. Marsden here immediately."

"What is it?" Jane asked, almost in tears, as Sir Henry hurried to the door.

"I'm not certain yet. What I do know is that you must not neglect your own health. Marsden tells me you haven't had breakfast yet, although you've been up for hours. Yes, I know you aren't hungry, but you must keep up your strength."

Once again Jane found herself bustled out of the room. "As soon as you've had something to eat, you may return," Hortense said reassuringly.

That was the last time for several days that anyone stopped for more than a scratch meal. By luncheon, Mark's fever was raging, and he was moaning constantly.

"We've got to bring that fever down," said Hortense, a determined look on her face. She turned to the housekeeper. "Send someone to bring in some snow, the cleanest they can find. Enough to fill a large tub."

"Snow? But lying so long in the snow probably gave him the fever," Jane said.

"Possibly. But unless it breaks soon, his reason may be in danger."

"His reason?"

"Fevers can do strange things," Sir Henry said, his voice sad. "And we never had enough ice to help in India." He crossed to the bed and ran a cloth moistened with water over Mark's dry lips. "It's the only way."

Jane, her protests dying on her lips, helped Hortense prepare the snow packs they put on Mark's head and wrists. As they melted, she replaced them with others and patted him dry. When those didn't drop his fever as fast as she wanted, Hortense had the hip bath filled with cold water chilled by snow. For once Jane didn't protest as Hortense ushered her from the room.

By the time she was allowed back in, she had almost worn a path in the hall with her pacing. "Is he better?" she asked anxiously.

"He's cooler," Hortense said, refusing to give her a direct answer. "The next few hours should tell the tale."

As the hours passed, it became obvious that Mark was growing worse. When he had opened his eyes that evening, everyone had sighed in relief. But the relief was short-lived. Catching sight of Hortense, Mark had cried, "Mama, I hurt. Make it go away. Please, Mama."

The three around the bedside exchanged worried looks. "Start those snow packs again, Sir Henry. Jane, you see if you can get him to drink some broth," Hortense said, marshaling her troops like a general.

In spite of everything they tried, by the next morning even Jane was ready to admit defeat. "Let's call back the doctor. I'll keep out of his way. I'll even apologize if he wants me to," she said, her voice pleading.

"I suppose we have no choice," Sir Henry said reluctantly.

"No, you were right. All he would do is cup him and fill him with laudanum. And that's not enough," Hortense said, surprising both of them.

"You don't mean there's no hope?" Jane asked breaking into sobs.

"Calm yourself. You'll just get him upset. No. I've sent Marsden for a local woman who treats the tenants."

"What?" Sir Henry frowned.

"I knew what you'd say, Henry. But our people trust her with their lives. Why shouldn't we give her a chance with Mark? At least let her look at him."

Jane, in agony at the thought of losing Mark, urged him to agree. "Please, Sir Henry! What can it hurt to try? If she can't help, then we'll call the doctor." The tears she had been holding back rained down her cheeks and made spots on her crumpled and water-stained dress.

"I suppose it can't hurt," he agreed.

By the time the woman arrived, Mark was more restless and had begun to cough weakly. As she watched the coughs wrack his body, Jane paced beside the bed. "Why? Why did I have to annoy him?" she muttered.

"What?"

"It's all my fault." Her whispered words brought looks of concern to the man and woman who now watched her. Totally oblivious to them, Jane stopped and took Mark's hand in hers, flinching as she realized how warm it was. "Why do we always have to quarrel?"

The door opened, and a small brown wren of a woman slipped quietly to the bedside, followed closely by an enormous man carrying a willow basket. Any other time Jane would have laughed at the contrast. Now she stepped back and asked, "Can you help him?"

"Help? Maybe. Good-looking man." The woman put her hand on his burning forehead and then raised his closed eyelids. Silently she inspected him, listening to his rough breathing. "Leave. Come back shortly."

Reluctantly the three obeyed. When they returned a short time later, they noticed changes immediately. Mark lay supported by pillows in a sitting position. On the fire rested a large pot filled with water and herbs. And the little woman was preparing a poultice of some kind.

"Don't bother me now," she demanded as she kept working. Finally she applied it to Mark's chest.

"A new one every time it grows cold. Inflammation of the lungs. Give him this every time he wakes up. Keep the pot boiling and drop these in." Her orders flew so fast that Hortense asked her to stop so that they could write them down.

"Someone with him constantly. And do this several times a day." To Sir Henry's horror she pulled Mark upright and began to pound on his back. But after being torn by coughs Mark seemed to rest more easily.

"Lots of fluids. Force him. Hold his nose. Broth. Barley water." She turned to go, motioning for the man who had waited silently.

"You'll be back, won't you?" Hortense asked.

"Send if you need me." She turned and walked out the door, followed by her shadow. Startled as they were, they had no time to wonder. Dividing up the duties, Hortense set up shifts to carry out the herb woman's instructions. Together the three of them prepared the next poultice, making certain they all understood the directions they had been given.

With Smythe to help her, Jane took the first watch, sending Hortense and Sir Henry to bed. Although she was supposed to call them in four hours, she let them sleep longer, only calling them when she could no longer stay awake.

In spite of her exhaustion, Jane slept only two hours, returning as Mark began rambling once more. She had not taken time to bind her hair, and it hung down her back in a brown cloud, her close-cropped front curls giving her a tousled appearance.

"Whore!" Jane drew back in horror as the word flew out of Mark. "Involved with a married man."

"Married man?"

"Going to tell. Old Beasley won't like it, Lucinda."

"Lucinda?"

"Someone in his past. He's talked about her for about an hour now," Sir Henry explained, drawing Jane over to the table where the supplies for the poultice were arranged. Hortense put a new compress on Mark's head and ran a wet cloth over his dry, cracked lips. "Let Hortense see to him. She'll calm him down."

"He's worse, isn't he?"

Sir Henry didn't try to lie to her. "Some. But he can breathe more easily now."

"He's going to die, and it's all my fault."

"What are you talking about?" he asked.

As she worked on the next poultice, Jane explained what had happened two days earlier.

"And that's all?"

"All? Isn't it enough?" she asked, filled with guilt.

"Jane, I'm certain that Mark was not blameless in this argument. Stop trying to keep all the guilt for yourself."

"But he's so ill. And if we hadn't argued?"

"He might have gone anyway. Here, give that to me." He took the finished medication and put it on Mark's chest. "Go on, talk to her, Hortense. Did you hear?"

Nodding, the older woman walked toward the stand where Jane rinsed her hands. "I thought you were going to sleep longer."

"I couldn't." Jane turned to face the older woman. "Is he going to die?"

"Not if we can keep him from it. Gloomy thoughts like that can't help, though. Maybe you should go back to bed."

"No."

The day quickly fell into a routine: fill the kettle, add the herbs, make a poultice, pound Mark's back, and then take a walk in the hall. After the heavy odor of the herbs, they needed fresh air. Once Jane raced down to the front door and opened it, welcoming the cold crisp January air.

As it became more evident that the crisis was approaching, everyone hovered close by. The red silk draperies of the bed hung limp in the steam-filled room, and Jane's dress, another gray wool, steamed in the dampness.

Only Sir Henry was forced out of the sickroom for any time. Because the district had learned of the accident, he was sent to receive the guests. His normally brown skin pallid, he explained and quickly sent the visitors on their way.

Only Lieutenant Dancy refused to be treated so summarily. He asked for full details. "Perhaps the magistrate should be called in?" he asked, his handsome face marred by a frown.

"For a riding accident?"

"A riding accident! I had understood it was a robbery."

"A robbery?" Sir Henry stared at him in amazement.

"A rumor, no doubt."

"No doubt." Hastily Sir Henry got rid of him, pleading duties in the sickroom. He walked up the stairs, a frown on his face. "A robbery?"

The sickroom was in turmoil when he returned. Smythe and Jane were trying to hold Mark still while Hortense struggled to get his medicine down.

"No," Mark said, his voice slurred. "No more drugs. I'll not go. I'm a gentleman. Let me see the captain. How dare you?" His scream filled the room, causing both Jane and his valet to spring back.

"Don't let him go. He's delirious," Hortense said, her voice shrill.

"Here, let me," Sir Henry said, reaching the bed. "Attention, sailor." The other three stared in amazement as Mark's pain-wracked body stiffened. "Open that mouth and take your medicine."

Mark, reacting to the authority in the older man's voice, did as he was told. Again racked by coughs, he leaned back on his pillows. "I can't go back up there. I can't," he tried to say as he gasped for air. "My hands." He held them out in front of him. Across the palms were thin scars as if they'd been cut. "I'll fall, I'll fall!" he cried. Then his voice grew heavy, resigned. "Yes, sir, I'm going." His voice was little more than a whisper. "Hold on. Don't slip. No, no! Ohhh!" Once again his screams rang out. Then for a time he was silent.

As the watchers breathed a sigh of relief, he began again. "My leg. No, you won't cut it off. No! Don't let them!" he pleaded. "I'll set it myself if you won't." Then his voice grew cold. "Oh, Lucinda. How delightful you look tonight. Is this the man you're cuckolding now? What happened to Robert?"

He paused as if listening to a reply. "I knew her before her first marriage, sir. Did you? . . . A duel over her? Never. She's not worth soiling my hands or yours either, sir. Ask her what she knows of press gangs. As, look at her pale."

"Press gangs," Jane asked, horrified.

"I'll explain later," Sir Henry promised.

As he rambled, Mark had pulled himself upright. Finally e slumped against the pillows again. Hortense drew a deep reath. "Listen," she said.

"I can't hear anything," her cousin Henry said.

"He's breathing normally. I think the crisis is past." Hortense at on a chair near the bed, suddenly exhausted. For the first ime in hours they heard the clock on the mantel strike. It was wo.

"Morning or afternoon?" asked Sir Henry, his voice re- ealing his own tiredness.

Smythe crossed to a window and pulled back a curtain. 'Morning, sir.''

They all watched him for an hour longer, replenishing his oultices and forcing him to swallow his medicine. "You two ;o off to bed. Smythe and I can manage now," Jane suggested. Jnder protest but realizing the wisdom of her suggestion, the)ther two left.

As the sun came up, Mark opened his eyes and stared in amazement at his usually orderly room. Then he caught sight)f Jane, her chair drawn up to the side of the bed and her 1ead resting on her arm. Her eyes were closed. "Jane?" he asked, puzzled by the weakness in his voice.

Immediately her eyes opened, and she rose to put a hand to 1is forehead. "Time for another poultice, Smythe," she called.

"Jane, what is happening?" Mark asked.

"You're awake," she said slowly. Then her voice rang)ut. "Smythe, let everyone know he's awake."

Watching in amazement as his valet hurried out, Mark coughed. Once more overcome by weariness, he closed his eyes and drifted off to a peaceful sleep.

As soon as someone came to relieve her, Jane, too, went to bed. For the first time in her life she slept the clock around.

CHAPTER
12

That first day Mark spent more time asleep than awake. He was still weak; at first all he could do was eat some soup and drink some lemon water. Almost before he was through he was asleep again, a deep, healthy sleep. While Jane enjoyed her first restful sleep in days, Hortense kept watch over Mark.

The next day when Hortense entered Mark's bedroom for the third time in an hour to find Jane pacing again as though she were a tiger in cage, she decided to put her to work. With the help of a maid and footman, Jane removed the damp and bedraggled hangings and hung the replacements, a rich gold velvet. Twitching the last length of fabric into place, Jane smiled. In spite of the acrid smell of herbs that still hung in the air the chamber was much more pleasant.

When Betty arrived a short time later under strict orders not to leave her mistress's side, Jane did not even utter a protest. She simply picked up one of the books she had brought to read and curled up in a chair. For some time the only sounds were the crackle of a page as Jane turned it or the snip of Betty's scissors as she trimmed a length of thread.

Then the rustle of sheets and a soft sigh drew Jane toward the bed. "Get a footman," she said quietly. "And tell Mrs. Marsden to send up some broth."

Putting her hand to Mark's brow, Jane was happy to find it cool. Before she could lift it, it had been captured by his weak one.

"Am I delirious? Or are you here?" he whispered, his lips dry and cracked. "No, don't go," he said as she stepped toward the table to get him a drink.

"I'm not. Here, take a sip." Nothing had ever given Jane as much satisfaction as Mark's plea had done. Her heart beat like a coal miner's hammer. She lifted Mark's head carefully and held the cup to his lips.

"Oh!" he sighed and tried to ease his head back to his pillow. "Ouch!"

"Don't try to move."

"What happened?"

"An accident."

"An accident?" Mark's voice was slow and slurred, his tone bewildered.

"After we fought. Oh, Mark, I didn't mean to make you angry, really I didn't," Jane said, tears dripping down her cheeks.

"Never angry at you," he whispered, trying to brush her tears away with a hand that was weak and shaking.

A voice behind them startled Jane and made her pull away. "So this is how you take care of your patient. You weep all over him."

Jane blushed, "Cousin Hortense, I didn't mean . . ."

"You just go along to luncheon, miss. I'll take care of this young man. We'll talk about the other later," Hortense said, waving Jane toward the door. "See that your mistress is more presentable before she joins Sir Henry at luncheon, Betty." She frowned at the gray dress, practically a uniform, that Jane wore. "Find her something cheerful." Mark smiled weakly as Jane was swept masterfully out of the room.

After luncheon Sir Henry and Hortense closeted themselves

with Jane in the library. "Now that Mark is recovering, some things must change," Sir Henry said forcefully.

"Things?"

"Don't play games with me, Jane."

"Games?"

"I have told him about the scene I interrupted this morning," said Hortense gravely. "Really, Jane, how could you be so lost to propriety?"

"What are you talking about?" Jane was confused, and her voice showed it.

"That scene with Mark." Hortense took a few steps toward the fireplace and then turned back to face Jane. "Are you trying to compromise the man?"

"What?"

"Hortense, I'm certain Jane meant no impropriety. We are all very glad that Mark is getting better, aren't we? I'm certain that's all there was to it," said Sir Henry, trying to soothe both women.

"I'm not even certain I understand what you're talking about," Jane said, a mask of indifference hiding her bewilderment.

"The handholding! Alone after sending your maid out of the room! Even when he was unconscious, your helping to nurse him was somewhat improper. Now that he is himself again, Jane, you really must think about your actions more. Why, already some of our neighbors have asked why you were permitted to ride with the men looking for Mark," Hortense told her. "What do you suppose the servants talk about?"

"All we are asking is that you think about your actions. We wouldn't want your good name smeared," Sir Henry said hastily.

"Just how can I prevent that?" Jane asked coldly.

"Remember to visit Mark only when someone, preferably Hortense or I, is present," Sir Henry said calmly. "And you can take over receiving the guests. Since Mark has taken ill, we've had more visitors in a day than in a usual week. Lieutenant Dancy has been here every afternoon.''

With all the effort she could muster, Jane kept her despair and hurt from showing. By blinking rapidly she cleared her eyes of tears. ''In your home, Sir Henry, I will do as you ask,'' she said so softly that he could hardly hear her.

Sir Henry and Hortense exchanged conspiratorial glances. Before Jane could leave, the door opened. ''Lieutenant Dancy,'' Marsden announced.

That afternoon Jane smiled in all the right places, responded with the correct replies, and knew nothing of what was happening. How she got through the visit without destroying them all she never knew. But she did.

Finally she could go to her room. Dismissing her maid, Jane stood looking out over the gray landscape. ''No, I won't cry,'' she promised herself. ''But why did he do this?'' He had seemed to understand how she felt about Mark. She knew he had.

Had she really been so obvious? Thinking about the way she had demanded she be included in the rescue party, the way she had acted when they had found Mark, Jane had to admit that her actions had been questionable. ''But why now?'' she wondered as she relived the scene in Mark's bedroom. Maybe she did have her arm around his neck. She was just helping him get a drink, wasn't she?

At that, Jane's innate honesty forced her to admit that helping Mark had not been her only motive. She did love to run her hands over those shoulders. Even when she had been changing the poultices, she had. She blushed as she remembered. Not even to herself would she finish that thought.

Her anger subsiding, Jane breathed deeply. ''At least they didn't forbid me to see him,'' she said happily. She crossed to the bellpull.

A short time later she and Betty slipped into the quiet bedroom where Mrs. Marsden sat knitting. ''He's awake, miss. He's just gotten comfortable again after a nice hot cup of soup. He's getting better every minute," she whispered.

Jane tiptoed over to the bed. "He's asleep again, Mrs. Marsden. Is he supposed to sleep so much?"

"No, I'm not," Mark whispered, opening his brown eyes and staring at her reproachfully. "Why did you leave before, beautiful lady?" His deep voice was still husky.

"Luncheon," she began.

"I'm glad you're back," he added, closing his eyes again. In a few minutes she could tell by his breathing he was asleep again.

She crossed to the chair by the fire and picked up her discarded book. "He's improving, isn't he?" she asked.

"Sleep is the best thing in the world for him, Miss Jane."

Somehow Jane made it through dinner that evening calmly. When they were in the small salon once more, she turned to Sir Henry. "What did Mark mean by press gangs and his leg?" she asked.

Sir Henry sighed. He fiddled with the fob on his chain and straightened the sleeves of his black evening coat before he answered. "No one else is to know about this. Do you agree?" He looked pointedly at both women.

When they both nodded, he began. "When Mark was eighteen, he was visiting a school friend in London. Because of the boy's sister, Lucinda, Mark was captured by a press gang and sent to sea."

"What? How could they?" Hortense cried.

"Why didn't he say something?" Jane asked.

"They kept him drugged. The men who gave him over had stripped him of everything valuable, even his coat. He had no way to prove his identity."

"How horrible. Something should be done about those gangs. Why, Mrs. Marsden told me that we almost lost a footman to one last month. If he hadn't had on livery . . ."

"That's just the point. They choose only those who seem to have no records, no way of striking back. They steal men and leave their families to starve." Sir Henry had a bleak expression on his face. "And those numbskulls in Parliament don't care."

"But how did Mark escape?" Jane asked, bemused.

"He didn't." Sir Henry paused, reached for his brandy glass, and downed it in one gulp. "After his accident they discharged him."

"Accident? What accident?" Jane asked, her voice anxious.

Realizing that he could not gloss over the details as he had hoped to, Sir Henry explained. "One winter day about six months after he had been impressed, the mate ordered Mark aloft. The rigging was icy, and before he had climbed twenty feet, Mark had cuts in the palms of his hands. When he reached the first sail, he paused." Sir Henry stopped himself and looked at the two women carefully. "You do know this is only what I myself have heard?"

"Go on please, Henry!" Hortense asked.

"Mark tried to get the mate to let him come down, even showed him his palms, he says, but the order was not changed. Slowly he made his way higher. Then it happened." Sir Henry mopped his brow with his handkerchief.

"What happened?" Jane demanded.

Sir Henry's voice was husky as he continued. "He slipped. His hands, wet with blood, slipped on the ice and he fell. Somehow, he never knew exactly how, he held on to the rope for most of the way down. When he finally let go, his leg took the brunt of the fall." Sir Henry brushed his handkerchief hastily across his eyes.

"The rest?" Jane asked, remembering the nightmares of Mark's fever.

"Nothing definite. Except they wanted to amputate and Mark would not let them."

Jane shut her eyes at the thought of that strong body under the surgeon's knife. "Thank you, God, for sparing him that," she breathed silently.

"When they got back to England he was invalided out. No need of a sailor with a bad leg in the navy."

No wonder Mark was moody, Jane thought as she sat in

front of her dressing table having her hair brushed. "And all because of some woman. No wonder he doesn't trust us."

"What did you say, miss?"

"Nothing, Betty. Just braid my hair and go to bed yourself." Jane smiled at the young girl. As she lay in bed some time later watching the play of fire shadows on the wall, she resolved to remember what Sir Henry had told her. "And I thought I had problems," she mumbled as she pulled the covers close around her.

Her resolution was sorely tested over the next two days. She had thought her father had been a bad patient, but Mark was worse. As he stayed awake longer, he wanted someone, preferably Jane, with him constantly. Still too weak to do more than lie in bed, he complained about his meals and his medicine.

When Lieutenant Dancy called, as he usually did each afternoon, both Jane and Hortense breathed a sigh of relief. But for Jane the lieutenant presented a different kind of problem.

"Lieutenant Dancy," she said, a smile lightening her face as she followed Hortense into the room.

"Miss Woodley." He bent low over her hand. Quickly remembering his manners, he turned toward Hortense. "And Mrs. Morgan. What a delightful pair you make."

He watched Jane arrange her dress carefully as she took her place on the settee and eyed the aquamarine-and-diamond pendant she wore. "How is the patient today?" he asked as he took his place beside Jane.

"Better. Definitely better."

"But he may be dead very soon!" Hortense whispered to herself.

"What did you say? He's not dying, surely?"

"No, but sometimes I would like to strangle him where he lies," Hortense explained.

"Oh! A bad patient?"

"The worst." Jane's and Hortense's voices blended into

one. The two women looked at each other and laughed weakly. Quickly they turned the conversation to the events of the district.

"And when will you be returning to grace our entertainments, Miss Woodley?" the officer asked.

Jane glanced over at Hortense, who seemed oblivious to the problem. She cleared her throat, but Hortense was in her own world. Why did this man insist on singling her out? He was handsome, and it was flattering to know he cared. However, no matter how hard she tried, she couldn't care for him. She smiled and said, "I'm not certain. Until Mr. Courtland is fully recovered, Sir Henry and Mrs. Morgan feel we must be close at hand." She gazed up at him, an earnest look in her wide gray eyes. "You do understand, don't you?" Somehow she had the feeling that it was important to keep the officer interested.

"Of course." He smiled at her, revealing a dimple any girl would be proud of. "Has Mr. Courtland explained how the accident happened yet?"

"Until today he's hardly been awake long enough to say anything," Hortense said. "And today all he's done is complain."

"He did ask me something when he first awoke," Jane said casually.

"What did you say?" The man's voice was so sharp that the two women turned to look at him curiously. "I just want to make certain there was no breaking of the laws," he added hastily.

"You mean you think it might have been deliberate?" Hortense asked.

"No, not really. It was just a thought." He smiled as if to reassure them. "I understand you were there when he was found, Miss Woodley. How exciting for you."

"Exciting? It was the most frightening experience of my life," Jane said, trying to hide her fears. She glanced at Hortense for help.

"Come, sir. Enough of this depressing subject. Mark is

getting better. Tell me about Lady Brough's musicale."
Carefully Hortense tried to lead him to another subject.

Had Lieutenant Dancy stayed only the prescribed thirty
minutes she might have been successful. He didn't. His visit,
at first a welcome relief, seemed endless as he asked them
one question after another.

"Hortense, have you seen . . . Oh, Lieutenant Dancy,"
Sir Henry said. "Good afternoon, sir. Jane, I hate to disturb
you, but Mark is asking for you," the older man explained.

Making her excuses, Jane slipped from the room. A whole
hour wasted, she thought. Her departure was a signal for the
lieutenant to leave. "Tell Miss Woodley I'll call again soon,"
he said.

"Probably tomorrow," Hortense said as the door closed
behind him.

"Very determined, is he?"

"And very nosy, too."

"What do you mean?"

"You should have heard the questions he asked us. Where
was Mark found, had we been able to discuss the accident
with him, why was Jane along?" Hortense paused. "Henry,
is there something you're not telling me?"

While Sir Henry was soothing Hortense, Jane was using
Mark's weakness to change his attitude. Before he had a
chance to complain, she was there, fluffing his pillows,
straightening his bed. Leaning over him, she held the glass
for him to drink. That evening under the watchful eye of
Hortense she fed him his first solid food in some time.

Mark, still weak, did not think about how he was failing
Sir Henry. He simply enjoyed being the focus of Jane's
attention.

After Mark drifted off to sleep that evening, a conference
was held in his sitting room. The participants were Sir Henry,
Hortense, Jane, and Smythe.

"Certainly, sir. I see no difficulty at all in caring for Mr.
Courtland," said Smythe

"He shouldn't be left alone," Jane said, trying to persuade the others to let her sit up with Mark.

"You heard Smythe. He can manage on his own. Mark will probably sleep through the night," Sir Henry said firmly.

"Besides, you'll be needed to keep Mark occupied tomorrow." Hortense smiled as she put the final stone in place.

"Then one of you."

"Nonsense, my dear. Smythe will have a camp bed in the room. That will be sufficient." Sir Henry refused to listen to any more of her protests. "I'm for bed. Let's go and let Smythe get some rest too." He swept them into the hall.

She was going to have to have lessons in argument, Jane decided, if she was to prevent Sir Henry from manipulating her. He was too good at it. Resentfully she prepared for bed.

Usually a sound sleeper, Jane was restless that evening. When she woke up for the second time in an hour, she stretched and eased out of bed. Sliding her feet into slippers, she pulled her dressing gown about her and picked up a candle. With any luck she could be in and out of Mark's room without anyone but Smythe noticing her.

She opened the door to the hall cautiously and slipped outside. Quickly she made her way to Mark's door and opened it.

She pulled it shut behind her and tiptoed toward the camp bed where Smythe lay. "Smythe?" she whispered, putting a hand on his shoulder. "Smythe?"

CHAPTER
13

Behind Jane a spoon clattered to the floor. She whirled. Cautiously she approached the bed. Holding the candle in front of her, she searched the room carefully. There was no one there. Just before she reached the foot of the bed, a dark figure jumped out of the hangings and wrenched the candle from her.

"Stop! What are you doing?" she cried. As the figure, a man she thought, swept past her, he pushed her into the curtains at the end of the bed. A few seconds later she felt a draft and heard the door slam shut.

Coughing and swinging wildly, Jane untangled herself from the heavy velvet draperies and stumbled to her feet, falling against the side of the bed. Before she could break completely free of the velvet in order to follow the intruder, someone had her by the hand.

She started to scream, but a hand clamped down over her mouth. "Wait. Light some candles before you chase after him," Mark said, his voice shaky.

"Mark?" Jane pulled his hand away and felt her way to the table where they had kept his medicine. Finding a candle, he made her way to the fireplace and lit the taper. After hrowing some logs on the dying fire, she hurried back to Mark's side.

"Are you all right?" she asked, holding the candle so that he could observe him closely.

"Just winded. He had a pillow over my face." Mark paused, torn by coughing.

"A pillow? Are you certain?"

"As I can be," he said, his tone rather dry. She straightened his pillows and blanket, allowing him to straighten his nightshirt.

"Well, I don't understand why Smythe didn't hear him. Oh, my goodness, Smythe!" Jane hurried to the camp bed hat blocked the entrance to the room.

"Is he alive?" Mark asked anxiously.

"Yes. He doesn't seem to be injured. Wait! Here's a bump. That person hit him."

"Jane, you'd better alert the household. That man could be anywhere."

Grimacing as she thought of Sir Henry's and Hortense's reactions to her presence in Mark's room, Jane tugged the bell-pull. She lit the branch of candles on the mantel and then bent over Smythe again. "He seems to be breathing normally."

Mark leaned up on his elbow to watch her. She was so lovely with that long braid hanging over her shoulder. The soft folds of her blue dressing gown swathed her from head to toe. He longed to remove it, along with the nightgown whose lace just peaked out at the neck.

His dreams were shattered a few minutes later when Sir Henry arrived. "Jane, what is happening? And what are you doing here at this time of night?" He frowned at her. He looked so peculiar with his pale, bare legs sticking out from under his silk dressing gown and with his nightcap askew that Jane had to hold back a laugh.

Mark, however, saw nothing to laugh at. "Thank heavens she was here! Had she not come in I would be dead by now."

"Dead?" asked Hortense, who obviously had taken some time to arrange her nightcap and select her most becoming dressing gown.

"And Smythe, too. Jane, look at him again to see how he's doing?"

"Smythe? What's the matter with him?" asked Sir Henry, still confused.

"He was hit on the head." Jane bent over the camp bed. "He seems to be all right except for that."

"Will no one tell me what is going on?" Hortense demanded, her nightcap sliding over her eyes.

"Yes. I too would like to know," Sir Henry added. By that time Marsden and his wife had arrived.

"Sir Henry, you should have someone inspect the house immediately," Jane said, realizing the intruder could be hiding in another room.

"Of course." He turned to give the order and then swung back. "And what shall I tell them to look for?"

"An intruder. He was dressed in dark clothing. He slipped past me and into the hall," Jane said impatiently. "Mark wouldn't let me follow him."

"Follow him? Nonsense." Sir Henry turned to his butler. "Rouse your most trusted men and search the house thoroughly. Then make certain the house is secure."

Mrs. Marsden moved toward the camp bed. "I'll look after Smythe now, Miss Jane," she said quietly. Crossing to the bed, Jane took a position near Mark.

Hortense, who was stunned by the thought that someone had entered her home without permission, sat in a chair staring at the fire.

"Well, are you going to keep silent forever?" Sir Henry asked. "What are you doing here, Jane?"

Realizing that the time had come for her reckoning, Jane cleared her throat. She began fiddling with the fringe on her dressing-gown sash. Then Mark captured her hand. His comforting touch gave her the courage to explain. How she could be so strong when it came to him and so frightened when she was involved she couldn't explain.

When she began, her voice was a whisper. "I couldn't sleep."

"You couldn't what?" asked Hortense, leaning forward to hear better.

"I couldn't sleep. I was worried about Mark. I thought no one would know if I quickly ran down here to check on him," she said quickly.

"Humph!"

"I know what you told me, but I didn't think anyone would see me," she said defensively. "And no one would have if that person hadn't been here."

"Yes, tell us about that person," Hortense suggested.

"I came in and stopped to make certain Smythe knew I was there. But I couldn't wake him up. Then the spoon dropped."

"The spoon?"

Mark interrupted. "The person had a pillow over my face when Jane came in. A few minutes longer, and I would have been gone."

"But who was he? How did he get in? And what happened to him?" Sir Henry asked impatiently.

"I'm not certain about the first two, but he left through the hall door," Mark said. "When Jane tried to rouse Smythe, she startled my attacker so much he hit the table."

"Something hit the floor, and I came toward the bed," Jane said, caught up once more in the terror she had felt.

"After blowing out the candle, he got away. Maybe the servants will find him."

"Did you see his face?"

Both of them shook their heads. "It was too dark, and he was wearing a mask," Jane said.

"A mask?" Sir Henry's tone was thoughtful.

"Do you mean to say that . . . that assassin was here

deliberately to harm Mark?'' Hortense asked indignantly.

Before Sir Henry could answer, Marsden was back. He bent to whisper in Sir Henry's ear. "Out with it, man. Everyone will know soon enough as it is," Sir Henry said loudly.

"There is no sign of the intruder anywhere."

"I knew he would get away. You should have let me follow him. I knew you should."

"And have him kill you? Not while I could prevent it," said Mark weakly. "Besides, he would have slipped away by the time you reached the hall. You were fairly entangled in the bed hangings."

Marsden cleared his throat pointedly. "Go on, Marsden," Sir Henry said, sending a stern look at the two squabbling young people.

"The French doors in the large drawing room, the ones that lead to the rose garden, were open, sir."

"Open? Were they forced?"

"No sir."

"Then he had to have help within the household," Sir Henry said quietly.

"Sir!"

"I know, Marsden. I don't want to believe it either, but what other explanation can you offer?" The butler was silent.

Hortense, who had been listening quietly, stood up. "Henry, something is going on. First Mark's accident and then an intruder. We've never had this much excitement before."

Henry, Jane, and Mark exchanged rueful glances. Before they began to explain, though, Sir Henry turned to the Marsdens. "Please see that Smythe is taken care of. Send for the herb woman if necessary. But I do think he would rest better in his own bed, don't you agree?"

With the help of two of the footmen, Smythe was soon safely in his own bed with the Marsdens looking after him. Then Sir Henry turned to Mark. "I suppose we'll have to tell her."

"I don't think we can avoid it."

"Tell me? Tell me what?" Hortense asked, nervous and distraught.

Mark pulled on Jane's hand. "Water, please." He took a sip and coughed weakly. "I think tonight and my 'accident' happened because of what I saw at the barn."

CHAPTER
14

The silence in the room was almost deafening. Mark's words seemed to hang in the air, creating specters that the others had never dreamed of. In the glow of the candles and the firelight, the room seemed to shimmer as if Mark's words had set in motion something that could not be stopped.

Sir Henry was the first to find his voice. "Your accident? What could tonight have to do with that? You were thrown from your horse."

"Was I?" Mark asked sardonically. He pulled Jane closer to him, indicating that she should sit on the edge of the bed beside him. With a defiant look at Hortense, Jane climbed the step and took her seat. Hortense closed her eyes and sank back into her chair by the fire.

"You'd better have a seat too, Sir Henry," the injured man suggested. With everyone seated, Mark leaned back on his pillows. "My accident was no accident," he said.

"What? But we found you where your horse had thrown you," Sir Henry explained.

"You found me where someone had dumped me," Mark corrected him.

"Go on, Mark," Jane said quietly, her heart beating furiously. Hortense, her nerves already agitated by the events of the evening, could hardly breathe.

"Coming back to the Abbey, I decided to stop by the barn to check its roof." Mark looked from Sir Henry to Jane carefully. At their nods, he continued. "As I got closer, I saw the snow had been packed down by hoofprints. It looked as if a hunt had taken place there. Not certain if anyone was still there, I got off my horse and made my way cautiously to the door."

"So cautiously that you were almost killed," Jane muttered, her face set.

"Why didn't you ride to the Abbey and get some help?"

"I didn't think about it. I was right there. The tracks were there, but I didn't see any horses or men. I really didn't think about the danger."

"Didn't think is probably right," whispered Jane, but not so quietly that Mark couldn't hear. The hand that had been stroking her braid gave it a good tug. "Stop that!" she said.

"What? What are you talking about?" Sir Henry asked.

Hortense, whose sharp eyes had noticed what was happening, said firmly, "You get off that bed and come sit by me."

Jane flashed a look at Mark as if to say "Look what you've done" and settled herself more firmly on the bed. "I'm fine right here, Cousin Hortense," she said, smiling sweetly.

Sir Henry, impatient over the delay, rose and crossed to the bed. "It's late, and I hope to get some sleep tonight. Could you please continue with your story?" He frowned at Mark, who nodded. Having made his point, he seated himself again.

"I was investigating the tracks. Holding my horse, I crept closer to the door. Hearing nothing—you know how thick the walls of that barn are—I opened the door." He paused and looked at Hortense. She was leaning forward as though to catch every word. "The place was full."

"Well, that was not unexpected, surely?" Sir Henry asked.

"Yes, it was," Mark reminded him. "The barn should

have been almost empty. All that should have been left was the seed.''

"Seed? Please explain. I don't understand what you are talking about," Hortense said.

"The seed grain Mark bought in Holland," Jane began, and then put a hand over her mouth.

"In Holland?" Hortense's voice was a screech.

"Well, you've done it now," Mark said disgustedly.

"Mark, don't blame Jane. In a few minutes Hortense would have known the whole anyway." He turned to his cousin and said crossly, "Hortense, calm yourself. Do you want to wake the entire household again?"

"Smugglers! I've been living in a house with smugglers! No wonder your accident was no accident. Some of your villains wanted to get back at you, no doubt. How could you? I'll never be able to hold my head up again. I suppose everyone knows." She pointed her finger at Jane. "You knew.''

"Hortense, be quiet!" Sir Henry's command voice cut through her excited ranting. Startled, she closed her mouth. "If you will listen, I'll explain."

Once more Sir Henry and Mark told of their attempts to locate grain for the tenants, the business in London, their final realization of their only chance. Like Jane, Hortense was sympathetic, but she was still upset. "I helped to deliver smuggled grain," she moaned. "From now on I can expect to hear a knock at my door. I am a criminal.''

After listening to her ranting for several minutes, Sir Henry had heard enough. "Hortense, be quiet! It's over and done with, and your comments won't change anything."

Mark cleared his throat hesitantly. "No it isn't," he said quietly.

"Isn't what?" Jane asked.

"Isn't over."

"Not over? What do you mean?" Sir Henry frowned.

"That's what I've been trying to tell you. When I entered

the barn it was full. Not only was there the seed, but I found brandy and sacks that looked as if they contained fabric.''

"Brandy?"

"Fabric?" The other three looked at him with renewed interest.

"There were other bundles too. I had just started to investigate when I was hit," Mark explained.

"Hit? By whom?" Jane asked.

"I don't know. I didn't see anyone. But if the goods are found in that barn it could be dangerous for all of us." Mark leaned back weakly on his pillows. "You need to send out someone trustworthy to check."

"I'll go myself," Sir Henry promised. "Then you think the attack tonight is linked to what you saw in the barn."

"Yes. Who knew about my injuries?"

"The whole district." Sir Henry shrugged his shoulders. "You know how servants talk."

"And my recovery?"

"The same. There's been someone here from almost every landowner in the district each day to check on you. You're very popular." Sir Henry smiled at him fondly.

"Especially with Lord and Lady Brough," Jane added wickedly. "The lemons for your lemon water were sent over just yesterday."

Mark frowned at her and then began to cough. Hortense glanced disapprovingly at Mark. She stood up. "Everything else can wait until tomorrow. Mark needs his rest. He is gray with weariness."

"But we can't leave Mark alone," Jane said.

"I'll stay with him," Sir Henry promised. He crossed to the bed. Before Jane could protest, he picked her up and swung her to the floor, placing a kiss on her brow.

Mark felt as though he had been stabbed. How could he have forgotten Sir Henry's plans? He closed his eyes and sank farther into his pillows. As tired as he was, sleep was not easy to find that night.

*　　*　　*

Both Jane and Hortense had trouble falling asleep too. Jane, filled with excitement at the way Mark had held on to her, considered ways she could be with him and still keep her promise to Hortense and Sir Henry.

Hortense's thoughts were not so pleasant. Smugglers! All her life she had heard what low men they were. Now to find that her cousin, the owner of the house in which she lived, the man who provided her such a generous allowance, was a smuggler was more than she could bear. Mark Courtland, too. And her own involvement kept her sleepless. Finally she too sank into a sleep punctuated by nightmares.

Sir Henry spent the rest of the night reviewing the list of people who had inquired about Mark. Some, financial backers in their grain deal, he eliminated immediately. But when Hortense came to relieve him immediately after breakfast, his list was still long.

Ignoring Hortense's demands that he get some rest before he went off playing hero, he paused only to don riding dress and his greatcoat. Earlier he had sent Marsden to the stables with a message. By the time he arrived there, the horses were already saddled, and three men waited impatiently.

As he briefed them carefully, Sir Henry checked their faces. Their astonishment seemed genuine. Giving the signal, Sir Henry mounted, admitting to himself that he was getting too old to enjoy this type of action.

Although the trip had seemed endless when they were bringing Mark to the Abbey, it took only a half an hour of hard riding to reach the barn.

Sir Henry signaled the others. As his men pulled up around him, he said quietly, "Let's not go in blindly. Proceed with caution. Look for hoofprints, any sign that will tell us who was involved."

Slowly they made their way over the rise toward the gray stone barn. "Sir Henry, look," the first groom called. "Hoofprints, lots of them."

"And wagons too!" another man called. "They all seem to be heading away from here."

"Whoever rode those horses had to be coming from the barn," one man said. The closer they came the more they knew how accurate he was. By the time they had reached the barn, Sir Henry was sure that the smuggled goods were gone.

In spite of his feelings, Sir Henry refused to take needless risks. "Slowly, men. Remember, keep calm." He made his way to the partially opened doors and slipped inside. One after the other, the other three followed.

"Leave the doors open," Sir Henry said quietly when he realized they were alone. As the daylight streamed in, he saw what he had feared—an empty barn. Even the seed was gone. The long night without sleep was beginning to tell on him. "Dammit! It's not fair!" he muttered under his breath. "And who will go this time?"

The ride back to the Abbey was longer than going, for they refused to push their horses. Sir Henry made his way reluctantly to Mark's rooms. "It's gone," he said once he had sent the footman on an errand.

"Gone? The brandy?"

"Everything." the older man said emotionlessly.

Mark sighed and closed his eyes. "Gone."

"Don't worry about it now." Sir Henry said. "I'm off to bed." He smothered a yawn. "If you can, try to remember what was there."

All that day Mark slept off and on. The events of the evening before had been more exhausting than his system was ready for. Jane, who looked in on him several times, always found him asleep. The dullness of her day continued till dinner. Since Sir Henry chose to dine in his room, Jane had to face Hortense alone.

The older woman made no secret of her disapproval of Jane's actions. She began with the clear soup and continued through the pudding. "That you were in Mark's room is positively scandalous. I do not care whether you saved his life or not. You shouldn't have been there. Do you understand?" She paused to allow the servants to present the next course. Jane, her eyes fixed on her plate, moved her food from one side of the plate to another.

As soon as they left the room, Hortense continued, "What the servants must have thought! When the Marsdens entered the room and you were sitting on Mark's bed, well, I could see their raised eyebrows even if you couldn't. I suppose every household in the district knows what kind of woman you are now. Do not be surprised to find that you are not included in the next invitations."

Jane gritted her teeth and let Hortense ramble, her worry about what Mark would do to replace the seed insulating her from the barbed comments. Why did Sir Henry have to report what he found so accurately?

"Such behavior." Hortense picked up her lecture again as she lifted her spoon to take the first bite of pudding. "And after your promise."

"My promise?" Jane asked wryly.

"That you would not be alone with him."

"I didn't break my promise. Smythe was there," Jane said smugly, pleased that she had an opportunity to contradict Hortense.

"Humph! An unconscious man."

"Well, I didn't know he was unconscious. I even stopped to wake him up." Jane was so righteous that all Hortense could do was fume.

When supper was over, Hortense stood up. "I think an early night would be appropriate for both of us. Goodnight." She was out of the room before Jane had a chance to reply. Glancing about the empty room, Jane sighed and made her way up to her suite.

The next morning nothing seemed quite as bleak as it had the day before. As soon as breakfast was over, Sir Henry closeted himself with Mark, once again in the hands of a fully recovered Smythe. "Good, Mark. This will help," he said as he looked over the list of goods that Mark had compiled. "I'll dash off a few notes. See if anyone has heard of anything. Some of this merchandise should be easy to spot."

He paused and smiled at Mark, who was twisting, trying to raise himself to a sitting position. "You just get plenty of rest, my boy. I've got everything under control."

Watching his friend walk briskly out the door, Mark muttered, "Get plenty of rest! Ha! What does he think I've been doing?"

"Did you say something, sir? Is there anything I can get you?" Smythe asked, his self-esteem still smarting from the way he had allowed Mark to be attacked.

"Nothing, Smythe." Watching his servant put the shaving materials away, Mark noted the slight droop of his shoulders. "Well, if it's not too much trouble . . . " he said hesitantly.

"Anything, sir. Anything!"

"That milk pudding you served me when I took that fall last spring. The one you made yourself? I think I could eat that if I had some." Mark smiled at his valet.

"But I would have to leave you alone, sir," Smythe protested.

"The bellpull is within reach. I'll be fine."

Reluctantly the valet allowed himself to be persuaded. "If you're certain. You'll call if you need anything?"

Mark watched in satisfaction as the door closed behind Smythe. He stretched and flexed his muscles. After a few minutes of twisting and turning, his sheets were tangled around him. Mark looked longingly at the chair beside the fireplace. He was so tired of lying in bed.

For a few minutes he lay there motionless. Then a smile lit his face. Cautiously he sat up and swung one leg over the edge of the bed. The other soon followed. Disdaining the use of the step, Mark slid off the bed. As he hit the floor, he had to grab the bed hanging to keep from being a heap on the floor.

Even the little energy he had used had left him drained. That chair seemed so far away. Resolutely, he straightened, still holding on to the velvet draperies. Cautiously he moved toward the head of the bed and the sturdy table beside it. If he could only hold on to something, he would make it.

A few minutes later he started as the door flew open. "Smythe, I've come to entertain your master. Is he awake? I've brought some cards." Jane said happily. Then she caught sight of Mark halfway across the room, his nightshirt barely covering his knees. "If Cousin Hortense ever finds out about this . . ." she whispered.

"Jane?" asked mark, his heart beating rapidly. The promise he had made himself went completely out of his mind. He forgot how weak he was and let go of the cabinet. Halfway through his turn, he began to sway alarmingly.

"Here, let me help." Jane rushed to his side, putting her arm around his waist. Mark leaned heavily against her, his arm encircling her shoulders. As she supported him, he took a breath of her clean, jasmine-scented hair.

"Hmm. You smell so good," he whispered.

Jane blushed as pink as the roses embroidered on her dress. "Hush. Let's get you back to bed now. What do you think you're doing, trying to get up?" she scolded.

"I had to do something. I'm tired of just lying in bed."

"You have something to do—get well. And don't think you're going to have a chance to do this again until we tell you you're ready."

As they neared the bed, Mark pulled away from her. "I can walk by myself," he said just before his knees started to give way. Trying to reach the bed, he took a hasty step, only to catch his foot on the rug.

"Mark!" Jane cried as she tried to grab him.

CHAPTER

15

With Mark's heavy weight pressing on her, Jane felt her feet slipping on the rug. She struggled backward, trying to support both of them. Feeling the bed behind her, she sagged against its edge.

Mark, using the bed hangings to help him, pulled himself more upright, sliding along Jane's trapped body. He paused and looked into her wide gray eyes.

Without thinking, he pressed closer, his hands running down her back and sides. She shivered and drew a quavering breath. Dark brown eyes held gray ones as his hand reached to caress her cheek.

"Jane," he whispered as he bent his head toward hers, his eyes holding hers captive. His first tentative kiss led to another. She responded to each new caress with enthusiasm. When Mark drew back to catch his breath, Jane sighed and followed. Soon, without either of them realizing what had happened, they were on the floor by the bed, arms holding each other close, legs entangled. His hands completely free at last, Mark cupped one breast as he bent once more to kiss her. Their lips parted; they kissed, Mark's tongue teaching

Jane new sensations. Jane's hand found its way to the nape of his neck, playing with his disheveled curls.

"You're beautiful. So beautiful," he whispered as he feathered light kisses over her face and throat. She was so sweet, so responsive.

Jane for the first time since her mother's death had lost the feeling of loneliness. "Mark," she whispered. "Oh yes." Then she was once more lost in the new sensations. Her hands slid into the open neck of his nightshirt and down his back, stroking the broad shoulders, reveling in his whispered encouragements.

Soon even the most passionate kisses weren't enough. Mark moved closer to Jane, searching out the buttons that ran down her back. Filled with an aching, a fire that was new to her, Jane sought to move even closer. Her eyes widened as Mark pulled her under him, his aroused body pressed into hers sending ripples of delight through her. As his hand released the first button, she shivered.

"Don't be afraid, my love," he said as he kissed her once more, his tongue teaching hers the moves he wanted her body to make.

Jane, caught in a sea of sensations, of pure enjoyment, didn't answer but initiated a kiss, her tongue revealing she had learned her lessons well. Mark returned to her buttons, his mouth leaving a soft line of kisses on her throat, pausing for a moment to nibble on an earlobe.

Jane followed his lead as though in a dance. His caresses teaching her a new sensation, sensations she wanted to share, Jane kissed his throat and ran the tip of her tongue around the outside of his ear.

Caught in the net of their own emotions, they didn't hear the door open, didn't even respond to the first words. "I am very disappointed in you, Smythe. How you could leave your master unattended?" Hortense approached the bed rapidly, still scolding the servant.

As she drew closer and her voice grew louder, the pair on the floor lay as if turned to stone, Jane's face hidden in

Mark's neck, waiting for retribution, which was not long in coming. Hortense rounded the end of the bed, almost tripping over the lovers trapped there.

"Mark, dear boy, have you . . . Mark! Jane!" Her scream was loud enough to alert every maid and footman on the floor. Smythe dashed toward the bed, stopping in dismay at the sight of the couple entwined there.

Hortense's shrieks brought a host of servants crowding around the door until Smythe shut it. "Send someone for Sir Henry," he said forcefully.

"Sir Henry?"

"What's wrong?"

"Is Mr. Courtland dead?"

"All of you, back to work. Everything will be fine," Smythe said, dismissing them. Reluctantly, they made their way back to their tasks, the few who had had the luck to be close enough to see spreading the word to those who hadn't.

When Smythe returned to his master's bedroom, Hortense was standing in the middle of the room, obviously drawing a breath so that she could begin ranting again. Cautiously Mark sat up, leaving Jane free. She stood up, shaking her disheveled skirts into place, trying to smooth the wrinkles from the soft wool. Her cheeks flamed.

"Help me up, please," Mark whispered, pulling on her hand. The strength that had been so evident a few minutes earlier had gone, leaving him weak and shaking.

Smythe hurried to his side. "Here, sir, let me help." Carefully he and Jane lifted Mark to his feet and guided him back into bed. Jane, outwardly calm, was shaking. She smoothed the coverlet over Mark's chest and fluffed his pillows, her actions automatic. Her eyes were a dark gray, haunted by despair.

As she turned to face Hortense, Mark caught her hand, "Jane, I'm sorry," he whispered. His actions trapped her close to his bedside.

"I'm sorry" rang through her mind. He regretted what he had done. Tears welled up in her eyes and threatened to overflow. All she wanted to do was get away, to be alone in her agony.

Although it seemed like hours since Hortense's entrance, it had only been minutes. Hortense, her hand covering her eyes, slumped in the chair near the bedside. When she sat up ready to face the situation again, the first thing she saw was Jane standing beside the bed, her hand clasped tightly in Mark's. "How could you?" Hortense asked angrily.

Jane blushed furiously. Mark, more confident than he had felt in a long time, said, "Mrs. Morgan, I can explain."

"Explain! Explain! I know what I saw. What the servants saw. We'll be the talk of the neighborhood before evening. I can just see it now. Our names stricken from every invitation list in the area. I shall have to leave the country."

"Leave the country? But you didn't do anything," Jane said, trying to soothe her.

"No, but I was your chaperon. Oh," she moaned, "to think that a girl I sponsored should act this way! I'm ruined, ruined!"

Jane opened her mouth, but before she could utter a word, Hortense had cut her off. "Don't say a word, you wicked girl. I should have known what would happen. Won't the gossips love this!" She crossed to stand in front of Jane. Shaking her finger in the girl's face, she said, "Why, only last night you promised. Why should I have believed you after the scandalous way you entered Mark's bedchamber before? And in his weakened condition!" She whirled and marched back to her chair. "I can no longer be responsible for you. You will have to leave."

"Leave?" Jane said, thoroughly distraught. One tear slid from the corner of her eye down her cheek. Her hand gripped Mark's even tighter.

"No," he said firmly. "I'm the one to blame. If anyone leaves, it will be me."

"Nonsense. It's her reputation that has been ruined. Leave she will," Hortense said firmly. "I'll not have a strumpet living in my home."

"A strumpet? How dare you call Jane that?" Mark tried to get up, but Jane pushed him back.

"Your house?" asked Sir Henry quizzically, his black eyes snapping. He had entered a few moments before. "That will be all, Smythe. Thank you."

"Smythe?"

"Yes, Hortense, Smythe."

She sank farther back in the chair, her mind replaying with horror every detail of the scene they had played before the valet.

"Now what has happened?" the older man demanded, his shoulders straight, his back ramrod-stiff. "One at a time, please."

Mark glanced at Jane, who nodded. "Smythe had gone to fix me his special milk pudding. I was tired of lying in bed, so I decided to walk around the room."

"Pull yourself around the room," Jane said quickly. "Sir Henry, he could barely stand up even with the furniture to lean on."

"Humph! Standing up indeed! Not when I arrived, anyway."

"Hush, Jane. You too, Hortense. Go on, my boy."

"Jane came in to play cards with me."

"So that's what you call it," Hortense said snidely.

Mark shot her an angry look and continued, "I was startled and began to fall. Jane was helping me back to the bed when I fell."

"And that's why you were on the floor, rolling around, your arms around each other, kissing? Ha!" said Hortense righteously.

Mark intertwined his fingers more closely with Jane's, refusing to look up. But his cheeks were almost as red as Jane's.

"Well, is there any truth in what she says?" Sir Henry asked quietly.

"And ask him what he was wearing," Hortense suggested.

"A nightshirt."

"And a short one at that. Even as a married woman I was

shocked. Scandalous! And she no better, with her dress unbuttoned. It still is," Hortense pointed out smugly.

Mark pulled Jane closer and turned her away from him. Slipping his hand under her disheveled hair, he reached for the first button.

"Stop that! How dare you!" Hortense cried.

"Hortense, be quiet," said Sir Henry sternly. He watched as Mark fastened the last button on Jane's dress and smoothed her hair, caressing her cheek as he did so. Jane, her cheeks still red, reached up to capture his hand once more.

"How dare you, Henry! I know what I saw." The outrage in Hortense's voice was very evident.

Sir Henry smiled thoughtfully and nodded his head. "Yes, I'm sure you do," he said soothingly. "But there are some facts you don't know."

"What?" The other two looked at him strangely, not certain what was going to happen.

"I told them we should tell everyone, Hortense. But they wanted to wait."

"Wait? Wait for what?"

"For Mark to get well first."

Mark and Jane exchanged a questioning look, still puzzled. But at least Hortense was no longer raging.

"Just what were they going to tell me?" she asked coldly.

"Why, only that Mark had asked my permission to marry Jane, and that both she and I agreed."

"Marry?" The three voices rang out in chorus.

CHAPTER

16

For a few minutes there was only stunned silence as the other three occupants of the room stared at Sir Henry. Jane and Mark glanced at each other and then quickly away, each not certain what the light in the other's eyes meant.

Hortense was the first to find her voice. "Well, I certainly wish someone would have the courtesy to inform me," she said, her voice once more a languid drawl. "After all, I have been sponsoring the girl. I really must congratulate you, Henry. When you first suggested . . ."

"Hortense," he said, a smile hiding his gritted teeth, "shouldn't Mark be the one you congratulate?"

"Of course. I will later. But you really are . . ."

He cut her off again. With both Jane and Mark staring at him strangely, he asked desperately, "Don't you want to hear why we didn't tell you?"

"Naturally she does," Jane said smiling. "And so do I," she muttered to Mark.

"Yes, of course. Now, Mark, I want to hear all the details. Where did you propose?"

Mark gulped and started a coughing spell. "Very convenient,'' Jane whispered as she pounded him on the back. ''Perhaps Sir Henry should continue, since you are having such difficulty,'' she suggested.

''We can wait, can't we, Hortense?''

''But you tell such a good story,'' Jane said, for once glad to see her old friend in difficulties. There was something strange in his announcement.

If looks could strike people down in their tracks, Sir Henry's would have eliminated Jane. He glared at her and then smiled. It was the kind of smile that Jane associated with a hungry wolf. She stared at him apprehensively.

Sir Henry pulled his olive-green coat straight and crossed to the mirror above the fireplace to straighten his cravat. In those few seconds he tried to marshal his thoughts, to pull a story together.

''Henry, stop fiddling with your clothes! Are you going to tell me how this engagement happened?'' She looked at him defiantly. ''Or are you trying to fob me off with some lie?''

''Lie?''

''It is rather strange to me that no one mentioned this engagement the whole time Mark was so ill.''

''That was the reason.''

''What?''

''Jane didn't want to distract anyone's attention from Mark. With him so ill she felt we should wait.''

''How commendable of her. And just when did this engagement take place?'' Hortense smiled sweetly at her sparring partner.

Jane opened her mouth to make a comment, but Mark put his hand over her mouth. When she looked at him indignantly, he whispered laughingly, ''Shh. Let's see how he gets out of this.''

''Why, Hortense, surely you remember?'' Sir Henry said calmly.

''Remember? Remember what?''

''The day of Mark's accident. Jane mentioned that Mark wanted to talk to me.''

"Did you?" Mark asked Jane quietly.

"Yes."

"That sly fox." Mark's admiration was evident as he beamed at his friend.

"You told her you hadn't seen him." Hortense was not going to let him get away with anything.

"I lied."

"Henry!"

"Well, we were going to tell you at dinner. Have a celebration, as it were," he improvised quickly.

"And that's the reason I insisted on helping to find Mark," Jane added helpfully, only to have her friend glower at her and Hortense inspect her as if she were some new species that had just been identified.

"I must admit it sounds plausible. It might just work." Hortense stood up carefully and looked at the young couple, their hands still clasped. "Hmm. Engaged. A few discreet notes to the right people. Yes, that might be the answer." She walked leisurely to the door, her lilac taffeta skirt swishing around her. She paused with her hand on the doorlatch and glanced at the three conspirators. "You do realize that with all this gossip the wedding must be as soon as possible."

Before anyone could answer her, she had slipped out the door, closing it carefully after her. As soon as she was alone, she skipped once and then headed sedately to her room.

The scene Hortense left behind was anything but peaceful. "Why did you tell her that we were engaged?" Jane positively shrieked.

"What did she mean, married at once? Sir Henry, I refuse to do this," Mark said, searching his friend for the despair he would have felt if he had had to announce Jane's marriage to someone else.

"Refuse?" Jane asked quietly. She retreated to the window in confusion.

"Mark, what are you saying?" the older man asked, his black eyes flashing. "No gentleman would put a lady in such a position without offering to do the honorable thing. I'm shocked at you.''

"No, I didn't mean that. Really. I am pleased to be engaged to Jane—Miss Woodley. But you, you . . .'' The excitement of the last hour finally caught up with him; he broke into a paroxysm of coughing. The whistling sound as he tried to suck air into his lungs frightened his two companions.

"Here, help him sit up," Jane tried, pulling Mark upright.

"Where's that medicine? Did Hortense take it with her?"

"It's over there." Jane pointed to the table. "Bring some of that lemon water too."

By the time they got Mark settled comfortably again, neither Sir Henry nor Jane had any energy left. Breathing sighs of relief, they sank into the chairs.

After a few minutes, Jane asked quietly, "What is our engagement going to solve? As soon as I break if off, Hortense will be as indignant as ever.'' Mark, still breathless, nodded his agreement. "Besides, you heard her. We need to get married immediately.''

"Just what were you doing when she walked in?'' Sir Henry asked. Mark glanced at him quickly, but the only emotion he could detect was curiosity.

Jane looked at Mark and blushed a pink that would have put the pinks in the gardens to shame. She shivered slightly and clasped her hands tightly in front of her to keep them still. The tip of her tongue wet her still-tender lips. She glanced at Mark, her heart beating faster, and looked away just as quickly when she saw the passion in his eyes.

Mark too was caught up in his memories. She was so soft, so sweet, so responsive. He held her glance for a moment and then looked at his friend. The rich color his face had worn a few minutes before drained away, leaving him pale. How could I have done it? he asked himself.

"Well, is someone going to tell me, or shall I ask Smythe?'' Sir Henry asked.

"We were kissing,'' Mark said hastily.

"Kissing? Hortense was that upset because of a kiss?"

"Maybe not." Jane kept her eyes firmly on the floor. She whispered, "I think it was because we were on the floor."

Although Hortense had mentioned it earlier, he had only noticed her tone, not the words. "On the floor!" Sir Henry's booming voice echoed throughout the room, rattling the glasses on the table.

"I fell," Mark said with a wheeze.

"And I tried to catch him."

"Interesting. Most interesting. I always miss the excitement," Sir Henry said with a frown. "That does make things a bit different."

"Different?"

"How?" The two questions came at the same time.

"Think of the way you were dressed, Mark. And to be caught in a passionate embrace—I suppose it was passionate?" he asked clinically.

Jane refused to look at him. Mark, an embarrassed smile on his face, nodded.

"Well, I see no other choice."

"Choice? What choice? Sir Henry, please be less cryptic." Jane asked, a frown crossing her face.

The older man looked at the two of them carefully.

"You were going to explain," Mark reminded his friend.

"Yes." He looked at Jane and Mark closely. "In this case Hortense is right. I'll make arrangements for you to marry as soon as Mark recovers."

For a minute neither Jane nor Mark could speak. Jane's eyes were huge, her brows lifted in surprise. Slowly her eyes began to sparkle, and a soft flush brightened her cheeks. Mark's wife—the thought sent shivers through her. Hoping to see a similar reaction, she glanced at Mark shyly.

"Of course. If we must," the younger man said, a deep frown creasing his forehead. Jane's hopes came crashing down. She turned quickly and smothered a sob.

Even Sir Henry was taken aback. "Not only is it the

perfect solution to your problem," he told them, "but it also will help cover our search."

"Explain," Mark said, his face still grim. He still could not accept what had happened.

"With your marriage you'll need to finish Courtland Place much faster."

"Yes, but I don't see what that has to do with the smugglers."

"You're going to need fabrics for draperies, for furniture. And probably your wine cellar will need to be restocked. Isn't that right?" Sir Henry asked smugly.

Mark nodded his agreement slowly. Then he said, "They wouldn't offer us the goods outright. You know that."

"No, but merchants in this area might have access to them."

"And I'll need lots of new clothes. Most of them I'll send to London for, but for ribbons, bonnets, gloves, and more personal items I can shop around here," Jane said.

"More clothes? You just bought a whole new wardrobe. Why do you need to get more? I'll buy you some after we're married," Mark said, concerned over her using Sir Henry's money to pay for their wedding.

"No, it's a perfect idea. Linens too, Jane. Maybe some lace. Whatever you can think of. You and Hortense put your heads together and make sure everything is complete. Send the bills to me." In spite of Jane's protests and Mark's anger, he refused to change his mind.

"It would be more appropriate if I paid for everything," Mark stated firmly.

"And deprive a guardian of a rare pleasure? Nonsense. I'll take care of it."

Jane cleared her throat and said decisively, "Neither of you will have anything to do with it. I'll see to it myself."

Mark and Sir Henry exchanged glances and smiled indulgently. Jane glared at them both. Suddenly, the highs and lows she had been through emotionally that morning left her feeling drained. She closed her eyes and sank down in her chair.

Sir Henry said quickly, "We'll talk about this again later. Come along, Jane. Let's leave Mark to rest. A little rest wouldn't hurt you either." As usual, he didn't give her a chance to respond but practically lifted her from her chair and swept her from the room.

CHAPTER

17

"We need to talk," said Jane tiredly as Sir Henry hustled her out of Mark's room. She was so exhausted she slurred the words.

"Talk? Certainly. But not right now. Jane, you've been under a strain. You go straight to your room and rest. We'll talk later." He silenced her protests. "No, my dear, don't try to talk now. I promise we'll discuss everything later. You go straight to bed. I'll have your maid bring your luncheon to you."

Jane stared at him in a daze. It was only luncheon? She felt as though she had lived several lifetimes already that day. Too emotionally exhausted even to think of arguing with him, she gave in, allowing him to escort her to her rooms.

"Don't let me see you before dinner," he said forcefully. "I want to see roses in those cheeks again."

Roses, she thought as she leaned against the door. He wants me glowing with happiness when I'm being forced to marry someone who doesn't want to marry me. Without trying to undress, she crossed to the bed and climbed up on it.

The events of the morning ran through her mind as though they were pictures in a book whose pages she was turning rapidly. His kisses were so sweet, his hands so warm. But her own reaction puzzled her. How did these things happen to her?

All she wanted was to enjoy life, to have a little excitement. In a moment of self-revelation she stopped herself. What she had really wanted was to be a part of everything. She hated being on the outside looking in. The parties Hortense had taken her to had been wonderful, but they hadn't filled that need. She was accepted, praised. Still, on the inside she had felt alone.

Only with Sir Henry did the feeling disappear. She knew he cared for her, cared more than her own father had done. What would she have done without him? She wouldn't have had this kind of problem in Bath. There would have been no Mark in Bath.

Staring at the blue canopy above her head, she wasn't aware of the tears that trickled helplessly down her cheeks. He had to help her. She couldn't do this to Mark. She'd go away. "The house in Bath," she whispered reassuringly to herself.

For a while that morning she had thought, had dared to hope. The tears became a flood as Jane admitted finally that what she wanted most in the world was not parties, not excitement, but someone to love, someone who would love her. "Oh, Mark," she sobbed. "How am I ever going to be able to leave you?"

She dashed the tears from her cheeks, trying to gain control of herself, but they kept flowing. As hard as the decision was, she knew that it would be better to live alone, isolated from society, than to marry Mark when he didn't want to marry her. "He would come to hate me," she said quietly. "Oh, why did they have to come in then?"

If she had only had more time, maybe he could have learned to love her. He was attracted to her. The memory of his quiet support during Hortense's harangue brought a revival of hope. It was short-lived. She also remembered his "I refuse." Sir Henry would help her; he had to. Sobbing quietly, she sank into a restless sleep.

The man whose support Jane was counting on was gleefully planning the next step in his coup. "That announcement must be on its way immediately," Sir Henry said, smiling broadly.

"Please tell Mr. Courtland that I offer him my congratulations, sir," said Mr. Herndon, Sir Henry's bailiff, who also was pressed into service as his secretary on occasion. "Miss Woodley seems such a lovely young lady. Such a credit to you."

Sir Henry laughed. "I want the announcement in the London papers by the end of the week." They weren't going to get out of this engagement if he could help it. As he thought of Mark's refusal, a frown creased his brow for a moment. He refused to worry about it too long, though. Those two were perfect for one another. Just perfect.

"Mr. Herndon, on your way out, would you ask Marsden to give a message to my cousin? I need to see her before luncheon."

A short time later, the door opened. "Henry, what is it now?" asked Hortense, her tone somewhat tart.

Seating her carefully, her cousin said sternly, "First, you must never mention that I planned this marriage. By heavens, Hortense, I thought you would destroy everything."

"Me? You didn't see what Smythe and I were witness to!"

"Passionate, hmm?"

"Downright *bawdy*, Henry," she said, surprising him. Before his laughter died away, she said, "All right, Henry. I'll keep your secret. But that couldn't be the only reason you wanted to see me."

Controlling himself with a firm rein, he said, his voice still shaking, "We've got to make certain there's no way either of them can back out."

"Back out? Not if I have anything to do with it." Her eyes

flashed, and her voice picked up speed. "Why, that would be disastrous. She'd be ruined."

"Indeed. Now, what steps can we take to ensure this doesn't happen? If I know Jane, she's probably trying to find a way to convince me right now."

By the time luncheon was over their plans were made. Leaving Hortense to enlist Mrs. Marsden and his bailiff, Sir Henry made his way up the stairs. Drawing a deep breath, he scratched on the door to Mark's suite.

"Is he awake, Smythe?" Sir Henry asked in a hushed voice as he walked into the room almost on tiptoe.

"Yes, sir. I was just on my way to find you. Mr. Courtland wishes to see you." Seating Sir Henry in a chair close by the bedside, he bowed. "I will be downstairs should you need me. Can you reach the bell?" he asked his master. Assured, he made his way out of the room in his usual dignified manner.

Now that his friend was there, Mark didn't know how to begin. His guilt threatened to overwhelm him. "Sir Henry—"

"Mark—" The names overlapped each other, and both men fell silent, each waiting for the other to continue. Finally, Sir Henry took the lead. "Mark, my boy, what was it you wanted to see me about?"

How could he be so cheerful? Mark wondered as he cleared his throat. "I just had . . ." He broke off, coughing. His nervousness was causing his dry throat. "Water," he said when he could gasp.

After putting the glass back on the table, Sir Henry returned to his chair. "I think you've had too much excitement. I'll come back later," he suggested.

"No. I'm all right. Really." Mark pulled himself upright on his pillows. His shoulders were straight, his back as stiff as he could make it. "About this morning," he began hesitantly. "Oh, Sir Henry, I'm sorry. I know what she means to you. But I can't . . ."

"Can't what? You're not trying to back out of the marriage,

are you?'' The look in the older man's eyes was as angry as Mark had ever seen it.

"No, sir. I'll marry her whenever you say." Mark looked closely at his friend. The only emotion he could read in his face was one of relief. A doubt entered his mind, but Mark quickly brushed it away.

"Good. I've sent the announcements to the papers, and Hortense is sending out invitations to an engagement party as soon as you're better." His most pressing worry solved, Sir Henry leaned back in his chair and smiled.

Mark tried again. "I'm sorry I disappointed you, Sir Henry."

"Disappointed me? How?"

"By acting the way I did."

"Nonsense, my boy. Your feelings for that lovely thing just carried you away. Can happen to anyone. Just wish it hadn't been so public."

"Not that. I mean, yes that. Damn." Mark stopped, too confused to think clearly.

"Out with it, my boy," Sir Henry said. "Never knew when you couldn't get your idea across."

Mark took a deep breath and said quickly, "I apologize for stealing the girl you had planned to make your wife."

"My wife?" Sir Henry went into gales of laughter. Mark, ready for a diatribe on his betrayal, was stunned. "My wife, you thought?" His friend was overcome again.

After a few minutes Sir Henry had himself under control. Mark, badly shaken, glowered at him. "I don't understand what's so funny," he said nervously.

"Me? Marry Jane? Come now, my boy. I'm old enough to be her father."

"But, but . . . her clothes, all those presents?"

Realizing the depths of his friend's feelings, Sir Henry sobered. "I care for her. I won't deny that. But as the daughter I never had," he explained. "I'd have done more and sooner if her father had allowed it. That man only thought of two things: himself and money."

"Money?"

"He was a wizard at the Exchange. Turned his inheritance into a fortune and wouldn't spend a penny on anyone but himself."

"Then Jane has been—"

"Spending her own money. Of course. I thought you knew."

"No." Still shaken, Mark asked, "You're not just saying this so I'll feel better, are you? You really don't care that I'm going to marry Jane?"

"Care? My boy, I'm delighted!" He paused and looked at Mark sternly. "You do care for her, don't you? I'll not have her hurt."

Mark's voice was fervent as he said quietly, "I love her. The question is, does she love me? Sir Henry, if she doesn't—"

The older man interrupted briskly, "She does. You should have seen her when we thought you were dying."

Mark too was overcome by memories. Her lips had been so sweet, so yielding. He shook himself and continued, "If she doesn't, I won't have her forced. We'll have to find another way."

Sir Henry agreed, to keep Mark at ease. "How soon can you arrange a meeting with your lawyer?"

"My lawyer?"

"For the marriage settlements. I warn you, my boy, I will be relentless."

"I should be able to come across quite handsomely. The repairs have taken quite a bit of my ready cash, but she'll have a handsome jointure."

Sir Henry looked at him peculiarily and then cleared his throat as if embarrassed. "My boy, that wasn't what I had in mind." He paused uncomfortably, unsure just how to proceed. "As I said, Jane's father was a genius when it came to making money."

"Good. I'm glad she'll have some of her own."

"Mark, Jane is worth eighty thousand pounds."

Mark looked at him, stunned. "I'll be thought a fortune hunter," he gasped.

"Nonsense. You have a sizable fortune of your own. Come now, my boy. We have other problems to discuss," Sir Henry said sternly.

Mark, his pride stinging and his feelings more than a little hurt, nonetheless put his personal feelings aside. He asked, "What problems?"

"The smugglers! Had you forgotten them?"

"Not likely. Tell me what you've discovered."

The last two days had not been easy ones for the older man. And admitting that he had no leads was not comfortable. He squirmed in his chair a few seconds and then rose to stand at the foot of the bed. He looked at his friend sadly. "Nothing," he said unhappily.

"Nothing? But you said . . ."

"I said we needed to talk. I sent out several expresses yesterday. If the people are in London, we should have replies soon."

"Those do-nothings. Humph!"

"Not the Home Office. I wrote to Bow Street."

"Bow Street? Are you trying to have us transported?" Mark asked nervously.

"Of course not. But we need help. Someone has been trying to murder you."

"But a Runner's just as likely to discover our crime as well. Being transported is not the way I want to begin my married life." He paused and then asked, "Jane? Does Jane know about this?"

"No. I had to talk to you first," his friend said reassuringly.

"Me? Why?"

"I thought the Runners could be disguised as workmen employed to finish your house."

The simplicity of it appealed to him, and Mark gave the idea careful thought. "We'd have to let Adams in on it. Otherwise it wouldn't work. And get to Jane. She'll give the show away if we're not careful." Love her though he did, he had no illusions about his darling's temper. And when she was angry, she sometimes spoke before she thought.

"Yes, of course." Sir Henry looked at Mark and grimaced. "I suppose that means Hortense too."

Hortense, he discovered, was no problem at all. Even the thought of Runners did not interrupt her plans for the engagement party and wedding. Jane, however, was a different story.

Immediately after tea that afternoon, he received the message he had been expecting since he left her at her room. She was waiting for him in the library.

Although she was wearing a vivid blue-green dress, her face was pale. Her hair, usually a combination of curls and a sleek knot, had been ruthlessly tamed and slicked back. The style made her eyes, shadowed with worry and tears, seem larger than ever.

She had been standing at the fire, staring pensively into it. As soon as she heard the door open, she turned to face him. He was startled by the bleak look on her face.

Hurrying toward her, he said soothingly, "Jane, my dear, tell me what is wrong."

His sympathy broke the firm control she had on herself. Big tears began to pour down her face again, and her body was wrenched by sobs. Not knowing what else to do, he took her in his arms and patted her shoulder comfortingly.

Just then the door swung open and Marsden appeared. His eyebrows raised, he backed out of the room following his master's silent command.

Hearing the door shut, Jane tried to control her crying. "Who was that?" she asked, her voice shaking.

"Marsden. By the time he gets downstairs and tells Smythe, I'll have to reassure Mark again."

"Mark?" Jane broke into fresh tears.

After a few minutes, Sir Henry's shoulder was wet. Determined to discover what had set her off this time, he reached up and gave her a little shake. Startled, Jane drew back, her breath catching in her throat. Her sobs slowed.

"Better?" he asked quietly. She nodded. "Then you sit down and tell me what's troubling you."

Quietly Jane did as he suggested. For a few moments she just sat there staring at her clasped hands. Then, drawing a shuddering breath, she looked up. Echoing Mark's words, she whispered, "I'm sorry I disappointed you."

"What are you talking about?"

"The way I behaved with Mark, Mr. Courtland." Jane refused to meet his eyes, keeping hers firmly fixed on the lovely oriental rug.

He crossed to stand beside her, putting his hand under her chin and forcing her to meet his eyes. "Nothing you have done disappointed me, my dear. Surprised me, perhaps." He hurried on as he saw a bleak look develop in her eyes. "In fact, I'm pleased. Your marriage to Mark will keep you close by." He patted her hand reassuringly.

"Marry Mark? Oh, Sir Henry, that was only a story to placate Cousin Hortense, wasn't it?" She looked at him, frantic in her need for reassurance.

"A story? Not likely, my dear. I've already sent the notice to the papers," he said firmly.

"The papers? Oh, how could you? How could you?" Jane jumped up, her voice cracked from her tears. She walked to one side of the room and back again, unconsciously pacing. "Get them back!" She whirled to face him. "Send in a retraction. Do something!"

"Jane, stop this minute. Look at me," Sir Henry said commandingly. Startled, she halted. "That's better. Sit down again, and let's discuss this."

"You can stop the announcement, can't you?" she asked hesitantly.

"No."

The words sent chills up her spine. Tears threatened to overflow again. Angrily she reached up to dash them away. "What am I to do? What am I to do?" she whispered.

"You're going to marry, raise a family, and live happily ever after," he said heartily.

"Live happily ever after with a man who doesn't want to marry me?" she asked bitterly. "I know firsthand what it's like to live where you aren't wanted. I'll not do it again."

Sir Henry stared at her in confusion. Then a smile crossed his face. "Jane, what are you talking about?"

"You heard him." Her voice was expressionless.

"Heard what?"

"Him refuse to marry me. Oh, later Hortense made him change his mind, but I heard his first reaction: 'I refuse.' No, I won't go through with it." She jumped up from her chair only to drop back in surprise as Sir Henry grabbed her shoulders and sat her down.

"Of all the hardheaded, confused pairs I've ever met, you two are the worst." He frowned at her fiercely. "Mark refused to marry you, did he?"

"Yes." Her answer was defiant.

"That's why he held your hand so tightly, wouldn't let you leave his side?"

The confusion that had held her captive earlier returned. "I suppose he thought honor-bound to protect me," she began.

"Protect you?" He paused and looked at her. "Just because he is honorable? Not quite!" She stared at him, her eyes wide and thoughtful. He stopped for a moment. Taking a different approach, he asked, "And what are your feelings for him?" Jane hesitated. "Well, what have you to say for yourself, miss? Be honest now."

In a voice that was so soft that it would not even qualify as a whisper, Jane finally said, "I love him." The words seemed even more daring than she had imagined. "But I won't marry him if he doesn't care for me. And he doesn't."

"Doesn't he?" her friend said, a smile breaking across his face. "That's why he apologized for stealing my bride-to-be?"

"What?"

"He thought we were going to marry."

Her heart beating so rapidly that she could hardly take a deep breath, Jane asked, "Why did he apologize?"

"For caring for you and not being able to control himself."

"Oh!" The joy that she had thought lost forever came flooding back. Her cheeks bloomed with color, and her eyes sparkled.

Some of her joy dimmed as Sir Henry reminded her, "But make no mistake about it. Under the circumstance, neither of you has any choice. You will marry as soon as Mark is strong enough."

CHAPTER

18

The preparations for the last party were minor compared to what Hortense had in mind for the engagement party and the wedding. Although Jane escaped having to write the invitations, she couldn't escape the planning. She was never alone.

Immediately after dinner, Hortense trapped her. "We have so little time we must get an express off to Madame Camille immediately. Have you any ideas about your wedding dress? How fortunate that she has your measurements. Do you have a list of what you require? Sir Henry and I insist that you have at least twelve of everything."

Jane stared at her in amazement. "How quickly are we talking about? Two months, three?"

"Two or three weeks, depending on Mark's recovery." Hortense's voice was as calm as if she had said a year. "I thought we would have your more personal garments made nearby. Remember to include more elaborate ball gowns on your list. As a married woman, you'll need a different style."

"A wedding in two or three weeks? That's impossible!"

"Nonsense, Jane. Difficult, perhaps, but not impossible."

Jane realizing that protests would do her no good under

Hortense's onslaught, went obediently to sit beside her. Her exhaustion somehow gave a certain distance to the proceedings and made them easier to bear. All through the lists of morning dresses, afternoon dresses, tea gowns, ball gowns, gowns for evenings at home or small dinner parties, Jane convinced herself that it was a dream or happening to someone else.

The wedding gown was a different matter. "Think of the look in Mark's eyes when he sees you in it. I can still remember the way my husband smiled at me. Ours was a love match, much like yours and Mark's." Hortense dried her eyes prettily with the scrap of lace she called her handkerchief.

A love match? The idea still bothered Jane. No matter what Sir Henry said, Mark had refused. Would a man in love do that? Before she could give that idea the time it needed, she was forced back into the present.

"Once your decision about your dress is made, I suppose we will be finished for tonight. Have you found a design you like?" Hortense asked.

Almost without thinking, Jane held up the plate she had in her hands. The dress was simple and elegant. The dominant element was the sweeping cape with a fur-lined hood. Hortense looked at it critically and then nodded. "Unusual. Hmm. Yes, I think it will do nicely. Velvet, I think. Don't you agree?" Jane's hesitant nod seemed the least of Hortense's worries. "Yes, worn with your hair down, it should be just the thing. Practical, too. Stone churches are very drafty in February. You may set a style for winter weddings." Hortense positively glowed as she bid Jane goodnight.

Even before Jane was down the next morning, Hortense was busy. Grooms traveled the countryside leaving the invitations for everyone. If some gossip accompanied the card, no one complained.

Breakfast over, Jane was once more immersed in plans. She remembered the boxes she had packed. "Cousin Hortense, is there a room I can use to go through my boxes?"

"How long will it take?"

"A day or two." Jane's heart twisted as she thought of what those boxes represented.

Hortense, her face thoughtful, was mentally reviewing suitable spots. She smiled. "Tell Marsden to have them brought to the ballroom. I'll help, and we'll get a footman or two. Perhaps we can get it done more quickly."

The thought of Hortense's sorting through her treasures gave Jane pause for a moment. She had to admit, though, that the idea had merit. Nodding, she hurried off in search of the butler.

Some time later as she looked at the pile of boxes before her, she wondered why she had been so willing to let Hortense help. The woman was merciless. Because of the older woman, the pile of discards was growing faster than the ones to save.

Then they reached the boxes of linens and crystal. These her father had kept, not realizing perhaps how much they had meant to her mother. Then too he would have had to buy replacements. A few memories had been better than money to invest, Jane thought cynically.

As Hortense began unpacking the carefully wrapped stemware, she was in rapture. "Venetian glass. So lovely. Look at the colors." Glass was a passion of hers.

"My mother's uncle sent it to her as a wedding present. She often said that every glass probably had an exciting story to tell." And some not so happy too, she thought, losing her slightly wistful smile as she thought of the times she had tried to celebrate one holiday or another.

"How could I forget?" Hortense asked as if to herself. "Jane, repack this immediately. We have no time to dawdle."

Surprised, Jane picked up the glass and rolled it carefully in its packing. Hortense hurried on to another crate, explaining as she went, "We must be ready to receive guests. Probably not this afternoon, but certainly tomorrow."

"Guests? Why?"

"Why, to find out about your engagement. Everyone must have received the invitations by now."

Feeling her cheeks grow warm, Jane kept her face down as she began to open yet another box.

Hortense looked around the ballroom carefully. "Shall we have these taken to Courtland Place, or is there something you wish to keep here?"

Jane paused for a moment and looked around her slowly. With these she could set up house anywhere. Hesitating over the last commitment, she frowned. Taking a deep breath, she sighed and closed her eyes. "Have them sent." The threadiness of her voice caused Hortense to look at her sharply. For once she didn't say anything, leaving Jane to her memories.

Before they had finished their inspection, Smythe appeared. "Mr Courtland would like to see Miss Woodley this afternoon if it would be convenient," he said formally.

Without even consulting Jane, Hortense answered, "Tell Mr. Courtland we will be there for tea."

"We?" The valet was visibly taken aback.

"Naturally I will accompany her."

Jane, her temper flaring, bit down hard on her tongue. Just a few more weeks and she would be—a wife. A wife. The images conveyed by that word were somewhat frightening.

Jane went about the tasks Hortense set for her dutifully. Her thoughts, however, were on the meeting that afternoon.

The anticipation which both Jane and Mark had felt soon gave way to resignation. Hortense dominated the conversation. Only when Mark presented Jane with her betrothal ring was she quiet.

Mark leaned over and picked up a velvet box that lay on the table closest to his bed. Breaking into Hortense's detailed plans for the party and their wedding, he asked Jane, "Would you come here, please?" He gestured to the spot she had occupied the night of the intruder.

"Totally improper. And if you were a gentleman, you

wouldn't even suggest it,'' Hortense said in her most con-
demning tones.

"We are betrothed," he reminded her.

"In my day there would not have been any of this flirting,
much less sitting on the bed.''

Mark ignored her and smiled at Jane. He held out his hand.
Taking it, she climbed the step and sat on the bed.

"I have something for you. I hope you like it," he said so
quietly that Hortense had to strain to hear. Mark handed Jane
the blue velvet box, worn with age. ''It was my grandmother's.''

Releasing the catch, Jane opened the lid. There on a bed of
white satin lay a dazzling aquamarine surrounded by a blaze
of diamonds. Stunned, Jane could only stare as Mark lifted it
and slid it on her finger. ''Just perfect. It reminded me of
you,'' he whispered before he placed a kiss on her palm.

Looking up from the ring, Jane stared transfixed into Mark's
deep brown eyes that were beaming with his love. Jane
leaned closer to him, not quite sure what she planned to do
but drawn like a magnet. ''It's wonderful, just wonderful,''
she whispered.

Hortense intervened. "What a beautiful ring! Let me see it,
Jane.'' At the sound of her voice, Mark fell back on his
pillows, disappointment radiating from his whole body. Jane,
startled, sat up straight and held out her hand. Glancing at
Mark, she smiled ruefully and shrugged her shoulders.

Shortly after that Hortense disturbed both of their worlds.
''Tomorrow, Mark, I believe you may go downstairs for a
short while in the afternoon. Smythe told me your morning
walk went well,'' she said as though conferring a great
honor.

Jane looked at Mark reproachfully. He had been up and not
told her. ''Smythe said you were busy,'' he explained. She
slid off the bed carefully, her eyes fixed firmly on the floor,
dashing Mark's hopes. If they could only talk alone, she
thought.

To be so close and then so far away depressed Mark. Only when Jane walked slowly back to the bed to stand looking at him did his sense of loss lift. Surprising both Mark and herself, Jane stood on tiptoe and whispered, "My ring is beautiful. Thank you." Leaving a hint of a kiss on his lips, she was out the door before Hortense could begin to complain. To Mark the room seemed much brighter.

The next day was a busy one. From the time that morning calls were proper there was a parade of visitors. Most were simply curious. A few such as Lady Brough and Miss Westmoreland were slightly hostile.

After thirty minutes of Lady Brough's "Well, in the circumstances, I suppose there was no other choice. But if she were mine to chaperon . . ." Jane was ready to scream or throw her first temper tantrum. Keeping a false smile on her face, she bit her tongue and dispensed tea as though she didn't hear a word of the conversation.

Finally she held out her hand. "Isn't this the most beautiful ring?" she asked, knowing how much the question would grate on the visitors' nerves. "Mark said it reminded him of me. Isn't he sweet?" Somehow she managed a blush. "It's even more special because it belonged to his grandmother." Without her trying, a dreamy look settled over her face.

By the time she was free, Mark had been downstairs and returned to his room. Jane's only contact with him was an after-dinner visit, again carefully chaperoned by Hortense. Determined to talk to him, Jane allowed Betty to ready her for bed and climbed in. As soon as the house was quiet, she would go to his room. Despite her best intentions, she fell asleep waiting for the servants to go to bed.

The next day was no better. They got to see each other at breakfast, but Sir Henry and Hortense were present. After the meal, Hortense spirited Jane away to the nearest town, determined that not another day would go by without their orders being placed. For Mark the day was equally exhausting because he was in conference with their lawyers working out settlements.

When Jane returned, hoping for an opportunity alone with Mark, she was met by Marsden. "Lieutenant Dancy called, miss. He was most unhappy not to find you here. He'll return tomorrow."

Dancy. Somehow Jane had been expecting him. The thought of the coming interview filled her with apprehension. He had heard. She tried to reassure herself. She hadn't made any promises. They were just friends, but a warning kept pounding in her mind, driving out all thought of a discussion with Mark.

Mark, his good humor slightly dented by the financial discussions he had just been through, sent word before dinner that he had retired for the night. As he lay in bed staring at the velvet curtains and watched the clock on the mantel tick slowly through the hours, he admitted his foolishness. Jane, even if accompanied by Hortense, would have made the evening pass faster.

After his long meeting the day before and his sleepless night, Mark chose to remain in bed until after luncheon. Then he made his way to the small salon, where Hortense insisted on helping him to a chaise. Smiling at Jane, he moved to one side and gestured to her. Before she could reply, Marsden was there. "Shall I show Lieutenant Dancy in here, ma'am?" he asked.

Hortense took a look at Mark and said, "No, we'll receive him next door. Wait just a moment before you show him in." She and Jane opened the connecting door and took their seats, leaving the door ajar.

Jane took a deep breath and fixed a smile on her pale face. "Lieutenant Dancy," Marsden said quietly.

It wasn't going to be pleasant. Jane knew that from the first moment she saw the scowl on his face. The first few minutes were formal as they executed the ritual of a call. Underneath the calm, even Hortense could sense strain.

As he reached the point of his call, the officer said to Jane, "I must wish you happy, I believe."

In the silence that followed his statement, Hortense rushed in. "Isn't it wonderful! Have you ever known such a perfect match? Sir Henry and I are delighted, simply delighted."

By supreme effort he erased his frown, smiling coldly at her. The look he sent to Jane was anything but pleasant. Hortense, hoping to ease the tension, rambled on.

Once again Marsden interrupted. "There seems to be a problem, ma'am. May I see you belowstairs for a moment?" Fortunately for both Marsden and Dancy, an unexpected delivery had arrived. After exchanging an enigmatic look, neither glanced at the other. As he showed his mistress to the delivery man, Marsden patted the pocket where the guinea lay. A man disappointed in love deserved a chance to speak to the woman alone.

Hortense, on the point of leaving the room, motioned to Jane to join her. "I'm certain Lieutenant Dancy will be a perfect gentleman. However, remember Mark is only next door," she said quietly. "Or should I send Marsden for Sir Henry?"

"I'll be fine," Jane whispered, wondering if the shaky feeling she had was some sudden illness. Turning back to her guest, she was startled to see him sitting on the settee, where she and Hortense had been sitting. Cautiously she took a chair opposite him.

Mark, stretched out on the chaise in the next room, chafed at the thought of Jane alone with someone else. He swung his legs to the floor and was ready to stand up when the noise from the room captured his attention.

"How can you do this to me?" the lieutenant asked, his voice almost a shout.

Mark had to strain to hear Jane's quiet reply. "I wasn't aware that I had done anything that required giving you an explanation."

"From the first moment I saw you, I knew you were mine. I even told you."

"When?"

"At the ball."

"I thought you were only flirting."

"You were the one flirting."

Mark could tell from the footsteps that the man was up, prowling like a caged tiger. "I had it all planned. After some useless preliminaries, we would marry. With your money I could—"

"My money?" asked Jane, startled.

"You didn't think it was a secret, did you? I'm certain Mark Courtland has plans for it too."

Muttering a curse under his breath, Mark stood up and made his way slowly toward the door. Before he reached it, Jane's temper exploded.

"You were going to marry me, were you? Have I ever given you the right to think I might agree? How dare you make assumptions based on your wishes only! Let me tell you, sir, that even if I weren't marrying Mark Courtland, you'd not be anywhere on my prospective husband list."

James Dancy crossed to stand in front of her. He pulled her up in front of him, his hands holding her firmly. "How dare I? Would I have given you the choice? You should have been mine. Oh, I had my doubts the night I saw you in his room. But I knew I could win you, make you mine in time!" He punctuated his comments by grabbing her shoulders and shaking her fiercely.

The cold voice from the door broke through the anger that gripped Dancy. "Let her go." The fierce look Mark sent the man made him take a step back and drop his hands. "I believe your visit is over." He pulled the bell and waited until Marsden appeared. In those few minutes the room was filled with an icy quiet. "Lieutenant Dancy is leaving, Marsden. He won't be returning. Will you, lieutenant?"

Looking into those eyes, the eyes of a man controlling himself only by extreme effort, Dancy took more steps back. Jane, released from the tension of the last few minutes, ran to Mark's side. Pulling her close to him, he slipped an arm around her waist. He looked over her soft curls to the vengeful eyes of his rival. ''Goodbye, lieutenant.''

Muttering a curse under his breath, Dancy stormed toward the door. He stopped on the threshold. ''Be careful, Courtland. I have more power than you think.'' He smiled cruelly and followed Marsden from the room.

CHAPTER

19

Thoroughly shaken by her encounter, Jane nestled against Mark. As her anger and fear ebbed away, she felt his shaking. "Come. Sit down," she said, trying to lead him to the closest chair.

"Not in here." He turned toward the open door. Eager to make her escape from the memories the room held, Jane supported him carefully. Although he could have managed slowly by himself, Mark leaned on her slightly.

"Why did you get up? I'm certain that wasn't wise. If you're not careful, you'll be sick again," she said. Her scolding, though anxious, was soft and gentle. "Now you sit right down there and put your feet up."

Mark sank back on the chaise but didn't release her hand. He looked up. "Sit with me," he said softly. Glancing hesitantly at the doorway, Jane looked at him and smiled. He moved over as he had done earlier and drew her down beside him.

Leaning back, Mark drew Jane close beside him, forcing her to move her legs beside him. Breathing in her sweet scent, he held her quietly until his shaking had stopped and her tension had slipped away. She was so sweet. The thought of Dancy's hands on her made Mark's arms tighten about her.

Jane, too, was content to be where she was. Those arms around hers made her feel so protected and secure. Fascinated, she watched the vein in his neck pulse. Timidly she put up a hand to caress his jaw and tucked her head in the space between his shoulder and neck.

Pulling back a bit, Mark stared at her somberly. She was such a darling. Pulling her closer, he buried his face in her curls. As Mark held her as though he never planned to let her go, Jane breathed in his clean, masculine scent. Freeing one of her hands, she slipped it around his neck.

After a few minutes Mark bent down to whisper in her ear. But Jane was moving too. As she lifted her head, she clipped his jaw with the top of her head. "Ouch!"

"Mark, are you hurt? Should I call Hortense?"

"If you do I'll never forgive you," he said, rubbing the sore spot.

Surprising Mark and herself, Jane reached up and kissed the spot. "My mother said kisses always make a hurt feel better."

"I have to agree," he said quietly into her ear.

Once again they sank into silence. This time it was a pregnant silence, a silence of two people with so much to say they didn't know where to begin.

Suddenly restless, Jane pulled away and sat up, facing Mark. Mark too pulled himself up facing her. "Did you agree?"

"They're not forcing you?" The questions overlapping, they stopped. After staring at one another for a few minutes, Mark took a deep breath and pulled her close to him again.

"Jane, I'm sorry," he began. Jane's heart was beating so hard that Mark could feel it pounding. She sighed wistfully.

He started again. "I'm sorry that you had no choice. If this marriage is in any way repugnant to you, say so. I'll find a way to get you out of it." He waited with bated breath for her reply. If she told him she wanted to get out of it, he'd be lost. If only Sir Henry was right.

"Me? You're the one who is trapped. I told Sir Henry that you shouldn't be forced into this. I know you don't want to marry me." Her voice shook with her effort to control it. In spite of the tingling sensation she had where his lips and hands were caressing her, she was filled with despair.

Mark paused in his exploration of her ear and asked, "What did you say?"

"You don't want to marry me."

A crack of laughter echoed around the room and jarred her where she lay, her ear pressed against his chest. "Do that again," she said, fascinated.

"What?"

"Laugh. It sounded so wonderful. I could feel it."

"Jane, Jane. You are enchanting." Mark's arms closed more closely around her in a tremendous hug. "When I'm not still so weak, I'll do better," he said in a promise he fully meant to carry out.

"Weak?" she asked breathlessly. Had he been any stronger she might have been crushed. She had no complaints, though. Once again she snuggled her head into his shoulder.

"Jane?"

"Hmm?"

"No one is forcing me to marry you," Mark said quietly.

Jane leaned back to look at him. "That's why you refused?"

"No, silly!"

"I'm a silly? I don't understand. You said, 'I refuse.' "

"Not you. I would never refuse you."

"My hearing must be going then," she said wryly.

"Stop twisting what I say!"

"How can I help it, Mark, when you contradict yourself?"

"Hush." He bent down and kissed her softly. "What a nice way to keep you quiet," he whispered as he kissed her again.

"No!" Jane turned her head, pulling her lips away from his. It was the hardest thing she had ever done.

"Why not?" Mark was determined to continue his sensual assault on her. He kissed the tip of her nose.

"Mark! We need to talk. With our luck, Hortense will be here in a few minutes," she said as calmly as she possibly could with her pulses racing.

Mark pulled away from her slightly. "You're right," he said quietly. "Will you let me tell you my side."

"Yes."

Mark took a deep shuddering breath and reviewed what he had already said. "Remember the first night we met?" Her eyes opened wide as his demanded an answer. She nodded.

"I heard Sir Henry mention an engagement."

"What?"

He laid a finger on her lips and continued while the tip of his finger traced their curves. "Sir Henry told me that neither of you was serious. Was he right?"

"Certainly! Mark, how could you think that I was engaged to Sir Henry when I was trying every way I knew how to get to know you?"

He blushed, something that he thought he had forgotten how to do. This was the part of the story that he was most worried about. Suppose she refused to listen? He took a deep breath and plunged ahead. "I thought you were going to marry him but were willing to have an affair with me." He waited for the explosion of temper he was sure would come.

She surprised him. Instead of anger her eyes filled with tears, her chin quavered. "How could you believe that?" Her voice broke, and one tear trickled down her cheek.

"Sweet, don't cry. Please don't cry. You don't know what it does to me," Mark whispered softly as he caught her close, kissing the tears away.

"What made you do it?" Jane asked, once more in control of herself and feeling wonderful.

Hesitantly Mark began his story. Although Jane had already heard most of it from Sir Henry, she stayed quiet, nestling close to him as his voice roughened with emotion. Slowly, painfully, Mark told her of his disillusionment, end-ing with his capture by the press gang. As he fell silent, Jane reached up and kissed him gently. Mark took advantage of her sweetness to capture her lips again.

Reluctantly, she pulled away. "And you never saw her again?" she asked quietly.

"Yes, I did. In fact, she has become one of the fast set, a member of the Prince's rakish crew. You probably saw her yourself last winter."

"Oh. Does it still hurt?" Jane asked, dreading his reply.

"Hurt? No. Only when I think what a gullible fool I was." He smiled down on her ruefully. "Turnabout is fair play," he said. "Tell me about you."

While they were talking, Hortense opened the door. Deeply engrossed in each other, Mark and Jane didn't even see her. She frowned and started to enter. Glancing at their serious expressions, she hesitated. Sighing, she quietly went on her way, closing the door carefully.

This time it was Mark who placed a comforting kiss on Jane's lips as she told of her mother's death and their relocation. Even though she glossed over some of the details of her life with her father, Mark heard the grief in her voice. "I was so lonely," she whispered. His heart ached for the unhappiness she had had to suffer.

"I'm here. You won't be lonely again," he said, his voice as solemn as though he were making a vow. His arms tightened in a comforting hug that caused her pulse to race.

She pulled back away from him, a hand resting lightly on his chest so that she could look into his face. "Were you ever lonely?" she asked wistfully.

"Many times, especially after my father died. And at school. But most of all in the navy." His voice had fallen until Jane was not certain he knew he was still speaking out loud.

"What was it like?" she asked. "Besides being lonely?"

"Hell." The word burst from him. Seeing her eyes widen, he hurried on. "Oh, it was exciting at times, but I had never seen such brutality as I witnessed there. Some men enjoy watching others suffer.'' His eyes darkened with remembered pain.

"Sir Henry said you hurt your leg in the navy. Was he right?''

"Yes." That one word told her that he would say no more. Sorry to have disturbed such bad memories, she lay quietly, one hand stroking his shoulder.

After a few minutes, Mark stirred and sat up straight. "Have I told you I think you are wonderful?'' he asked. Pleased, Jane blushed and shook her head. "Well, you are.'' He pulled her close again. When a few minutes had passed, he shook her slightly, causing her to look at him in surprise. "Well, don't you have anything to say to me?'' he asked rather sternly.

Before the passionate look in his eyes, Jane blushed and looked away. "Lost your voice, have you?'' he said teasingly.

Gathering up her courage, Jane whispered, "You make me forget that I was ever lonely." Embarrassed at the words that seemed too revealing to her, she hid her face in his shoulder.

For a few minutes he sat there with her in his arms. Then she felt him stir restlessly. He pulled away and stood up. He walked to the window to stare out sightlessly. Disturbed, she swung her legs over the edge of the chaise and straightened her dress, staring at him warily.

After a few minutes he crossed the room and sat on the foot of the chaise. Looking at her somberly, he picked up her hand, his fingers running over the ring he had given her.

Now, she thought, now he'll tell me he loves me. Her lips parted slightly. She leaned toward him, ready to pour out her own feelings.

"Jane." He paused and revised what he was going to say. "Jane, we're going to be married soon.'' He looked at her closely, noting the disappointment she tried so hard to hide. He hurried on. "I think our marriage can be successful. Do you agree?''

She nodded hesitantly, her throat too choked for her to speak. "Then, Jane,'' he said hesitantly as he closed his eyes and prayed, ''will you do me the honor of becoming my wife?''

Her eyes flew open and stared into his. She cleared her throat and tried to answer him, but no words came out. ''If you say no, we'll find some way out,'' he said, his voice deep and rich, his eyes haunted.

Finally she forced out one word: ''No.'' Mark's shoulders slumped; he dropped her hand and turned away. Before he could get up, Jane had his hand once more. ''I didn't mean what you think,'' she said hurriedly. ''I meant no I didn't want any other way.'' She smiled at him shyly. ''Mark, I would be very happy to be your wife.''

Breathing a sigh of relief, he smiled, a rich, warm enveloping smile that made Jane tingle to the tips of her toes. ''Come here,'' he said huskily.

Without hesitation, Jane threw herself into his arms, almost knocking them off the chaise. ''Feisty little thing, aren't you?'' Mark whispered laughingly as he rearranged them so that could not happen again. Jane blushed but did not pull away.

''You're sweet, so sweet.'' His whisper and the way his teeth nibbled at her earlobe sent shivers up Jane's spine. She was warm, and a strange ache made her press closer to him. ''Aren't you going to talk to me?'' he asked as his kisses feathered across her forehead.

''Talk?'' The word was little more than a sigh.

''Tell me if I please you?''

She shivered and said bravely before her courage disappeared, ''You do. You know you do.'' As he pulled her closer to him, she sighed and closed her eyes, raising her parted lips to meet his. Her arms crept around his neck.

CHAPTER
20

Even though they were caught up in themselves, in the sensations they were creating, Jane and Mark jumped when they heard a cough. Panting slightly, they pulled away from each other and looked cautiously at the door.

It was closed. At one side of the room, carefully looking out a window, stood Sir Henry. Jane blushed a fiery red. Giving her skirts a shake, she rose, pushing Mark back onto the chaise when he tried to follow her. She crossed to the fireplace.

Watching her stare into the flames, Sir Henry smiled. He turned toward Mark and raised an eyebrow. Mark stared back at him enigmatically.

"Jane has agreed to marry me, Sir Henry. Will you wish us happy?" Mark asked quietly.

"But it was already settled," the older man said, surprised.

"By you. But not by Jane." Mark smiled at her. The soft richness of his voice sent a shiver of delight through Jane. He had such delightful means of persuasion.

"Well, both of you know your happiness is important to

me. I'm glad she agreed.'' The abstracted look Sir Henry wore made Mark frown.

Smoothing his thick hair, Mark got slowly to his feet, carefully crossing to stand near Jane and the fireplace. ''Come back and sit down,'' he whispered.

Startled, she looked up. Still blushing, she allowed him to lead her to a small settee. His hand holding hers tightly, Mark asked, ''Are you here simply as our chaperon, Sir Henry?''

''Chaperon? Not I.'' He walked to a chair near them and stood leaning against its back, his worry clearly marked on his face. He cleared his throat nervously. ''I received a letter in answer to my expresses today.'' He took out his handkerchief from an inside pocket of his claret-colored coat and mopped his forehead nervously. Then he took his seat.

''Well?'' Anxious to learn what Sir Henry's contacts had discovered, Mark leaned forward as if to urge him on.

''It's not good news.''

''I rather gathered that,'' Mark said dryly.

Sir Henry glared at him and then relented. ''It's all so frustrating. No one even wants to bother with us.''

''Didn't I try to tell you that those people in London cared only for themselves? The only way they'd be interested in our problems is if they were actively involved. Otherwise we'll be ignored.''

''That's not it,'' Sir Henry said more bitterly than Mark had ever heard him. He crossed to the fireplace. ''Blast it, Mark! They refuse to believe that there are any smugglers.''

''What?''

''That's right.'' A defeated slump to his usually straight shoulders, Sir Henry sighed. ''Even the Runners declined to take our case.''

''I can't say I'm sorry about that,'' Mark said quickly. ''I could see all of us being transported.''

''Yes. I don't plan to spend my honeymoon on a boat to the New World,'' Jane said, her cheeks once more flushed.

Mark placed a kiss on Jane's palm. ''There must have been

some reason given. Or was it a blanket refusal?'' Mark asked, his interest firmly on the problem.

"According to London and the navy we have the quietest stretch of seacoast in England. The navy said every time they've been alerted it's been a false alarm.'' His voice was ironic. "We've had two instances of smuggled goods during the last two months, and we're a quiet seacoast. I wonder what they call busy.''

"Repeat that, please!''

"We're too quiet for smugglers.''

"I suppose that's why we have a troop of soldiers patroling the area too?'' Jane asked.

"The disquieting thing is that these people are right,'' Sir Henry said, returning to take the seat near theirs.

"Come now, Sir Henry. You know better than that,'' the younger man scoffed, his face showing his confusion.

"Mark, let him explain,'' Jane said quietly, her eyes watching the older man carefully. "Go on, Sir Henry.''

Patting his forehead again with his handkerchief, Sir Henry leaned forward. "When I sent out those expresses to London, I also sent out some men to try to uncover some information around here. Using your engagement as an excuse, I instructed Mr. Adams and Herndon to start making inquiries about extra wagons and teams that we could rent to carry supplies. To our surprise there was no difficulty except in choosing whose we would use.''

"What did you expect to happen?'' Jane asked, her face thoughtful.

"Smugglers have to transport their goods some way. Usually they borrow teams and wagons from farms in the area, sometimes with the farmers' cooperation, sometimes without.''

"But all the people in our district have equipment that can be rented. I understand,'' Mark said quietly. He turned to Jane, who still wore a puzzled look on her face. "If a farmer had made arrangements with the smugglers, he would have had to turn us down.''

"Unless the smugglers were expecting us to do something

like this," she said, her voice and face pensive. "They had several days while you were ill to prepare."

"Hmm. That idea has merit. Even then there is another problem." Jane's sigh echoed in the room. Sir Henry leaned forward and patted her hand consolingly. He said, "Jane, we will find a solution to the problems, I promise you."

"Until we do, Mark is in danger," she said sharply. "I just know it."

"You're right. That's why I needed to talk to you."

Mark, who had been abstracted for a few minutes, asked suddenly, "Did any of the farmers mention missing animals?"

"No, we thought of that too. Nor were there any but the usual signs of harnesses on them." After a few minutes of silence, Sir Henry asked, "Jane, when you went shopping yesterday, were you able to find any of the items we discussed?"

"No. Most of the merchants complained that they hadn't seen French lace or velvet for a long time. We went to several places. Do you think they could be lying to us?"

"No, more than likely they are telling the truth. I even had Lord Brough put out some feelers, but they yielded as little as ours."

"Lord Brough?" Jane's eyebrows tilted upward.

Mark sent his friend a look that said, "Now look what you've done," and explained, "He's one of our partners in the grain venture."

"Do his family know?"

"Naturally not. If I didn't have such a nosy love, you wouldn't know either." Mark softened his words by kissing her softly on her cheek.

"Oh," she whispered, forgetting about their problems for a moment. Her eyes widened, and a smile softened her face as she realized he had called her his love.

"Either there is a tremendously large organization held together by fear, or there's another explanation," Mark said as if he were talking to himself.

"You can eliminate the first. Someone would have given

that away. The only fear I've found here has been of starvation, and that's gone now," Sir Henry said firmly.

"For the moment. If we don't find that seed before planting time, the problem may be more severe," Mark reminded him. "I'll go back to Holland if I have to, but I'd rather not."

"If you go, I go," Jane said firmly, delighting Mark by her militant attitude.

"No one is going anywhere. At least not now," Sir Henry reminded them. "Let's consider some other possibilities."

"We know we have smugglers—ourselves and someone else. London doesn't agree. Right?" Jane asked.

The two men nodded their agreement. "Somehow those same smugglers have managed to dispose of a large shipment of goods without anyone else but Mark knowing about it. Is there any logical explanation for that happening?"

The two men looked at each other questioningly, running the problem through their minds. "How would you go about hiding something like that?" Mark asked as if to himself.

"Especially with that troop of Dancy's careening over the countryside," Sir Henry added. "Too bad we can't tell him about the problem. He's bound to have seen something."

"Dancy would like nothing more than to see my head on his platter or the gallows if he could manage it. He wouldn't help even if he could." Mark stretched his legs and stood up.

"Why?" Sir Henry asked.

"It seems the man had decided to marry Jane." Mark smiled down at his darling reassuringly.

"What? The man never requested permission from me."

"He felt he didn't need to," Jane said, frowning. "He had told me, and I was supposed to obey."

"That good-looking upstart didn't try anything, did he?" asked the older man, his gaze switching from Jane to Mark.

"When Hortense left us alone, things got rather unpleasant. But Mark rescued me," Jane said, her eyes dreamy.

"What do you mean, 'unpleasant'?"

"Nothing."

"Nothing? You mean his shaking was nothing? Perhaps I should have waited longer to rescue you?" Mark's eyes were snapping as he stared across the room at the softhearted creature who had promised to marry him.

"The bounder!" Sir Henry's eyes flashed black fire.

Jane jumped up and crossed to stand in front of Mark, her hands on his chest. "Nothing because you rescued me. I simply didn't want Sir Henry to worry. You were there, and I am safe."

"I don't like that man. Never have," said Sir Henry almost under his breath.

"I agree." Mark drew Jane back to the settee, settling her carefully before he took his own seat close beside her.

"But he's not our problem. We could leave the area," Sir Henry said quietly.

"Run away? Never!" Mark's usually soft voice had a biting edge to it. Jane glanced at him, half-pleased with his courage and half angry at his foolishness.

"Then we must redouble our efforts. Let's review what we know. There may be something we've missed," the older man said.

"Maybe you were seen when you brought the grain in, Mark. Start there." Jane smiled up at him encouragingly.

Step by step, Mark led them through the voyage to Holland and back. "We were almost home when we were sighted," he explained.

"Sighted? From land or sea?" asked Sir Henry, his mind ready to snap up any new details.

"A cutter flying the Union Jack and a troop of horsemen, I assumed it was Dancy, on the cliffs."

"Both of them? Where?"

"Up the coast. I planned to hug the shore until I reached home. As it was, I found a hidden inlet and anchored there till morning."

"Were you anywhere near your docks? Could they read the name of your boat?"

"No. Everything was disguised that could be."

While Sir Henry sorted Mark's answers, Jane had some questions. "Mark, think about the night you were hurt. What did you see to make you suspicious?"

"Hoofprints in the snow."

"How many?"

Mark thought for a moment before he answered. His voice was thoughtful. "I remember thinking that it looked as though a hunt had ended there."

"A hunt?" Jane asked quietly, not wanting to disturb his thought processes.

"Yes. It looked as though a large group of horses had been standing around waiting. The snow was packed down and dirty. The hoofprints overlapped one another."

Sir Henry looked at Mark closely. "Why a hunt? Couldn't there have been wagons and teams?"

"Maybe. But if there were, the prints were hidden by those of single horses. Lots of them."

"Lots of horses. Why didn't anyone see them?" Jane asked angrily. "Someone had to. You can't hide a large group of people."

"You're right, my dear. But let's hear him out."

"I crept up to the barn and opened the door. As soon as I went in, I saw the new bales and casks. I started forward and was hit from behind."

"Let's think about what you told us. You went in and saw the bales and barrels. What time of day was it?" Sir Henry's eyes glinted with excitement.

"Twilight." Mark paused, a thoughtful look on his face. "I see what you mean."

"I don't. Would someone explain it to me?" Jane demanded, her brows tilted in confusion.

"Sir Henry's just reminding me how dark that old barn usually is." Mark smiled at Jane ruefully.

"But you were able to see. Oh!"

"I must have been stupid to walk in like that."

"No, just not thinking clearly. Besides, at that time you

had no reason to suspect that anything was wrong.'' Sir Henry said reassuringly.

''Mark, dearest, don't be so hard on yourself. You couldn't have known.'' Jane captured his hand, holding it between hers and willing him to look at her.

Finally he did. A rueful smile crossed his face. ''It makes me so angry to think how easily I walked into that disaster. If I'd only backed out right away.''

''They'd probably have gone after you,'' Sir Henry said, forcing him to accept reality. ''Then they might have killed you instead of leaving you to freeze.''

At Jane's gasp, Mark turned and put his hand on her shoulder. ''It didn't happen.'' She kept her eyes fixed on the floor. ''Jane, look at me!'' He put his hand under her chin and forced her to look up. ''I'm all right, thanks to your careful nursing.'' Ignoring Sir Henry, he bent his head and kissed her softly, holding her until she nestled close against him.

''Is there anything else?'' their friend asked. ''Something you've forgotten.''

''He was unconscious after that. How could he remember?'' asked Jane, ready to defend Mark if need be.

''The next thing I knew was Jane bending over me, a worried frown on this pretty brow.'' He kissed her quickly on her forehead.

''Time enough for that after we've caught this gang. If we ever do.''

''We will, Sir Henry. Somehow.''

''What about the night the intruder got in? What happened then?'' Jane asked.

Mark thought for a moment and said, ''I was asleep. Then a pillow was put over my face. I fought, but I really didn't think I'd survive until Jane came in and the intruder fled. You were certainly the most welcome sight I had ever seen in that blue dressing gown, holding that candle out in front of you as though it were a sword. What did you plan to do? Set him on fire?''

''Look who's being silly now. All I wanted to do was to see what was happening.'' Jane's voice dropped off in surprise. Her eyes grew larger than either of the men had ever seen them. Quickly, she turned toward Sir Henry. ''Tell me once again what the letters from London said about us.''

Mark heard the ''us,'' and his heart beat faster. Quickly Sir Henry repeated what he had told them earlier. As he did, Jane's frown grew darker and darker.

Uttering a word neither man had any idea she knew, Jane exclaimed, ''Of course. It had to be he!''

CHAPTER

21

The two men stared at Jane in amazement, thinking the stress of the last few weeks had been too much for her. Her face was flushed. Her eyes sparkled as she reviewed once again the reason for her excitement. Too excited to sit still, she began pacing.

"Don't you see?" she asked Mark, who was just as puzzled as he had ever been.

"See what?"

"Remember what Lieutenant Dancy said while he was shaking me?" She stopped pacing to stand before him, her dark eyelashes fluttering up and down in her excitement.

"I wish someone would explain what is happening," said Sir Henry sternly. They ignored him as though they had not even heard him. "Is this a private discussion, or may I join?"

Mark, who had been frantically reviewing what he had heard, waved Sir Henry over to him. "Jane, I was so angry I don't think I heard anything but the tone."

"You had to. You just did. It's too important to trust just my memory." She paused and looked at Sir Henry thoughtfully. "Still, if what I remember is true, we should be able to find proof."

Sir Henry had heard enough. He pulled Jane around to face him, his hands holding her firmly by her shoulders. "Jane, as much as I love you, if you don't tell us what you're talking about soon, I may strangle you."

"And I'll help him," Mark laughingly agreed.

"Mark, you remember. Dancy said he saw me in your room." Her words turned the men into statues. As she watched the realization spread slowly over their faces, Jane grinned. "I'm right. I'm certain I'm right."

"You did it!" Mark said looking into her delighted gray eyes. He reached out and pulled her into a hug that would have lasted longer except for the fact that Sir Henry started pounding them on their backs. Before he let her go, Mark gave her another quick hug and whispered, "I can always count on you to rescue me."

Sir Henry, embarrassed by his own behavior, took his seat and urged them to take theirs. "Mark, will you testify that what Jane said is true?"

Mark, all of his energy seeping from him, leaned back in the corner of the settee, his face almost gray. "Testify, no. But I'm certain of what he said." He smiled at Jane weakly.

Worried by his sudden exhaustion, she put her hand to Mark's cheek. It was as cold as a sheet hanging in an early spring rainstorm. "He needs to be in bed," she said urgently. "Can you walk upstairs?" she asked Mark.

Although Mark nodded weakly, Jane decided differently. "Call Marsden for some footmen. I am so stupid. I should have remembered not to let him tire himself."

As soon as Mark was on his way up to bed, Sir Henry turned to Jane, observing her closely. "As much as I need the information you have, I think you should also rest. Now, don't worry about Mark." He laughed at himself ironically. "I'm a foolish old man if I think you'll obey that suggestion. Take yourself up and lie down. Don't come down for dinner if you don't want to. We'll meet in Mark's room later."

Like Mark's, Jane's energy had disappeared. Even moving her head to nod was difficult. She faced the stairs with trembling but determination. Step by step she pulled herself up to her room.

Later that evening, refreshed by a good nap, she made her way toward Mark's sitting room. She had taken great pains with her toilette and wore one of her most becoming gowns, a soft cream wool woven with rose, periwinkle, apricot, and pomona-green stripes around the rounded neck, under the puff of the sleeve, around her wrists, and at the hem. Her hair had been brushed until it glowed.

Glancing at a mirror in the hall, Jane pulled a curl back into place and patted the intricate knot at the back. Taking a deep breath, she closed her eyes momentarily. Outwardly calm, she scratched at the door, biting her lips to make them even more pink.

"Miss Woodley," Smythe said as he ushered her to a chair beside the settee on which Mark lay. Her eyes widening, Jane glanced around the room. "Sir Henry sent word that he had been detained. Will you have a seat?"

After a quick look at Mark, Jane kept her eyes firmly on the floor, embarrassed by the passionate look they had exchanged. "Have you rested?" she asked quietly.

"Yes, blast it. I'm so tired of being weak." He wondered what she would do if he pulled her into his arms. He fixed his eyes on her rosy lips, hungering for their shy touch.

"May I offer you some tea, miss?" Smythe asked, disturbed by the atmosphere. Although he hadn't wanted the job, Sir Henry had made him promise to chaperon them carefully.

Startled, Jane look up, surprising a wicked gleam in Mark's eyes. He was laughing at her. "No, thank you, Smythe. Will Sir Henry be here soon?" Her voice was colorless.

I've startled her, Mark thought ruefully before he said, "He won't be long. He said he's been busy investigating what you suggested."

Before Jane could answer, the door swung open, admitting Sir Henry. As Smythe bowed and prepared to leave, Sir

Henry detained him. "I think you deserve to hear this, Smythe. After all, you were one of his victims. Did you tell him?"

"Not yet," Mark said quietly. "I thought we needed more information."

Jane nodded her head. "Yes. What we have now will not convict anyone. Although his words tell us much, they certainly can't be used as proof."

"And I wouldn't let you use them in court anyway," Mark said firmly. Both Sir Henry and Jane looked at him, puzzled. "Can you imagine what the defense would do to your reputation?"

"Oh." A blush spread from Jane's throat to the top of her head, rivaling the rose stripe in her dress.

"I'm working on that. That is where Smythe will come in, too," Sir Henry said reassuringly. He turned to the valet. "We have reason to believe that Lieutenant Dancy was the intruder who struck you and tried to kill your master."

"But he is supposed to help uphold the law," the valet complained.

"Maybe." All three of them looked at Sir Henry, waiting for him to finish the thought. "What did London say about our area?"

"We had the quietest stretch of seacoast in England," Mark said quickly. Startled, he turned to Jane. "What did you say after Sir Henry told us that this afternoon?"

She thought for a moment. "Something about Dancy's troop, I think."

"The troop! Why do we need a troop of soldiers if we're so quiet?" Mark asked, his voice jubilant.

Sir Henry, his face pensive, considered the question carefully. Then he asked, "And why is Dancy so popular with the merchants here and in the surrounding counties?"

Without having to pause to think, Mark said, "Because he is always willing to provide an escort against highwaymen and riots for goods being sent to market." He paused and looked at his friend. "That's it, isn't it?"

"What? What are you talking about?" Jane asked.

"Very good, sir!" the valet said encouragingly.

"What a perfect situation," said Sir Henry. "People are so accustomed to seeing his troop escorting merchants and their goods they would never think to look for smuggled goods among them."

"You mean he does this in the daylight, right in front of everyone?" Jane asked, appalled.

"What better way?" The older man smiled. Jane shivered slightly looking at him.

"What's your idea?" Mark asked quickly, delighted at the thought of taking action.

"Smythe, we need some servants who can't keep their mouths shut. Think you can find them?"

"Certainly, sir," the valet said quietly, his eyes glowing with excitement.

Slowly, carefully, over the next few days they made their plans. Much to his disgust, Mark had to keep to his rooms. He had suffered a relapse and was lying in bed. His job was to compile the reports that came filtering back in. Day by day, the case was built.

While Mark was fuming at his inactivity, Jane helped Hortense prepare for the party. As the acceptances poured in, Hortense was elated. "Almost everyone has accepted," she said proudly. "Even Lord and Lady Brough." She looked at Jane sternly. "After the way you acted the last time Lady Brough was here, I'm surprised."

Jane smiled sweetly. No matter what Lady Brough wished, Lord Brough would be there. She asked casually, "Has Lieutenant Dancy replied?"

"That man! After what you told me about his last visit, I would think he would be ashamed to show his face here."

"Cousin Hortense, you know he sent both Mark and me very nice notes of apology."

"In my day a gentleman would never consider what he did, much less do it."

"Has he replied yet?" Jane asked again.

"No, and I hope he doesn't."

Jane frowned. What were they going to do if he didn't come? By the end of the week the question was answered. Dancy's acceptance had arrived.

While the final menu was approved and the brilliants repolished at the Abbey, Jane also had to help Mark with the decorating of Courtland Place. As soon as Sir Henry let him leave his room, he escorted Jane to his home, waiting anxiously for her reaction.

During the weeks of his illness work had progressed rapidly, especially with the extra help Sir Henry had provided. All that had to be completed was choosing paint, wall coverings, curtains, and fabric to recover the furniture. Jane, her eyes sparkling, enjoyed every minute of her first visit. As the housekeeper took her through the house, measuring windows as they went, Jane looked at each room critically; only the kitchen and servants' quarters caused her to frown in disapproval. She would have to say something about them.

"Well, what do you think?" Mark asked anxiously.

"It's beautiful. Truly beautiful." Jane made a complete circuit of the largest salon.

"You can order anything you like, change what's already been done," he said, smiling at her enthusiasm.

"Nonsense. If she were to do that now the wedding would have to be postponed for a year," said Hortense, who had declared that no young lady under her chaperonage would visit a man's house alone. Jane and Mark exchanged secret smiles, letting her ramble on.

"I had Johnson take the sample fabrics and wall coverings to the office. It and the library were untouched except by smoke. Mrs. Johnson will bring us a tea tray," Mark said.

For the rest of that afternoon he and Jane chose the hangings and furnishings for only the rooms needed immediately. The small salon was to be cream with lovely cream-and-gold hangings. For the dining room, they chose elegant amber, moss-green, and cream stripe paper with amber velvet drapes. For the walls of their suite, they selected a gray so pale it seemed like fog. Rose-pink hangings highlighted by robin's-egg blue were Jane's choice for her bedroom, and the blue with a more masculine burgundy for Mark. Their sitting room was gray with burgundy hangings and upholstery.

"Can this be finished soon?" Mark asked his agent when Adams joined them.

"Within ten days. Everyone is helping to get it ready. As soon as the fabric arrives, teams of seamstresses will be here," Adams assured them. "What about the other bedrooms?"

Mark looked at Jane, his eyebrow cocked. Catching her eyes, he motioned for her to give her ideas. "Paint them all cream. We'll see to draperies and hangings later. Or you could see what Mrs. Johnson has put by." With that last detail finished, the party got ready to leave.

Suddenly Jane stopped. "We must do something about those attic rooms," she said firmly. "And that kitchen."

"Whatever you like, my dear." Mark would have agreed to anything she said at that moment.

"Have Mrs. Johnson and Cook decide what they want in the kitchen. It may be better to wait until after the wedding to install everything. But let Cook and Mrs. Johnson decide. Get those upstairs servants' rooms painted immediately. Let them decide their own colors."

"Really, Jane. They'll be quite above themselves. What are you trying to do, spoil them for the rest of us?" Hortense asked petulantly.

"No, but I remember what it was like to want to change the color of the walls and to be turned down, time and time again," Jane said softly.

Mark put his arm around her to lead her out of the room. "Always thinking of others, aren't you?" he whispered in her ear. "I'm so proud of you." His words made her eyes sparkle, and she smiled up at him bewitchingly.

Two days before the party a large wagon pulled up to the delivery area and started unloading boxes. A short time later Betty found Jane in the library. "Oh, miss, come quick," she said as if she had been running.

"What is it, Betty?" Sir Henry asked, not happy to lose one of his planners.

"The dresses from Madame Camille have arrived. Mrs. Morgan thinks you need to try them on to see if any alterations are necessary."

"Clothes!" Sir Henry threw up his hands in disgust.

"Tell her I'll be up presently, Betty." She looked at her maid's disappointed face and smiled. "In the meantime, begin unpacking them."

"Oh yes, Miss Jane. Thank you."

"Sir Henry, you have no right to make fun of my clothes. The only time gentlemen notice a lady is when she is becomingly dressed," Jane said, laughing.

Mark leaned over her shoulder and whispered in her ear, "I know of one gentleman who prefers undress."

"Mark!" Her face a bright red, she turned her back on him. Composing herself with effort, she turned to Sir Henry and asked, "Is this going to work?"

"Probably."

"Remember, Jane, nothing is certain," Mark said quietly.

"I don't see why you should put yourself in danger again. The last few times you have almost been killed. If you were a cat, I'd say you had used up your nine lives." Although Jane had tried her arguments before and been unsuccessful, she refused to give up.

Before Mark could answer, Smythe slid into the room. "Any news?" Sir Henry demanded, his eyes snapping.

"They've taken the bait." The valet took a deep breath and smiled broadly.

"Good man. Tell us about it," Mark said, pounding his servant on the back.

To Jane, Smythe seemed to grow larger by the moment. Beaming proudly, he said, "Just like we planned. Alfie and Ross had a bit too much to drink and let it slip to some of those troopers that a second grain shipment will arrive in the early-morning hours after your engagement party. Even from where I was sitting, I could see their eyes light up."

"They didn't see you, did they?" Sir Henry asked.

"No, sir. Like you said, I sat in a dark corner with my back to the room. Anyone who was looking saw just another man who'd had a drop too much."

Mark patted the man on the shoulder and sent him on his way. Jane looked from one to the other closely. There was something they weren't telling her. "Everything is ready, isn't it?" she asked, her voice slightly husky.

"Of course. We have the men lined up, and Lord Brough has promised to present whatever we discover to the magistrate, who is a friend of his."

"And the grain?"

Mark frowned. "It should be here."

"Should?"

"It will be here," Sir Henry reassured her.

"Why you had to use smuggled grain, I'll never know. No one could tell the difference between English seed and Dutch. We could have put it in those empty sacks from before." Her eyes grew enormous. "Did those sacks give us away?"

"I doubt it. Jane, we'll have the goods. The only problem is that this time I contacted an acquaintance of mine from the navy to pick them up," Mark said quietly. "He'll deliver them while everyone is at the parties."

"Mark Courtland, if you do anything to harm yourself, I'll, I'll . . ." Jane stormed out of the room, rather shocked at her own strong feelings.

Her anger didn't last long. The sight spread over the bed in her room was one to charm any beauty-loving girl. Gown after gown in all her best colors lay there like a rainbow. "Oh, they're lovely," Jane said. "But however did she manage so many?"

"I'm certain we'll find out when we get her bill," Hortense said dryly. "Now let's see how these fit." After days of Hortense in her role as a general, Jane was pleased to hear her slow drawl.

Finally only the wedding dress was left to try on. Carefully Betty and Hortense's dresser lifted it over Jane's head and hooked it into place. "Perfect, my dear. Absolutely perfect!" Hortense reached out to smooth the ermine around the neckline into place.

"You don't think it's too low-cut, do you?" Jane asked, her eyes on a great amount of bare skin.

"Nonsense! With the cloak hardly anyone will notice."

Jane looked in the mirror and blushed, the red rising from the neckline to her face. Mark would notice. She knew he would.

As the time of the party grew closer, Jane grew more and more nervous. With the rumors that were rampant in the neighborhood, she'd have to behave very circumspectly; Hortense had made certain she was aware of that. And she'd have to face Lieutenant Dancy again. Thinking of her own hot temper, she knew she would have to watch herself constantly. The only time in those two days Jane felt free from fear was when Mark pulled her under the staircase for a quick kiss.

Nervous or not, Jane looked stunning as she and Mark helped greet the guests. To display her betrothal ring and Sir Henry's Christmas gift, Jane had chosen a dress in a light aquamarine worn over a slip of silver tissue silk. The neckline, as deep as that of her wedding dress, had a silver lace edge. Diamond combs that Mark had given her that afternoon twinkled in her hair.

When Dancy entered the ballroom, Mark was whispering in Jane's ear. Dancy, his face a thundercloud, controlled himself with an effort. Taking his place in line, he hid his feelings under a false smile. When he reached Jane and Mark, his congratulations were as warm as anyone else's.

As he had at the earlier ball, Mark led Jane into the first dance, once again a waltz. But this time he wasn't stiff. As they swept around the floor, Jane had to fight to keep the proper distance. "It's no fun this way," Mark complained. "Will you promise to dance only with me this evening?"

Jane drew back to look at him. "What kind of girl do you think I am, sir? I value my reputation more than that," she said teasingly. Then she smiled. Her mouth curved so sweetly that all Mark wanted to do was steal her away to kiss her until she was breathless.

Feeling very much as if she had been kissed, Jane bowed formally as the dance ended. "Cousin Hortense said not to give anyone more than one dance," she said, fluttering her eyelids.

"She couldn't have meant me. Let me see that program." He looked up and smiled. "You little minx." It was more than a name; it was a caress. "Don't let anyone take these away."

"The third waltz. Don't forget," she said as she turned to her next partner.

While Jane and Mark twirled around the dance floor, Sir Henry had another mission. Step by quiet step, he checked with his partners. Following his lead, they gravitated toward the whist tables he had insisted Hortense set up. On the surface the talk was of planting, crops, and politics. But everyone seemed to be just marking time.

The undercurrent of uneasiness pervaded the ballroom too, but not to the extent that it had the cardroom. Everyone seemed to be having a wonderful time. Miss Westmoreland was dancing every dance. Only Lieutenant Dancy stood glowering at the edge of the dance floor. Hortense soon solved that problem, sending him to ask one of the shy young ladies to dance. At first she thought he would refuse, but he bowed and moved toward the girl she had suggested.

Had Hortense known what he had planned she might have had second thoughts. Manipulating his partner into the same set as Jane and her partner, he took advantage of his opportunity. "I suppose you did not save a dance for me?"

Jane's startled eyes followed his as they separated and returned to their partners.

The next time they met in the figures she shook her head. "Five minutes, then?" Jane looked at him carefully and nodded her head.

"The punch bowl. After the next dance," she said quietly. His fierce smile made her shiver.

As Mark joined her for their waltz, he asked, "What did he want?" When she told him, he looked at her fiercely. "Why didn't you tell him no?"

"I didn't think it would be right. Mark, if he isn't the one we suspect, I wouldn't want to hurt him. It wouldn't be right to do so."

"Well, take Hortense along. Tell her you're afraid of him. I'll get Sir Henry, and we'll stay close." He pulled her closer than he should have; however, she didn't protest as they swung across the floor. She didn't want to tell Mark, but Dancy did frighten her.

The dance over, Mark escorted Jane to Hortense, who looked up startled. As he hurried away, Jane led the older woman toward the area where punch was being served.

Dancy had been waiting for her. When he saw Hortense, his blue eyes grew hard. "You needed protection, did you?" he asked bitterly.

"You must admit I have a right to be cautious."

He nodded his head. No matter what he did Jane saw in her mind a dark figure with a pillow over Mark's head. "I only wanted to apologize in person," he said quietly.

"You have our letters of acceptance."

"But yours was so cold."

"What did you expect? You assaulted me!"

"Jane, not so loud," Hortense said quietly. "You already have enough of an audience."

Jane looked around her at several young men, punch cups in their hands. Farther in the background she saw the figures of Mark and Sir Henry. She turned back to Dancy. "Do you have anything further to say, sir?" she asked. He shook his head. "Good evening."

As she walked toward Mark, her fiancé watched Dancy's face lose its usual good looks. His eyes flashing blue fire, Dancy seemed to be issuing a challenge. Quickly Mark smiled and took Jane by the arm. "Do you think your partner would excuse you from this dance?'' he asked wistfully. ''There is something in the library you simply must see.''

''Try another idea, young man. You may be engaged, but engaged isn't married,'' Hortense reminded him. Startled, he jumped. ''You just get back and find your partner, miss. And, you, sir, ask someone to dance.''

For the rest of the evening they did just that. As the hours neared the rendezvous, they exchanged worried glances across the floor. At supper, a magnificent meal that everyone else enjoyed tremendously, they could hardly eat. After the engagement had been toasted, the orchestra played the last dance. Jane, Mark and Sir Henry smiled as they said goodnight and counted the minutes before they could leave.

CHAPTER
22

Sir Henry headed up the stairs as soon as the last guest left. Then Mark kissed Jane on the cheek and said, "You help Hortense. I'll tell you about it when I return." Had he seen the look on her face as he ran up the stairs he would have worried.

A short time later the men met again in the entryway. To their surprise Jane was also there, dressed in a gray velvet riding dress, pulling her gloves on. Sir Henry smiled ruefully. "What do you think you are doing?" Mark asked her, his voice an angry snarl.

"I'm ready to go with you." Although she was quaking inwardly at the anger in his eyes, outwardly she was calm.

"Never." The thought of Jane in danger sent chills of fear down his spine. She could just stay at home as she should.

"Mark," Sir Henry said quietly. "We've got to be going." They turned to walk out the door, Jane walking with them.

Mark stopped. He stared at her. His fear for her safety added a harsh edge to his usually smooth voice. "I am not going to take you with me." His voice dropped to a low plea.

"Please, just go on back upstairs and wait until we come back. I can't stand to have you in danger."

"How do you think I feel? You'll be in danger too." Mark's elation at the thought of her worrying about him almost made him miss her next words. "I'll tell you what I told Sir Henry last time. You can go without me. But if you do, I'll follow you."

The older man chuckled. With that stubborn lift to her chin he had known what she was going to say. Deciding to stay out of this contest, he listened as they talked.

"We can't wait any longer. Are you coming, Mark?" Jane turned and walked to the waiting horses.

Sighing, Mark followed her. Grabbing her about the waist, he swung her around to face him. "You promise to do what I tell you?" At her nod, he swung her into the saddle. "You'd better. You'd just better." Jane flashed him an impish grin and waited impatiently as the men mounted.

The ride that night was similar to the search for Mark. But this time the air was softer, more springlike. Instead of fear her pulse hammered with excitement. The clouds that obscured the sliver of a moon made deep shadows over the fields, adding a sense of suspense to the already heady atmosphere. Once or twice she glanced at Mark, throwing him an impish smile.

As they drew closer to the barn, they slowed their horses. "Are you certain everyone got here?" Jane asked.

"According to Smythe, his group was to leave before midnight. The other men were to drift in slowly. They should be in place by now." Mark smiled wolfishly. "Dancy won't want to take a chance on interfering with the arrival of the goods. He'll wait until he sees the ship being unloaded."

"What about the lookouts? He's certain to have posted some," Sir Henry said thoughtfully. "Do we have our spotters out?"

"We do. Each man in Dancy's troop has had one or two unseen companions all week. His lookouts are in place, and so are ours."

"What about the real shipment?"

"It arrived safely this afternoon under the new kitchen stove and other household items." Mark flashed a quick smile at Jane. "Mrs. Johnson and Cook plan to worship at your feet daily," he teased.

"Quiet," Sir Henry said. "There's the barn. Let's get into place."

Before they had had time to do more than dismount, a groom was there to take their horses into hiding. Using the hedgerows for cover, they joined the others. Jane noticed a few raised eyebrows but refused to let them bother her.

Smythe hurried to their sides. "Dancy's lookouts arrived about midnight. They're in the rocks above the beach."

The sliver of the moon disappeared as they waited. The minutes ticked by slowly. Sir Henry leaned close to Jane and said mischievously, "I promised you'd have more excitement with me than in Bath."

"Next time I'll go to Bath," she quipped.

"Hush!" Mark's low voice sent shivers up her spine. "There's our signal. Is everyone ready?"

"Ready!"

Mark and the others waited patiently as the schooner, its decks loaded with cargo, dropped anchor. Then came the muffled curses as a line of men loaded the same cargo into a smaller boat. Soon those same men, working in a rhythm developed with long practice, formed a line to shift the goods up the hill to the barn. Working rapidly, they soon had everything safely stowed away. Taking their money, the leader said a few words to his contact, Smythe, and left. A few minutes later neither the shore nor the barn showed any sign of life.

"Dancy's lookout left when they started unloading the boat," came the whisper. Everyone froze. Suddenly someone coughed. Another person jumped. Mark checked the area closely and then stood up. He said quietly, "It will be some time before they can get here. Don't get nervous. If you talk, talk softly. They may still have a man at the shore."

Collectively, the men around Jane stretched. A sort of sigh ran through the group. Cautiously, Mark made his way from one group of men to another, reassuring them. As he took his place beside Jane once more, they heard horses in the distance. Somehow her hand was in his, and she was holding on as though she feared they would be ripped apart.

The night was dark; more clouds had overcast the stars. No one moved. As though they were afraid to make even the slightest sound, all of them held their breath for a moment, relaxing only as they realized that there really was a group of people coming.

Sir Henry, on the outside, was the first to see them clearly. It was a small caravan—three wagons, several pack animals, and more men on horseback. Not a uniform was in sight anywhere.

Although the group moving up to the barn was quiet, they had an air of unconcern about them that led them to make only a cursory inspection of the area. By the time they reached the barn, the lookout from the shore had joined them. Slipping up to a tall man mounted on an elegant black stallion, he gave his report.

Everyone watching held his breath, waiting for the ploy to be discovered. Sliding to the ground, the tall man looked around and gave a signal to dismount. The watchers heaved a sigh of relief.

After setting four lookouts and someone to oversee the horses, the tall man entered the barn, lighting a lantern as he went. Quickly he signaled the rest to follow.

As soon as they were inside, Sir Henry checked his men, making certain they were in place. Giving the signal, he sent them moving at their targets. Following Sir Henry's instructions, one man gagged each thief while another hit him over the head. The men in the barn heard nothing. When those men were hidden away, farmers donned their jackets and took their places.

Mark signaled the men to follow him, Jane's pleas to be careful ringing in his ears. He smiled at her and squeezed her hand. Before she could say anything else, he was gone, melting into the night.

Jane looked at Sir Henry, tears in her eyes. "Look at the men he's taken with him," he whispered. "He'll be fine." Slightly envious, he gazed at the barn where the darkened shadows hovered around the doors. Everything had to go well.

Almost before the men were in place, the door swung open. A lone man stumbled outside with a small cask. "Alfie? Where's my ol' friend Alfred?" he called. "Here's a drink just for you. They'll never miss it."

Before Mark's men had a chance to silence him, the door swung open again. The men lying in wait froze. "Quiet, man! Didn't you hear the captain? No drinkin'. He wants to see you," said a thick-chested man. His voice caused the hidden listeners to shudder, glad they were not the one it was directed at.

The drunken soldier paled. "No, I won't do it agin. I promise."

"He wants to see you. Now!" Shoving the now babbling man in front of him, the powerfully built man started to enter the barn. He stopped, his hands digging into the shoulders of the man in front of him. "You out there, keep a good watch, or maybe you'll be next." The threat in his voice made the listeners more determined than ever to succeed.

Taking advantage of the partly open door, Mark crept closer to check inside. While their leader sat on a keg, the rest of the men were clearing an area of the barn. One held the man who had come outside. His skin had the green-gray tone that tanned skin has when all the color seeps away.

He was whimpering. "No, you can't. I didn't mean it." No one but the leader was paying any attention. Mark was horrified to watch the man's shoulders shake, to hear his laughter.

"Hurry! We have to be gone soon," the cold voice snapped. The men cleared the area, cruel smiles on their faces. The leader stepped to a bale and picked up an object that made

Mark pale. It took supreme effort of will for him not to cry out in protest.

"One blow by all present. Isn't that what we agreed on?" the leader asked, turning to look at each of his men. It was Dancy. Mark pulled back hastily. The man seemed almost out of control. His blue eyes glowed with passion. Pleasure radiated from his smile, from the way he handled the cat-o'-nine-tails. He raised the whip and struck, tearing the man's cheek to ribbons.

Mark closed his eyes. But he couldn't shut out the noise, the moans of pain and pleasure. Scenes of his life in the navy haunted him, caused his gorge to rise.

The group away from the barn waited, perplexed. Those men should be loading, ready to leave. Just as they were about to leave their hiding place, the doors swung open, spilling light into the darkness. Hastily, they pulled back under cover.

Mark had just had time to jump out of the way. Taking refuge around the corner of the barn, he listened as Dancy started the loading process. "Get those kegs and barrels on first. Then make sure they're covered. Wouldn't want the good merchants of this train to be suspected of smuggling." He laughed loudly.

Mark signaled his men to get ready. As the first man lifted his load and walked out of the barn, they were on him. Using the technique they had perfected earlier, they gagged and disposed of two men quickly. Carrying the kegs to the wagons, Mark's men tried to make everything look as though it were going smoothly.

Their plan for bloodless victory might have worked had it not been for one of three men who brought their loads out next. "Hey there. Give us a hand, Tom," he called as he and his mate carefully lifted the cask of Oporto onto a wagon. As one of the men hurried to respond, keeping his head low as he did so, the thief heaved the cask into place. Catching sight of a strange face, he shouted, "Captain, watch out." Although the three were finished off quickly, Mark knew the danger had just gotten worse.

"Get those horses and wagons out of here," he shouted. "Surround this place!" Before he had finished speaking, men had leaped to the wagon seats, jumped on the backs of the horses, and were away.

Inside the barn, Dancy was cursing, his face livid with rage. Hearing the wagons pull away, he took his chance, plunging into the confusion. The remainder of his men followed him. As Dancy stopped short of the circle of men who waited for him, his men tried to fade back into the barn. The men who had been waiting beside the doors grabbed them and tied them tightly.

Dancy stood in front of Mark, his eyes gleaming with hatred and anger. "So you think you have me, do you?" Dancy smiled cruelly. "All these people just for us?"

"We couldn't afford to have you escape again," Mark said quietly, his hand keeping the others at bay.

"What gave me away?" Dancy asked curiously. His voice was so calm it sent a shiver through Jane. She hurried to Mark's side, careful to stay out of Dancy's range.

"Something you said to me," Jane said, her voice defiant. She looked at him coldly, the thought of his trying to smother Mark almost overcoming her with anger.

"Oh, yes. The innocent Miss Woodley." The accusation in his voice made more than one eyebrow rise. "How interesting to see you again this evening."

"I'd advise you to keep your gutter manners to yourself." Mark's voice was steel edged with ice.

The lieutenant turned his back on Mark, slowly going the full circle. As he saw the mix of gentry, farmers, and servants, a stormy look took over his face. When he reached Mark again, he frowned. "Really, Courtland, I had thought better of you," he said with a sneer.

"What do you mean?"

"Resorting to brute strength rather than calling me out like a gentleman."

"Are you a gentleman?"

The fire that had been raging beneath the surface broke free. For a moment it looked as though Dancy would strangle Mark. Gradually those watching could see an icy calm settle over him. "*Touché!*"

"Mark, let's take him prisoner and go home," Jane asked quietly. On his other side Sir Henry agreed.

Mark kept his eyes on his prisoner. "What did you have in mind, Dancy?" he asked coolly.

"A fight between the two of us."

"Weapons?"

"Fists." The lieutenant smiled; he was taller than Mark and had longer arms.

"You know that won't change what's to happen to you. They'll not let you go no matter what happens."

"Mark, you can't," Jane said pleadingly. "Think of me, of us."

"Yes, little man. Hide behind her skirts!" With Courtland's limp he should be able to defeat him easily, Dancy thought. And at that close range, he would be able to use him as a hostage. He smiled cruelly as he thought of Mark in his power.

Mark glanced at the men who surrounded him. From the look in their eyes, he knew what he had to do. Shaking off Jane's hands, he took a step forward. With a smile that matched Dancy's in bitterness, he said, "You have yourself a fight."

"No, Mark! Don't do it!" Jane screamed. Sir Henry pulled her back and cradled her head on his shoulder. He looked at Mark and nodded his head.

"You're going home. No, Jane, don't protest. Remember what you promised. This is one time I'll not listen to you," Sir Henry said firmly. Calling the two older grooms, he sent her on her way. The two men would never forgive Jane for causing them to miss the mill that everyone would talk about for years. As she mounted her horse, she looked at Mark sadly.

He hurried to her side. "I'll be all right. I promise you." He smiled at her, a look in his eyes that he reserved just for her. "Would I spoil anything before my wedding to you?"

"Just be careful, my dear." She leaned from her horse to kiss him briefly and then turned toward the Abbey, her shoulders drooping.

Mark turned back toward the circle of men eagerly. A wolfish grin made his face look dangerous. As he walked back, Sir Henry fell into step beside him. "Mark, watch out. He's planning something."

"Yes, and so am I." He stopped and looked at the man, who waited impatiently. "Strip down!"

"What?"

"Strip to the waist." Mark was already suiting his actions to his words, discarding his jacket and his shirt. He sat on the ground and motioned the nearest man to help with his boots.

Dancy looked at him for a moment and followed suit, cursing to himself. Although he sat down to remove his boots, he changed his mind. He rose slowly, staring at Mark.

They stood silently for a moment, each taking the other's measure. Slowly they started circling, each looking for an opening. Dancy attacked with a quick right to the jaw. Mark ducked and jabbed his fist into the iron muscles of the other's stomach. Dancy grunted and swung again. Mark stepped back.

Calmly, coolly, Mark began to hammer away at his opponent, taking hits but giving more than he received. Dancy began to swing wildly. Mark stepped back again, his face flushed. He was breathing hard.

Dancy smiled savagely and began another assault, pummeling Mark fiercely. Closing within the circle of those arms, Mark connected with Dancy's chin and sent him reeling backward, landing him on the ground.

As Mark stood above him breathing hard, Dancy's eyes narrowed. His hand slipped to his boot top.

"Mark, watch out! He has a knife," Sir Henry shouted. The others in the circle moved back, calling their encouragement. One man slid forward, his eyes on the slowly rising Dancy, and gave Mark a knife.

Once again they circled one another; this time there was murder in Dancy's eyes. He made a pass at Mark, laughing when a line of red showed on his chest. Drawing back, he slashed wildly. Jabbing at Mark, he passed him. He turned quickly, but not as quickly as Mark. While Dancy spun about, Mark from his vantage point lifted the heavy dagger and hit Dancy across the back of the head. He dropped like a stone.

"Fine fight, Mark. I was a trifle worried for a moment, but you came about nicely," Sir Henry said proudly.

"A trifle worried! Sir Henry, I was petrified," Mark said, breathing hard.

"If I had to explain to Jane . . . I shudder to think of it."

"Well, you won't have to, you old matchmaker."

Before Sir Henry could go on, Mark was surrounded by well-wishers. Seeing the tiredness in Mark's face, the older man made quick work of getting everyone started. "Get them all tied up and in the wagon. Who'll see them to jail? Good. Lord Brough, you'll present the evidence to the magistrate in the morning. Let's get those wagons loaded."

Mark breathed a sigh of relief and helped them load. As they wrapped the body they found in the barn in canvas, everyone's face sobered. Before long, though, the barn was empty again, and they all headed to their homes.

CHAPTER

23

Although Jane had waited downstairs until the men arrived, they had done little but smile at her and head for bed. When everyone woke late that afternoon, she was waiting impatiently.

Glossing over the details of the fight and the dagger, the men merely told her what had happened to the captured men and goods. Not certain she wanted to know more, Jane eyed them warily for a moment and then relented. Hortense shattered her calm acceptance. "Mark, you are so clever to disarm that man without any harm to yourself," she said, beaming at him.

"What do you mean, 'disarm'?" Jane asked, her eyes flashing.

"He knocked the man out and took the knife away."

"What knife?" Mark and Sir Henry were frantically trying to capture Hortense's attention, but it was too late.

"The one the lieutenant pulled from his boot. Smythe told Marsden, who told Mrs. Marsden, who told me, that it was the most exciting fight he had ever seen." Hortense, as usual when she was excited, had forgotten her drawl. "Can you imagine a man drawing a knife when the other man is unarmed?''

Drawing Hortense out of the room, Sir Henry left Mark to face a raging Jane. "You had to fight him. You men and your dratted honor. You could have been killed!" Tears started flooding down her cheeks.

"But I wasn't." Mark prudently kept his wound to himself. There would be time for that later. He sat close beside her on the settee and tilted her face up so that he could see her eyes. Her dark eyelashes glistening with teardrops fascinated him. Using his handkerchief, he patted them dry and kissed the tears from her cheeks. "If I promise that I will never do such a thing again, will you forgive me?" he asked in a low rich voice dark with suppressed emotion. She nodded her head. "Come here." He opened his arms, and she flew into them, happy for the moment to simply be close to him.

Over the next few days she was to remember that time with longing. After long deliberation, everyone decided that Mark should accompany Lord Brough to London—everyone but Jane and Mark, that is. Fighting their need to be together, even they had to agree that Mark was the one who knew what was happening. Sir Henry added the deciding factor. "If you're there, you can scoff at what Dancy's going to say about us. Brough will try, but he wasn't in the thick of things." Reluctantly they had to agree.

While Mark was in London, Jane was left in charge of Courtland Place. Accompanied by Hortense, she inspected the rooms daily and encouraged the staff. Although she enjoyed visiting the other rooms, it was their suite where she could be found most often, a dreamy look on her face. Sir Henry, who accompanied them as escort on many of their trips, beamed proudly as he watched her inquire about the progress and approve the decisions.

The servants at Courtland Place were devoted to her, not solely because she was Mark's choice. Her interest in them and planning for them made them feel important. As Mark had told her, Mrs. Johnson and Cook were delighted with the new kitchen. The others took advantage of her offer to have their rooms painted in their choice of color.

By the time Mark returned, Courtland Place was habitable. Jane breathed a sigh of relief as she thought of the clean kitchen and fresh rooms. Everything smelled so new. Dismounting from the carriage, she ran up the front steps of the Abbey and straight into Mark, who was waiting for her. She threw her arms around his neck, raising her lips happily.

"A bit too public, wouldn't you say, Hortense?"

"Do they kiss in private?" she asked ironically.

Blushing, Jane pulled away. She smiled as though her dearest wish had come true. Mark beamed fatuously.

"Come into the library and tell us about London," Sir Henry urged. Mark simply stared at Jane.

Finally Hortense took Jane by the arm and drew her down the hallway. "You want to hear about London, don't you, my dear?" Jane smiled and nodded. Mark followed her.

Seating Jane in a chair, Sir Henry turned back to Mark. "Let's have the details, my boy." Hortense took her seat and looked at him expectantly.

"There were more than a few shocks," Mark said quietly.

"What?"

"Explain!"

"With all the witnesses and evidence against them we convinced the government to send them to Newgate."

"And well they should," said Hortense indignantly.

"When we went to talk to the army about replacements, we were surprised."

"How?"

"Why?" Sir Henry and Jane looked at each other and laughed.

"Remember the answers to your letters, Sir Henry, and your question, Jane?"

"About why we had a troop of soldiers if we were so quiet?"

Mark nodded and continued his explanation. "Dancy and his troop were not soldiers."

"What?"

"How did they dare?"

"How did they get away with it?"

Trying to answer all three questions at the same time, Mark explained. "Dancy had been a soldier but had been cashiered. He was a by-blow of some lord who'd paid up for the last time. When he ran up debts, he turned to thievery."

"I always knew he wasn't good *ton*," Hortense said firmly, completely ignoring the gasps of the other three.

"How did he find his men?" Sir Henry asked.

"Most had been dismissed too. Posing as soldiers was to them an excellent opportunity to show up the government."

Sir Henry, his face serious, asked, "What did Dancy say about us?"

"Everything. Oh, don't worry. He wasn't believed. But he could have been. You were right in insisting that I go to London," Mark said, his face somber.

"What gave us away?" Jane asked.

"Those blasted sacks. Apparently at the Christmas melee Dancy found one and got suspicious. The rest you know."

"What will happen to them now?" Jane asked thoughtfully.

"Most told the prosecutors what they wanted to know. They'll probably be transported. For the others?" He frowned. "The confessions linked Dancy and some of the others to some unsolved murders and spying. It's probable they'll hang."

Mark and Sir Henry exchanged a sober glance as they thought of the body they'd taken from the barn. Thankful that Jane had been spared that, they turned the discussion to other subjects.

As the last details of the plot were unraveled, everyone began thinking about the wedding. As the day grew closer, Jane became more and more nervous. She knew how to housekeep, but could she be a wife? Because Hortense in a spirit of renewed chaperonage accompanied Jane everywhere, she had not been able to talk to Mark.

He too was having his doubts. As he watched her turn pale

and flinch as people discussed their marriage, he wondered if he should find some way to break it off. Then he remembered her soft kisses and the feel of her in his arms and hardened his heart.

Not wishing an elaborate spectacle, they had chosen a private wedding with only Sir Henry and Hortense as their witnesses. This was to be followed by a wedding breakfast for everyone in the district, hosted by Sir Henry.

As Jane dressed that morning, her cheeks matched the creamy whiteness of her gown. Betty rushed down the stairs, returning a few minutes later with Hortense's dresser.

Henshaw looked Jane over critically from the tousled curls to the elaborate coil of her hair on the nape of her neck. Despite Jane's protests, her cheeks were lightly dusted with rouge. Henshaw inspected her work, nodded her head, and left.

When Jane's cloak was in place, Betty drew the hood up to frame her face. She smiled at her mistress. Before Jane left the room, Smythe appeared, a box in his hand. "With Mr. Courtland's compliments," he said proudly.

Jane opened the box carefully, delighted by the charming bouquet of snowdrops, hothouse roses, and ivy. For the first time that morning she smiled as she breathed in their sweet scent.

When the door opened the next time, it was Sir Henry, waiting to escort her to the coach. Hortense and Mark had left a short time earlier. Hesitantly she took his arm, gripping it so hard he almost protested.

Settling her in the coach, he arranged her skirts and climbed in beside her. As he gave the signal for the coachman to begin, he turned to her. "Jane," he said quietly. His voice broke, and he began again. "My dear, no matter what happens in the years to come, remember I love you. You are the daughter I never had." He wiped his eyes with his handkerchief. "I'm just an old fool, I guess," he muttered.

Jane smiled up at him, tears brimming in her eyes too. "Sir Henry, I wish you were my father. I love you too."

Catching her close, the older man held her for a moment and then put her away from him. Pulling out his handkerchief again, he patted her tears dry, daubing at his own as well.

"I'm so frightened, Sir Henry," Jane whispered as they neared the church.

"Of Mark?"

"No."

"How do you feel about him, my dear?"

"I love him," she said quietly.

"And he loves you. Because of that your marriage will be a success. Trust yourself, and trust Mark." Straightening his shoulders, Sir Henry smiled at her and opened the door.

Unlike many brides, Jane remembered most of her wedding vividly. As they stood in the vestibule, her knees started to shake so badly that she clutched Sir Henry's arm to keep from falling. Her maid adjusted her hood and straightened a curl. Sir Henry adjusted the cuffs of his gray velvet coat one last time and straightened his cravat. Then the doors to the church swung open.

As Jane waited for Sir Henry to escort her up the white satin runner that ended at the altar, she stared at the man who waited for her. Never taking his eyes off her, Mark stood proudly. His snowy white cravat and dark blue coat outlined his impressive shoulders. Much to Hortense's despair, he and Sir Henry had chosen to wear pantaloons instead of court dress. A slow blush crept up Jane's face as she thought of the intimacies that that night would bring.

Sir Henry tugged at her arm and smiled. Jane held her head proudly, walking steadily toward her future. The rich organ music sent a thrill through her. As she came closer to the altar where Mark waited, her nervousness returned. Before the blaze in Mark's brown eyes, she dropped hers.

Although the ceremony was a simple one, Hortense and Mrs. Langley had decorated the altar lavishly with ivy and candles; an arched bank of candles gave the altar a halo, their bright brass candlesticks reflecting the massed flames. For a few seconds Jane was mesmerized by them. When the opening words of the marriage service were over and Sir Henry gave her hand to Mark, she was startled.

As they moved forward to stand before Mr. Langley at the altar, Jane kept her eyes on the floor, too shy to meet the fierce joy in Mark's. As they repeated their vows, she raised her eyes to his. Her heart pounded as he looked steadily, passionately, at her. His promises were made in clear, soft rich tones that seemed to lap Jane in velvet. Hers, although softer, were just as firm. As she watched Mark slide her ring carefully on her finger, she felt his hand tremble. Startled, she looked up and saw him blinking rapidly, his eyes misted.

Mr. Langley finished the words of the service and pronounced the blessing. For a moment Mark and Jane simply gazed at each other. Then, turning, they walked slowly up the aisle toward the vestibule. Pausing only a few moments to sign the registry, they were soon in their carriage.

The ride back to the Abbey was a quiet one. Mark, recognizing her nervousness, simply pulled her close to him, putting his arm around her and capturing her hands in his. As Jane realized that he only wanted to hold her, she began to feel less nervous. As Mark felt the tension slip away, he breathed a quick sigh of relief.

While Mark and Jane traveled in a peaceful silence, Sir Henry and Hortense in the carriage ahead were too happy to be silent. "Henry, I must admit when you broached the subject, I was a bit skeptical, but I'm proud of you. She was a beautiful bride."

"She was, wasn't she? I must admit, though, that they've given me one or two bad moments."

"Only one or two?" Hortense asked coyly.

"It gives one such a sense of accomplishment," he said happily, "such a feeling—"

"Of playing God?"

"Hortense!"

"Don't be getting a puffed head, Henry. I daresay Mark and Jane would have come to the same end even without your machinations," Hortense said flatteningly.

A mischievous look came over Sir Henry's face. "How old does a girl have to be before she's out?"

"Seventeen or eighteen."

"Hmm. That long."

"Henry, what are you planning?"

"I hope their first child is a girl." His eyes glinted as he thought of the years he would have to find just the right young man for her.

"Henry, stop grinning like that and come greet your guests."

The wedding breakfast was as elaborate as Hortense could make it. There were two soups accompanied by smoked sturgeon and mussels in wine. The second remove featured squab and duckling, lobster in an appropriate sauce, and baked trout. For the third she'd chosen barons of beef, roasted capons, and mutton with cucumbers served with the freshest of green peas (obtained only at great expense), salsify, and various salads. The last remove was a masterpiece; Alberto had outdone himself with a vast display of molded jellies, creams, meringue baskets of sweetmeats, an elegant butter cake, filled and iced, and his *pièce de résistance*, a lovely ice sculpture decorated with fruit.

As one dish followed the next, Mark put a variety of selections on Jane's plate, but she ate only a small amount. After watching her drain her wineglass once more, Mark signaled to the footman behind his chair. After that Jane drank lemonade and never noticed the difference. By the end of the meal, she was wearing a false smile and was so nervous she could not reply to the toasts that were proposed. Watching her carefully, Mark made his decision.

Standing, he replied to the last of the toasts and said goodbye. Helping Jane to her feet, he led her quickly into the hall. "May I offer you my congratulations, sir?" Marsden asked as he assisted Jane with her cloak and handed Mark his hat.

Mark smiled happily and nodded. Sweeping Jane outside, he helped her into the carriage that would take them home.

By the time they reached Courtland Place a short time

later, Jane's eyes were beginning to droop. Mark kept close
by her side while they greeted the servants who were lined up
to offer them their best wishes. Then he whisked her upstairs to
their suite.

Before Jane had a chance to say a word, Mark left her in
the hands of her maid. "Put her to bed for a nap, Betty. She's
exhausted," he said quietly as he opened the connecting door
to his bedroom. When he returned a short time later, Jane
was asleep. Smiling slightly, he pulled off his dressing gown
and slipped into bed beside her. He put his arm around her,
and she nestled close to him. Although he had thought it
would be impossible, he drifted off to sleep.

Some time later he stirred. Opening his eyes, he moved
cautiously, rolling over on his side. Jane was awake. Her eyes
were huge, her face solemn. Mark smiled and bent to kiss
her. Although she didn't pull away, her lips trembled.

Mark took a deep breath, willing himself patience. He
fluffed his pillows and sat up, pulling her beside him. "Have
I told you how beautiful you were today?" he asked quietly,
his lips making a foray down her neck. She shook her head,
afraid to speak. "I was afraid to look away, afraid you would
disappear, and I'd be lonely once more," he whispered.

"Oh!" Jane leaned toward him, her eyes soft. She let her
lips brush the pulse in his throat.

He cleared his throat, and she watched in fascination as the
cords in his neck tightened. He took a deep breath. "Jane,"
he said quietly, "I love you."

The simple words surprised her, and she sat there, her head
on his chest listening to his heart pounding. Just when he was
beginning to give up hope, she raised her head and smiled.
Her smile was so full of joy it seemed to fill the whole room.

"Jane?" he whispered quietly.

Her eyes never leaving his, she leaned closer and kissed
him on the lips. "I love you too," she whispered.

For as long as he lived, Sir Henry took pride in their happy
marriage, a pride that grew stronger as their children were

born. In his later years, he would put the two youngest—twins, a girl and a boy—on his knees while their older brother and sister leaned over his shoulders and tell the story of how he arranged their parents' marriage. And each time Jane and Mark heard him, they would smile, their eyes once again affirming their love.

SIGNET Regency Romances You'll Want to Read

(045)

☐	**THE REPENTANT REBEL** by Jane Ashford.	(131959—$2.50)
☐	**THE IMPETUOUS HEIRESS** by Jane Ashford.	(129687—$2.25)
☐	**FIRST SEASON** by Jane Ashford.	(126785—$2.25)
☐	**A RADICAL ARRANGEMENT** by Jane Ashford.	(125150—$2.25)
☐	**THE HEADSTRONG WARD** by Jane Ashford.	(122674—$2.25)
☐	**THE MARCHINGTON SCANDAL** by Jane Ashford.	(116232—$2.25)
☐	**THE THREE GRACES** by Jane Ashford.	(114183—$2.25)
☐	**A COMMERCIAL ENTERPRISE** by Sandra Heath.	(131614—$2.50)
☐	**MY LADY DOMINO** by Sandra Heath.	(126149—$2.25)*
☐	**THE MAKESHIFT MARRIAGE** by Sandra Heath.	(122682—$2.25)*
☐	**MALLY** by Sandra Heath.	(093429—$1.75)*
☐	**THE OPERA DANCER** by Sandra Heath.	(111125—$2.25)*
☐	**THE UNWILLING HEIRESS** by Sandra Heath.	(097718—$1.95)*
☐	**MANNERBY'S LADY** by Sandra Heath.	(097726—$1.95)*
☐	**THE SHERBORNE SAPPHIRES** by Sandra Heath.	(097718—$1.95)*
☐	**THE CLERGYMAN'S DAUGHTER** by Julia Jefferies.	(120094—$2.25)*
☐	**THE CHADWICK RING** by Julia Jefferies.	(113462—$2.25)*

*Prices slightly higher in Canada.

Buy them at your local

bookstore or use coupon

on last page for ordering.

More Regency Romances from SIGNET

Buy them at your local

bookstore or use coupon

on next page for ordering.

More Delightful Regency Romances from SIGNET

(0451

- [ ] **THE ACCESSIBLE AUNT by Vanessa Gray.** (126777—$2.25)
- [ ] **THE DUKE'S MESSENGER by Vanessa Gray.** (118685—$2.25)
- [ ] **THE DUTIFUL DAUGHTER by Vanessa Gray.** (090179—$1.75)
- [ ] **RED JACK'S DAUGHTER by Edith Layton.** (129148—$2.25)
- [ ] **THE MYSTERIOUS HEIR by Edith Layton.** (126793—$2.25
- [ ] **THE DISDAINFUL MARQUIS by Edith Layton.** (124480—$2.25)*
- [ ] **THE DUKE'S WAGER by Edith Layton.** (120671—$2.25)*
- [ ] **A SUITABLE MATCH by Joy Freeman.** (117735—$2.25)*
- [ ] **THE NOBLE IMPOSTER by Mollie Ashton.** (129156—$2.25)*

*Prices slightly higher in Canada
